The
Dashwood Sisters'
Secrets of Love

ROSIE RUSHTON

HYPERION ❧ NEW YORK

Printed in the United States of America
First Edition
1 3 5 7 9 10 8 6 4 2

Library of Congress Cataloging-in-Publication Data on file.
ISBN 0-7868-5136-8

Reinforced binding

Visit www.hyperionteens.com

*For everyone who finds
the true meaning of love—
and has the courage to live it.*

A tried and true secret of love:

If a woman doubts as to whether she should accept a man or not, she certainly ought to refuse him. If she can hesitate as to Yes, she ought to say No, directly.

—Jane Austen

PROLOGUE

*I*T WASN'T LONG AGO that photographs of the Dashwood sisters' ancestors—yellow with age, the occasional school picture of Ellie, Abby, and Georgie tucked into the edge of the frame—hung along the long, winding staircase at Holly House, the Dashwood family's home for generations. There were other photos, too— an aerial shot of the Holly House grounds, the girls' father at the ribbon-cutting of one of his many businesses, their mother in her wedding dress, a toothless Georgie on her first bike, Abby as Juliet at the local theater, Ellie winning a spelling bee.

But that was then. *Before.* Before the divorce and the terrible day that changed everything forever. And now, the pictures all lay packed away somewhere, too full of memories to find a place in the Dashwood girls' new home.

All, that is, except one: a portrait of their family—Dad,

Mum, seventeen-year-old Ellie, sixteen-year-old Abby, and thirteen-year-old Georgie—painted long after the last time they'd all been together. The Dashwoods had never posed for the painting; they couldn't have even if they'd wanted to.

Now it hung in their new hallway—miles away from the old Holly House stairway—and the girls realized that this was the way they wanted to remember their family. After all, it had taken a year for the Dashwood sisters to discover the secret of love, and now that they'd found it, they weren't about to let it go.

⚜ SECRET NO. 1 ⚜

Sometimes a broken heart beats louder than all the whole hearts combined

HI BABE! R U ON 4 2NITE? CROWD GOING 2 CLUB XS 8PM. B GR8 2 C U. XX

Abby Dashwood let out a squeal of delight, dropping her mobile phone on her bed and dancing around in her bare feet.

"This is it," she announced to Manderley, her somewhat overweight ginger cat, who was eyeing her critically from the chintz-covered window seat. "I just know this is it!"

She grabbed the phone and began stabbing madly at the keys.

SURE I'LL B THE—

No, that sounded like she was desperate to see him. Which of course she was but it wouldn't be smart to let him know that.

WILL C IF I CAN MAKE IT.

Should she put a kiss or not? Yes. No. Did the message sound too offhand? She held down the delete key.

SURE I'LL BE THERE. XX

After another moment of deliberation, Abby held the phone away from her, closed her eyes, and pressed the SEND button. Then she bent down, lifted the corner of her mattress, and pulled out her purple diary—the one no one knew about. She had a scarlet one that held boring stuff, like dental appointments and reminders about homework, and acted as a decoy if her inquisitive sisters or overanxious mother found it. But the purple diary held her secret, most intimate thoughts—stuff that her totally unromantic family would have mocked.

TODAY AT 8:58, she wrote, MY DREAMS CAME TRUE. FERGUS MORTIMER WANTS ME, DESIRES ME, YEARNS TO BE WITH ME . . . Okay, maybe that was a tad over the top, but she'd read somewhere that if you send out positive vibes to the universe, it gives you exactly what you want.

"Abby, for the last time, will you please hurry up? It's nearly nine o'clock!" Her mother's shrill voice wafted up the stairs.

"Okay, okay, I'm coming!" Abby hollered.

She kissed the page, and rammed the diary back under the mattress. Nine o'clock. In less than twelve hours, she'd be with him. Of course, there were a few minor obstacles to overcome in the meantime—like that she wasn't allowed out late during final exam week, that her mother would die a thousand deaths if she knew her sixteen-year-old daughter was planning to venture anywhere near Club XS, never mind inside it, and that she had to find a watertight alibi that wouldn't land her in trouble like the last time. But somehow she would do it. She had to. Her future happiness depended on it.

She slipped her feet into her new silver wedges, grabbed her bag, and crossed to the dressing-table mirror, sticking a large green flower clip into her flame-colored curls.

She blew a kiss at her reflection, and assessed her capri-clad backside before deciding the capris were way too last year. She unzipped her pants, hurling them onto the floor as she yanked garment after garment out of her wardrobe, all the while wishing she had the same beanpole figure as her sister Ellie. She cringed when she heard her mother's voice coming from downstairs again.

"Abigail, Ellie's getting the car out right now, and you will be in it within the next three minutes or else! This is your sister's day, remember?"

Abby groaned inwardly as she wriggled her backside into a pair of black satin trousers. Another complication. Mum would expect her and Ellie to have supper at home, eat birthday cake, make a fuss of Georgie. Her mother was big on the happy family bit, especially after everything that had happened. Abby let herself wish, for only a second, that things could go back to the way they used to be.

* * *

Are you daring?

In search of an adrenaline rush?

Well, now you've got it!

Two heart-stopping sessions of

Zorbing—Sphering—Call it what you will!

It's the newest,

fastest thrill on earth

and it's yours

with love from

Tom

"This is just the coolest present!" Georgie exclaimed, leaning on the garden gate and clutching the voucher in her hand.

"You really like it? You're not just saying that?" he asked, running slightly muddy fingers through his unruly, blond hair.

" 'Course not," Georgie assured him, flicking her ponytail over her shoulder. "It's awesome!"

That was the best thing about Tom—unlike her own totally boring, completely predictable family, he was on her wavelength. He always had been, ever since she'd wriggled through the gap in the stone wall separating their houses, and demanded that he let her have a go with his new bow and arrow. That had been several years ago, when he told her that six-year-olds couldn't shoot arrows, and she'd have to wait till she was seven and a half like him. Georgie, who'd never taken no for an answer in her life, and had no intention of starting then, wrestled him to the ground with the moves she'd learned at Kiddies Karate. He told her she was pretty okay for a girl; she spat on her hand and then helped him up with her sticky palm; and that had been that—they'd been best mates ever since.

"Georgie, I've got a confession to make. I didn't pay for it—my cousin Josh works at Sportsextreme, and he fixed it up for me."

"Who cares, as long as we get to do it?" Georgie grinned. She knew her sisters thought she was too old for tomboy activities, but she didn't care. Pushing the boundaries was her thing—not dressing up and worrying about what other people thought.

"Get to do what, dear?" Julia, Georgie's mother asked, panting slightly as she reached them. "Oh, another birthday card! How sweet of you, Tom dear. Do let's see, Georgie!"

She reached out and took the envelope from Georgie's hand.

"Mum, I . . ."

Her mother perched her new Calvin Klein spectacles on the end of her nose, read the fluorescent orange card, and frowned.

"Zorbing? Sphering? What is . . ." She turned the card

over to where there was a diagram of a person rolling down a hill inside a ball. "Georgie, you can't!"

Tom suddenly found something of enormous interest under his left thumbnail.

"Isn't that just the coolest thing, Mum?" Georgie smiled. "And it's totally safe, honestly."

"You're trying to tell me that strapping yourself inside an inflatable ball and rolling down a hill at high speed is safe? And besides, why would you want to?"

Georgie counted silently to ten in her head and took a deep breath. It was a trick their father had taught them to do when they were little that all three sisters had taken to heart.

"It's an experience, Mum, an adrenaline rush. Tom and me are going to do it together."

"Tom and I," her mother corrected her. Even the shock of her youngest daughter going zorbing could not dampen her passion for good grammar. She eyed Tom suspiciously.

"Does your mother know about this?" she asked, glancing over the garden wall as if hoping that Mrs. Eastment would appear and put a stop to the whole idea.

Georgie cringed with embarrassment. What kind of a question was that to ask a fifteen-year-old guy?

"Oh sure," Tom grinned, hooking his thumbs through his jeans belt. "My cousin runs it."

Julia swallowed hard and fixed a bright smile on her lips. "Really? How fascinating. Well, I suppose . . ." The sound of a car engine firing up inside the garage put an end to her musings.

"Ellie, no! Stop this minute! What are you doing?" She ran across the gravel drive toward the garage, her ample breasts bobbing up and down in alarm.

"Georgie," she called over her shoulder. "Come. Car—now!" When distraught, Julia tended to wind down to monosyllables.

"What's keeping her?" Ellie leaned on the horn of her bright red Fiat Uno as her mother wrenched open the door and sighed. "She's been getting ready for the last hour."

She zapped down the window and peered up at Abby's bedroom window.

"Mum, go and get her—we'll miss the train if she doesn't get a move on," Georgie complained, climbing into the back of the car. "Ellie drives so slowly. . . ."

"So I should hope!" their mother said sharply, clicking her seat belt in place even though the car was stationary. "She's still a learner driver, remember?"

"Not for much longer," Ellie grinned, unzipping her bomber jacket and hurling it onto the backseat. "Four weeks and three days, and these L plates can go out the window."

"Don't you be so sure, young lady," her mother teased, touching up her lipstick in the rearview mirror. "Not if . . ."

"Here she is!" Georgie interrupted, as the studded oak front door of the half-timbered house banged shut and her sister crunched down the gravel drive. "Come on, Abby, what kept you so long?"

Abby hitched her bag up onto her shoulder and clambered into the backseat of the car beside Georgie amid a cloud of L'Eau d'Issay.

"Couldn't find my new lavender mascara," she replied. "And then my lip liner smudged, and . . ."

"Abby, for heaven's sake," Ellie interupted, dropping the sun visor to cancel out the glare from the distant ocean. "We're going to London for the day, not parading down a catwalk."

"Whatever," Abby retorted, clicking her seat belt in place. "Some of us like to look our best even if it is only our kid sister's birthday."

"Even if the kid sister looks like she's about to go on a drill," interjected Julia, glancing in the rearview mirror at her youngest daughter. "Georgie, couldn't you have worn something a little smarter? Ellie and Abby manage to . . ."

"Mum, these are dead cool combats, okay?" Georgie stressed, ramming her baseball cap more firmly on her head. "Anyway, it's my birthday and I can do what I like."

"Ellie!" Julia Dashwood cried, grabbing on to the dashboard as the car lurched forward. "Gentle on the clutch!"

"Sorry," Ellie apologized to the car as much as to her

mother. She shouldn't be taking out her frustration with her family on Fenella the Fiat.

"And not so much of the kid-sister routine," protested Georgie, digging Abby in the ribs. "I'm thirteen today, remember?"

"Sorry," smiled Abby sweetly. "I keep forgetting. I mean, when I was thirteen, I'd already started dating. . . ."

"You started dating in preschool," Ellie muttered under her breath.

"Will you concentrate on your driving?" her mother shouted. "You nearly took the branches off that bush!"

Ellie drove slowly down the long rhododendron-lined driveway.

"Okay, we're on our way," Ellie chanted, trying to lighten everyone's mood.

"See you, house, at the end of the day!" they all cho-rused and then giggled in a slightly embarrassed way. It was a goofy tradition, but one they could never quite break. It had started when Abby was two and insisted on saying good-bye to everything before she went out—the cats scattered about the house, the doves in the dovecote on the back lawn, the stone cherub on the fountain, and of course, the house. Abby had been sure that Holly House had a heart, and so she had always told it she would be back. The habit had stuck, and now none of them wanted to be the first to break it.

"I wish the weather would warm up," Abby said. "Then we could mow the tennis court and put the nets up. I want to get some practice in."

"You what? You don't even like tennis," Ellie protested, slowing to a halt and pressing the remote control that opened the wrought-iron gates onto the road. The traffic was already beginning to build up as tourists sped along the coast road to enjoy the delights of Brighton on a spring Saturday.

"She does now," Georgie intervened. "She's in love."

"She's permanently in love," Ellie retorted, zapping the gates closed behind her, "but it doesn't usually involve her moving any faster than a slow amble."

"It's Fergus Mortimer," Georgie informed her. "He's a tennis whiz, and Abby fancies him."

"I don't!" Abby snapped.

"You do so," Georgie countered calmly. "You wrote 'Fergus 4 Abby' on your homework notebook and all over your biology folder."

"All of Abby's books are covered with love notes," Ellie commented. "So what's so special about this Fergus?"

"Will you three just stop all this chattering!" their mother exploded. "My nerves go through enough with Ellie's driving, without listening to all your nonsense."

Ellie bit her lip to stop herself replying. She knew quite well why her mother was on edge, and it had nothing to do with Ellie's ability behind the wheel. It was the fact that the girls were off to see their father. And Pandora.

"So where have you asked Dad to take us this year, Georgie?" Ellie heard Abby ask from the backseat as she pulled into the outside lane. "Not another safari park, I trust. Remember when Mum screamed because that buffalo stuck its tongue out at her?"

If Ellie hadn't been driving, she would have turned around and thumped her sister. How tactless could she get? Mum wouldn't need any reminders that this time last year, she and Dad were still together. Just.

Twelve months—just 52 weeks ago—they hadn't had a clue. Dad had, of course. All the time they'd been at the safari park, with him laughing and joking and taking photographs, he'd known he was going to leave them. And by the time the pictures were developed, he had.

"I've grown out of safari parks," Georgie retorted sharply, and Ellie guessed she was watching the same mental-movie in her mind as well. "This year it's going to be the London Dungeon first, then lunch at Piggy Passion's, and a ride on that new big-wheel thing that all the pop stars go on—what's it called?"

"The London Eye," her mother said. "Sounds like a fun day."

Ellie caught the wistful note in her mum's voice.

"Why don't you come too, Mum?" Georgie cried,

leaning forward as far as her seat belt would allow and tapping Julia on the shoulder. "It would be just like old times."

"Georgie!" Ellie hissed. "Shut up."

She knew Georgie meant well, but the hard fact was that nothing would ever be like old times again.

"That's sweet of you, darling," her mother said calmly. "But I don't think Pandora would relish my company, do you?"

She sounded amused, but Ellie could see the way she was clenching and unclenching her hands in her lap.

"But, Mum, that's the whole point. Pandora won't be there," Georgie insisted.

"Georgie, of course she will," her mother retorted sharply, flicking a stray hair from her shoulder. "Your father and Pandora are joined at the hip. With superglue."

It was almost a relief to Ellie to hear the note of acerbity in her mother's voice. There were times when she seemed to be almost too dignified to be true.

"Mum, I promise . . ." Georgie began.

"Georgina, leave it, okay?" Their mother only ever used their full names when she was about to explode, and it never failed to stop them in their tracks.

"Which way?" Ellie asked her mother. "North Street or along the seafront?"

"North Street," her mother replied. "You need practice in traffic."

Ellie took a deep breath and maneuvered her way past the Royal Pavilion, with its Indian-style turrets and enthusiastic clusters of Japanese tourists waving guidebooks, past the carpet gardens, and into her favorite area of town. Not that she dared to take her eyes off the road long enough to soak up the buzzy, Bohemian side streets of the North Laines with their artists' studios, funky nightclubs, and tiny shops selling vintage clothing. The narrow streets were a challenge even to the most experienced driver, and Ellie found herself holding her breath as if that would help the car squeeze past the pavement cafés with their tables spilling onto the roadway.

"Well done, dear," her mother said as Ellie turned into the station forecourt. "Pull up over there and give me the car keys." {13}

"Will you be okay, Mum?" Ellie whispered, grabbing her jacket as her sisters piled out of the car.

"Okay?" Julia replied brightly, leaning across to give her a hug. "I'll be hunky-dory. I've got those rosebushes to prune, then I'm having lunch with Fran at the new organic bistro down by the marina—Fresh and Fancy, I think it's called. . . ."

"Come on!" Georgie interrupted, hopping from one foot to another and grabbing Ellie's arm. "The train goes in ten minutes."

"Before you go," their mother said hesitantly. "You will give my love to—well, remember me to your father, won't you? Tell him the daffodils are all out and those cowslips he planted . . ."

Her voice petered out and she gave a brief wave, before firing the engine and driving off, narrowly missing a couple of seagulls pecking for scraps at the curbside. Ellie, Abby, and Georgie just watched her go.

🐚 SECRET NO. 2 🐚

There really is no accounting for taste

"It makes me so angry!" Abby yelled. They were halfway across the crowded station concourse when she swung around to face Ellie. "Why didn't she fight more for him? I mean, you can tell she still loves him to bits. Why did she let him go?"

Abby's voice rose to a crescendo, and a couple of pigeons stopped pecking around a rubbish bin and flew into the air in front of them.

"Abby, for goodness' sake," Ellie began, conscious of the glances of the other passengers hurrying for the London train. "Don't start all that again. It's over—and besides, there was nothing Mum could have done about it. It wasn't her fault that Dad fell in love with Pandora."

"Pandora seduced him, you mean! All those come-hither looks and giant silicone boobs!" Abby stormed, stomping into the first free carriage. "And of course she could have done something about it. If she'd been more—oh, I don't know—more stylish, more sexy, more in your face. . . ."

"Look, Abby, I wish Mum were here, I wish she and Dad were still together, I wish we were just a normal family like before, but we're not and . . ."

"Stop it. Shut up, and stop it right now!" Georgie's face was scarlet as she stomped down the gangway to the first row of vacant seats. "It's my birthday and I don't want anything to spoil it, okay? Can't we just spend the day with Dad and pretend . . ."

"What? Pretend he'll be coming home with us, pretend nothing's changed?" Abby mocked, slinging her bag onto the overhead luggage rack and slumping into a window seat.

"Abby, don't," Ellie said, slipping into her usual role of mediator. "Georgie's bound to feel a bit upset. . . ."

"Upset? I'm not upset!" Georgie stuck out her chin and bit her lip, which was a sure sign that she was.

"Anyway," Ellie went on calmly, "I guess Georgie's right. We've got Dad to ourselves for the whole day so . . ."

"Hardly," sniffed Abby. "Pandora, queen of all bird-brains, will be there."

"Oh, no she won't," Georgie declared smugly.

"Face it, Georgie, she will," Ellie agreed, peering at her reflection in the train window and musing for the tenth time that day on whether to get her shoulder-length hair cut really short.

"No. She. Won't." Georgie articulated each word as if talking to a pair of morons.

Ellie eyed her sister closely. "Georgie," she asked as the train pulled out of the station. "What exactly do you know that we don't?"

"Just that I'm a genius," she giggled. "Why do you think I chose the London Dungeon, Piggy Passion's, and the London Eye for my birthday?"

Abby shrugged and stood up to grab a bottle of Evian water from her bag.

"Because you are a hugely strange individual?" Abby suggested mischievously, unscrewing the cap and taking a large swig.

Georgie pulled a face.

"I chose them because no way will Pandora want to be a part of it. She's a total wimp when it comes to ghosts and ghouls—remember how she almost fainted watching *The Sixth Sense*? And she can't stand heights. . . ."

". . . and she won't eat anything that's not fat-free, gluten-free, and grown in organic soil on a south-facing slope of the Andes!" finished Ellie, bursting out laughing as the train gathered speed. "Georgie—you're brilliant!"

"This is true." Georgie grinned, scrabbling in her rucksack. "Want a potato crisp?"

"Dear me," teased Abby, "what would Pandora say? A *crisp*?"

"Don't you realize," chimed in Ellie, mimicking Pandora's shrill tones, "that mass-produced products loaded with salt and fat can wreak havoc on one's arteries, not to mention destroying the complexion and introducing toxins to the bloodstream?" Ellie giggled and reverted to her normal voice. "Give me a handful!"

Georgie tossed the bag of crisps onto Ellie's lap.

"Hot in here, isn't it?" Abby said, unzipping her cream leather jacket and flinging it on the spare seat beside her. "I'll have some too."

"Abby! That's my new top you're wearing! How dare—" Ellie's outburst came to an abrupt end as she choked on the crisps she had just stuffed into her mouth.

Her sister ran her hands admiringly across her chest.

"Looks good on me, doesn't it?" Abby grinned. "At least I fill it out!"

Even over the sound of her own coughing and the rattling of the train, Ellie could hear the titters of the two guys sitting across the aisle. Abby's chest was hardly something you could overlook at the best of times; in Ellie's new black-and-scarlet tube top it was totally in your face.

"I haven't even . . ." Ellie leaned across, grabbed the bottle of water on Abby's lap, and took a swig in an attempt to regain the power of speech. ". . . worn it yet!"

"I know," Abby grinned. "It's been hanging in your wardrobe for weeks, so I thought it deserved an airing."

"That is so rude of you!" Ellie hissed under her breath. "I was saving it for . . ."

"For what?" Abby demanded as the train plunged into the darkness of Clayton Tunnel. "You haven't been clubbing in ages, and you could count the number of parties you've been to on the fingers of one hand. I don't even know why you bought it in the first place."

"Because I am—I *was*—going to wear it to Verity's party next week," Ellie lied. In truth, she wouldn't have dared leave the house in it; she only bought it on impulse one day when Abby had been nagging at her to loosen up a bit. It had looked cool in the shop, and the assistant told her it enhanced her nearly nonexistent chest (though she didn't say it in those words, of course). Ellie glared at Abby, but her sister had already fished a magazine from her bag and was deeply engrossed in an article about snagging the perfect guy. Typical.

"Good magazine?" Ellie touched Abby's knee a few minutes later.

Abby smiled a little and nodded. That was so Ellie—always the first to make the peace after a row, always desperate to keep everyone happy. Sometimes Abby wished she could be more like her elder sister. It must be cool never to be so angry that you felt like your guts were going to burst all over the floor, never so miserable that you couldn't eat, speak, or sleep. But if Ellie never plummeted emotionally, she never flew, either. Seventeen years and three months and she'd never been seriously in love. And as far as Abby was concerned, that was majorly tragic.

The trouble was, Abby mused, staring out of the train window at the encroaching suburbs, Ellie lacked passion. She'd had a couple of boyfriends and apparently had snogged one of them in a fairly hands-on kind of way, but she was always so detached about them. You never caught Ellie writing "E ❤ F" all over her French folder, or skipping lacrosse practice to slip through the back hedge of the schoolyard and chat up the guys from Bishop Radford College next door. You never found her sobbing in a corner because a guy had ignored her at a party.

Even when Dad left to live with that little piece of lowlife, Plastic Pandora, Ellie had been all buttoned up and controlled about it. Georgie had cried and dropped her grades and gotten chubby from eating too much chocolate and cake; Abby had shouted and ranted at her father, thrown up a few times (stress frequently caused Abby to vomit), and bought her father a whole load of books written by psychologists about how tough divorce is on kids; Mum had sobbed for weeks. But Ellie had just sighed a lot and cooked the meals because their mum was falling apart and having migraines. In the end that had turned out to be a good thing since Ellie's cooking was so gross that Georgie dropped a bit of the cake-weight, and eventually their mother rallied enough to drive them to the Old Mill for supper rather than stomach another one of Ellie's meals.

"We're here!" Georgie's elbow driving into Abby's ribs broke her reverie as the train pulled into Victoria Station. "Come on. Quickly. Dad will be waiting!" Georgie was already scampering toward the train exit.

Abby stuffed her magazine back in her bag and stood up, irritated to find her stomach lurching in nervous antici-pation. She hoped Georgie was right, and that Pandora wouldn't be standing at the barrier, her arm hooked through Dad's, calling him Maxi Boy, as if Max weren't a perfectly acceptable name.

So Abby did what she always did in times of emotional crisis—pretended it was a movie and that she was the acclaimed and idolized star. Just thinking about it made her feel better: tragic, deserted child of millionaire leaves train, her eyes searching the platform as the wind catches her hair.

"There he is!" Georgie cried. "Hi, Dad!"

The pathos of the beautiful scene playing in Abby's head was shattered by the comic sight of their father, stand-ing at the turnstile, hands in the air, waving one of those happy birthday banners you stick on the wall at parties. He was chanting, "Here they come, here they come, here they come," like a drunken football hooligan.

"Dad!" Georgie hurtled down the few remaining meters of the platform and flung herself into her father's open arms.

Her father grinned, threw back his head, and burst into somewhat discordant song. "Happy birthday to you, happy birthday to you . . ." he warbled, totally oblivious to the smirks of passersby. Abby caught a whiff of pungent aftershave as she caught up with her sister.

"Dad, you're totally mad!" Abby planted a kiss on her father's cheek, love for her dotty father welling up inside her.

Her father gave her a hug, and Abby noticed that his hands were shaking.

"Not mad, just so pleased to see you all," Max said, pulling away from Abby and hugging Ellie. "Hi, sweetie. Congratulations on your French prize—what a triumph! And runner-up in the public speaking—is there no end to your talents?"

For a moment, Abby was overcome with jealousy. There she was, struggling to cram for her finals, struggling to pass, while everything Ellie touched seemed to turn to gold.

"Thanks, Dad," she heard Ellie say. "But it's Abby you should be congratulating—she was an absolute star as Juliet."

The jealousy vanished in an instant, and Abby impulsively squeezed Ellie's hand. Drama was her thing; she was good and she knew it. Which was just as well, really, since she had every intention of becoming the best thing on the West End stage since Dame Maggie Smith.

"I wish I could have been there, kiddo," Max said, "but as I said at the time, Pandy had one of her heads. . . ."

"I didn't know she had several," Abby murmured. "How unusual!"

Max threw her a sideways glance.

"Abby . . ." He cleared his throat and sighed.

"Shall we get a taxi, Dad? To the Dungeon?" Ellie poked Abby in the ribs and gave her a look.

"Good idea!" Max said, his good spirits returning in an instant as he steered them across the crowded concourse to the line of black cabs waiting outside. "And then we'll have lunch—I've booked a window table at Piggy P's."

"Ace!" grinned Georgie. "Can't wait."

"Isn't Pandora coming, Dad?" Abby asked, winking at Georgie.

"Afraid not," Max replied. "Thing is, she's got such a delicate stomach, bless her. Besides, the big wheel would get her vertigo going."

Georgie gave Abby and Ellie the thumbs-up sign behind her dad's back.

"But don't worry," he went on, "you'll see her when we go back to the apartment later."

"Go back?" Abby gasped. There was no way she could go tearing across London to her dad's flat when she had to be back in Brighton by seven-thirty to get to the club.

"I don't think we can do that," she began.

"Nonsense!" cried her father. "You couldn't come to London and not see our amazing new apartment, could you?"

"Watch me," Abby muttered.

"Besides, I've got presents for Georgie," Max added, "but they are too heavy for me to hike around town all day! So we'll go back for them later."

Oh, clever one, Dad, thought Abby wryly, as they clambered into the taxi. No way can we wriggle out of it now.

"Tooley Street, please—London Dungeon," Max instructed the driver before turning back to his girls. "Well now, isn't this fun? What did you get for your birthday, Georgie?"

"Sound system, mirror shades, baseball boots . . ." Georgie began.

Abby stared out of the cab window. There was zero chance socializing with Pandora was going to wreck her chances with Fergus. She had to make sure they were home by eight at the latest. She *had* to.

"Wow, I'm stuffed!" Ellie leaned back in her chair, rubbing her tummy. "That was a scrummy lunch. Thanks, Dad."

"The biggest meal I've had in a long time," her father grinned, standing up and fishing in his back pocket for his wallet.

"You do look thinner," Georgie ventured, as her father beckoned to the waiter.

"Great, isn't it?" Max replied. "Don't you think I'm looking good?"

To Ellie's embarrassment, he stood up and twirled around, right in front of the neighboring diners.

"Yeah, great," Ellie muttered hurriedly, even though she didn't mean it. She'd been looking at him all through lunch. His hair, which a month ago had been streaked with gray, was now a solid mahogany blob on top of his head, and his face looked gaunt and drawn.

"Pandy's put me on a fitness regime," he told them, handing his credit card to the maître d'. "No wheat, no dairy, lots of bean sprouts—and plenty of exercise."

That, thought Ellie, groaning inwardly, accounted for the trainers he was sporting with his jeans. They were so not Dad—he had always prided himself on his Italian loafers and highly polished English brogues.

"Pandy thinks that it's very . . ." Max began, only to stop in midsentence as the waiter returned to the table, his forehead puckered in a frown.

"I'm sorry, sir, but your credit card has been rejected."

"Rejected?" Max frowned as he stuffed his MasterCard

back into his wallet. "Can't imagine why. Not to worry, try this one."

He slapped his Visa card into the waiter's hand.

"Better get a move on, girls," he gabbled. "I've booked the London Eye for three o'clock."

He hustled them toward the door, tossing Abby's bag at her and shooing them with both hands.

"You three go out and hail a cab," he told them.

Abby and Georgie scuffled out to the street first, and Ellie's hand was on the doorknob when she heard the waiter's voice.

"I'm sorry, sir, but that card has also been rejected. I must ask you to pay in cash or with a guaranteed personal check."

Ellie hung back as her father fumbled in his breast pocket and pulled out his checkbook.

"Is everything okay, Dad?" she asked anxiously.

Her father laughed.

"Of course it is, sweetheart," he assured her. "Trouble is, you transfer funds from offshore accounts to pay bills and what happens? The idiots mess up the transactions. Nothing to worry about."

Ellie sighed with relief.

"That's okay, then," she said, slipping her arm through his. "Let's hit the big wheel!"

* * *

They were queuing for the London Eye when Abby whipped her mobile phone from her pocket.

"I won't be a minute, Dad," she said, edging away. "Just got to make a quick call, okay?

"Is that a new phone?" he queried, eyeing the tiny psychedelic-patterned phone in Abby's hand.

"Great, isn't it?" she enthused. "Mum got it for me after I did Juliet—it's a WAP. It does a whole load of stuff. You can send photos round the world, do e-mails, play games . . ."

"And send the bill for the whole damn lot to your father, I suppose?"

Abby's mouth dropped open.

"But then again, why not?" he ranted. "After all, I'm the bottomless pit of money, aren't I? Never mind the stock market crash, never mind falling interest rates. Good old Max, he'll sign the checks, never a murmur . . ."

"But, Dad," Abby burst out, her heart thumping in her chest as she realized that half the people in the queue were staring at her father. "You agreed—I mean, you've always paid our phone bills and you never said . . ."

Her father took a deep breath.

"'Course I have, love." He nodded. "And it's a great phone. I was only teasing you, silly. You've got to learn to take a joke."

Abby sighed with relief and began punching the keys.

"Do you have to do it now, Abby?" Ellie protested. "What's so important?"

Abby pretended not to hear. She was certainly not about to tell Ellie her master plan. It was far, *far* too good to risk sharing with her sister.

⚜ SECRET NO. 3 ⚜

Love is a bit like a doodle by van Gogh—
your lopsided circle could be a masterpiece to someone else

"Here we are!" Max cried as the lift juddered to a halt on the fifteenth floor of Wapping Heights, one of the most luxurious and exclusive buildings in London. "Just wait till you see the apartment. It'll blow your mind!"

Georgie sighed inwardly. Whenever Dad started to use what he thought was cool jargon, she got an ache deep down in her chest, a bit like the homesick feeling she'd had at Brownie camp when she was eight.

"Pandora, angel, we're back!" He ushered the girls through the tiny entrance lobby and into the huge sitting room. "Ta-da! What do you think?"

"Good grief, it's like an operating room!" The words were out before Georgie had time to stop them, but it didn't matter—Dad clearly didn't hear her. At that moment, Pandora came running across the clinically pristine room and hurled herself into Max's arms. She was wearing a pink-and-white lace dress with a fluffy cardigan and Perspex sandals and looked, Georgie thought, like a mobile meringue.

"Give your Pandy a kissy, then!"

Georgie's heart lurched, and she turned away. All the time they had been having lunch or fooling about at the shops, she had been able to pretend that nothing had really changed. She had even kidded herself that because Dad so clearly loved having them around, he'd wake up one morning very soon and come to his senses, tell Pandora that it had all been a huge mistake, pack his bags, and { 30 }come home to Holly House. But now, watching as Pandora wrapped herself around Max like a boa constrictor about to suffocate its prey, she was forced to acknowledge that a happy ending didn't look likely.

"Missed you, missed you, MISSED YOU!" Dad chanted, enveloping Pandora in a bearlike hug. He kissed the top of her bottle-blond hair.

"Missed yooooo too, gor-jus!" Pandora puckered her scarlet lips and made ridiculous kissing noises.

Abby nudged Georgie. "I think I'm going to vomit," she muttered in her ear.

"Make sure you do it all over her, then," Georgie whispered back, giving her hand a quick squeeze.

"So, what do you think?" Max finally managed to put three centimeters between himself and Pandora's enormous silicone-enhanced chest, and waved an arm airily round the apartment.

"It's very, um, white, isn't it?" Georgie remarked, gazing at the painted floorboards, bare walls, and billowing voiles at every window.

"And empty," added Ellie, perching awkwardly on the arm of a white leather sofa. She leaped to her feet as Pandora threw her a warning look. "Where are all your pictures and stuff?"

"We don't do 'stuff' anymore, do we, Maxi?" Pandora explained, flicking her immaculately manicured hand over the area where Ellie's backside had dared to touch the sofa. She had the kind of high-pitched voice that sounded like a tape being played at the wrong speed. "It's all about decluttering your surroundings, throwing out anything that doesn't enhance, uplift, and embrace your soul and spirit."

"So why hasn't she been chucked out, then?" Georgie hissed at Ellie.

"We've gone for the minimalist look, haven't we, Maxi darling?" Pandora twittered. "Just a few eye-catching features."

She waved a hand to indicate a vase containing one orchid (white), a few candles (white), and a large floor cushion that had the audacity to carry a splash of pink across one corner.

"My nephew Blake is very arty, bless him. He helped

me to capture the very essence of me in this place—purity, light, and freedom of spirit."

With more than a touch of rampant insanity, thought Georgie.

"Oh, speak of the devil!" Pandora giggled as the front door opened, and a gangly, sandy-haired guy in paint-spattered jeans and cowboy boots struggled in with a port-folio case and a huge camera bag. It occurred to Georgie that he looked rather too normal to be related to Pandora.

"Blake, just in time!" Max boomed. "Meet my girls. Ellie, Abby, and Georgie."

"Hey," Blake raised a hand and promptly dropped his portfolio case.

"Careful, Blake!" Pandora urged. "You'll chip the wood floor. Go and put that stuff away—you know I can't stand mess. And change your clothes—you look like a dropout."

Tell her to stuff it, thought Georgie savagely. Put paint on her stupid white walls, and see how she takes that! Sadly, Blake just nodded at Pandora and ambled out of the room.

"You never mentioned that you had someone staying," Ellie said to her father, as Pandora began anxiously rubbing invisible marks off the varnished floorboards. She wasn't sure quite why it mattered that this Blake was staying there, but it did.

"Didn't I?" Max murmured vaguely. "He's with us for a few weeks—he's got some problems at home. . . ."

"Max!" Pandora threw her father a warning glance.

Poor Blake, Ellie thought. Maybe that accounted for the rather dreamy, faraway look in those extraordinary gray-green eyes?

"Dad?" Abby asked, walking back toward her dad after checking on the invisible marks that Pandora was scrubbing at. "Where are all those things you brought from Holly House? I don't see any of them here."

She's right, thought Georgie. She glanced quickly around, searching for his collection of antique Toby jugs that they used to tease him about so much, the fading sepia photographs of Dashwoods of long ago parading in long dresses in the garden of Holly House, the lopsided head of Mum that he'd made when he first started sculpting. Come to think of it, thought Georgie, where was his potter's wheel, his kiln, all that gear that used to live in the old summerhouse behind the vegetable garden?

"You haven't chucked them, have you?" Ellie asked.

"No, darling, of course not, I—" Max didn't have the chance to finish his sentence before Pandora cut in.

"I had to be firm with him, silly old sausage," she tittered. "We don't want the junk from an old life cluttering up our new one, do we?" She didn't give anyone the chance to answer. "But then I thought, No, Pandora dear, you're being a real meanie. . . ."

"Clearly the first worthwhile thought to have crossed

your mind this millennium," Georgie quietly muttered and received a sharp nudge from Ellie.

". . . so we've turned the third bedroom into a little hidey-hole for your father, haven't we, babe?"

Max nodded.

"Come and look," he invited them, striding across the room, and throwing open a door. "Sweetheart, I expect the girls would like a drink."

"Sure," Pandora nodded, following Max and patting the odd stray hair back into place on his head. "What would you like—elderflower pressé, gentian and lime-flower cordial, or wheatgrass juice?"

"Um, could I just have a cup of tea?" Abby asked.

"Mango, mint, or chamomile with spiced apple?"

"Just regular tea?" Abby queried. "You know, in a tea bag. From India? Normal?"

"Sorry!" Pandora shook her head. "We don't do regular—too much tannin. It's so bad for the joints."

"Elderflower will be fine," Ellie intervened, desperate to avoid any more snide remarks from either of her sisters. "Georgie? Abby?"

"I guess," Abby sighed, pulling her mobile phone from her bag and flicking open the cover.

"I suppose," muttered Georgie, not because she didn't like elderflower—she did—but because she saw no reason to give in to Pandora's ridiculous fetishes.

Pandora nodded triumphantly, and tottered across the room to the kitchen. Georgie glimpsed a mass of gleaming stainless steel and an array of chrome-and-leather bar stools. It didn't look as if anyone had ever so much as eaten in there, let alone cooked.

"So you see," Max was saying, beckoning them into his den. "It's got everything important in it. Here are my photos of you three. . . ."

Aren't we important enough to be in the sitting room? thought Georgie, peering into her dad's den. At least it looked as if a human being occasionally sat down in it. And it wasn't white.

". . . and look, I've got my old desk, my CDs, and the paperweight Abby made at preschool and all my Holly House pictures."

Georgie gazed at the cluster of familiar photos on the pale gold walls. There was the one taken for Granny and Grampy's golden wedding when she was only five, the aerial shot of the house and gardens that Mum had done for his fortieth birthday, and her favorite, the one of all five of them with Bridie, their old flat-coat retriever in front of the Christmas tree. Bridie was dead now, and Georgie was convinced that the old dog had died of a broken heart after Max left them all.

"What about your potter's wheel and stuff?" Ellie butted in. "That's not here."

"No, I agreed to put it down in the caretaker's store-room, just until I find a little studio somewhere. Pandora's not keen on . . ."

"Speaking of wheels," Pandora interrupted, appearing at Ellie's elbow with a tray. "How was the big wheel?"

"Round," muttered Georgie. She looked across at Abby, expecting a thumbs-up for quick-wittedness, but her sister was standing by the window, fiddling with her mobile phone. "Oh, Dad, by the way, Mum sends you loads of love."

Okay, so she knew Abby had told Max that within the first few minutes of seeing him, but when she saw Pandora's pale face flush a livid purple, she knew it had been worth repeating.

"The wheel was great, thank you," Ellie said. "So, Dad, you're not going to give up sculpting, are you? I mean, you love it so much."

"Sculpting?" Blake reappeared in the doorway in clean jeans and a rugby shirt. He threw Max an admiring glance. "Max, you never told me you were into that type of thing. Can I see some of your stuff?"

"Well, I . . ." Max hesitated and Georgie couldn't help smiling to herself. Blake was in for a disappointment. Dad's skill at sculpture didn't quite match his enthusiasm; half the door stops at Holly House had started out as his attempts at Greek goddesses or birdbaths surrounded by overweight cherubs.

"He has no time for all that now, do you, Maxi Boy?" Pandora put the tray on the glass-topped coffee table and ran a hand over his shoulder, removing two stray hairs. "Our life is so full, what with tai chi on Mondays and Thursdays, and our shamanism sessions, and of course, the daily runs. . . ."

"Runs?" Georgie and Ellie gasped in unison. "Dad, *you* run?"

Even Abby stopped whispering into her phone and stared at him in astonishment. Georgie did her best to stifle her giggles.

Max nodded proudly, tapping his tummy.

"Now, then," Pandora announced, retreating into the kitchen again. "Do sit down. I've made a cake for Georgie."

For a moment, Georgie felt hugely guilty. She'd been thinking nothing but horrid thoughts about Pandora since they arrived, and now here she was, carrying a plate with an enormous cake.

"That's really kind, Pandora," Georgie said, and was rewarded with a quick hug from her father.

"Looks scrumptious," he enthused. "Can I have a slice?"

"I'll let you have the teeniest bit, honey, because it's gluten free and I've used soya instead of milk, and carob instead of chocolate, but remember to take it off your calorie allowance for today, won't you?"

If her father hadn't at that moment been rummaging in

a drawer and pulling out two parcels wrapped in fluorescent pink paper, Georgie would have been tempted to tell Pandora that calorie-counting was for dweebs with no self-esteem, but she didn't want to break the moment.

"Happy birthday, Georgie darling!" Her father slapped two hearty kisses on her cheeks and handed her the parcels.

Georgie ripped the paper off the first package and threw it on the floor. Immediately Pandora was at her side with a black garbage bag.

"Dad, that's ace!" She turned her brand-new skateboard over in her hands, spinning the wheels and running her hand over the deck. "I've always wanted an Alien Workshop board! Wait till Tom sees this!"

She dropped it on the floor and stepped on the board.

"No!" Pandora's cry of alarm ended in a high-pitched screech. "Not in here, for heaven's sake! You'll scratch the floor."

"Sorry," Georgie said, flicking the board with her toe and deftly catching it in one hand. Blake caught her eye and winked.

"Why don't you blow out your candles?" Blake suggested to Georgie. "Oh sorry, candle, singular." He eyed the pink-and-white-striped candle in the center of the cake solemnly.

"It's organic," Pandora murmured.

"The candle or the cake?" Blake inquired, and received a withering look from his aunt. Perhaps, thought Georgie, he's not that wet after all.

Georgie blew out the candle and Pandora began slicing tiny slices of cake onto paper plates.

"Open the other present!" Abby urged, glancing at her watch. "I really think we ought to get going soon."

"Oh, chill out," Georgie muttered, ripping the paper from the second parcel. "Wow!"

Her mouth fell open and she gazed awestruck at the digital camera in her hands.

"I thought you could take a whole load of pictures of all the things you get up to, and then e-mail them to me." Her dad laughed. "Come to think of it, get your sisters to snap you on the skateboard—action stuff, of course!"

{ 39 }

"I'll start practicing right now." She grinned, flicking through the instruction manual. "Give me five minutes. . . ."

"We haven't got five minutes," Abby protested, biting into her slice of cake. "If wedungoshasunim . . ."

"Pardon?" Ellie eyed her sister in confusion.

"I sheed, if wedongoshaysun . . ." Abby gave up, stuck a finger in her mouth and dislodged a lump of glutinous slop from her upper jaw. Pandora thrust a paper napkin under Abby's chin.

Georgie, who had just taken a bite from her slice of cake too, understood the problem. The cake—if you could call it that—was disgusting; it had the consistency of Play-Doh and the flavor of prunes mixed with licorice. No way could she eat it.

"Don't you like it?" Pandora looked hurt.

"Mmm, much too good to hurry," Georgie said with a smile. She dumped her plate and stood up. "Okay, I'm ready! Dad, you go over there by Abby, and Ellie, you sit in front, okay?"

Abby sighed and moved toward her father. Ellie took no notice. She was deep in conversation with Blake.

"Ellie!" ordered Georgie. "Over there."

She gestured toward the mock fireplace and held the camera to her eye.

"Wait for me!" Pandora dabbed at her mouth with a paper napkin and sidled over to Max, slipping her arm through his and gazing up at him with doe eyes.

Georgie bit her tongue. She didn't want the princess of plastic in the picture, but she could hardly say so. Reluctantly, she took the picture.

"Hey," she said, peering at the screen and vowing to delete it when Pandora wasn't looking. "Not bad. Now just Dad on his own. . . ."

"No, no," Pandora chirped. "Take one of all of us, out on the balcony. After all, I'm your new stepmother, aren't I? All one happy family together—that's what your Dad wants, isn't it, Maxi Boy?"

She grabbed Max by the arm and dragged him over to the balcony door, sliding it open and beckoning to Georgie and her sisters to follow.

"And you, too, Blake!" she ordered.

Blake shook his head.

"No way," he said. "I don't mind taking the shots but you're not getting me in the frame, that's for sure." He glanced at his watch. "Anyway, I'm out of here," he said. "Life class starts in half an hour."

"Life?" gulped Ellie. "Isn't that . . . ?"

"Nudes," laughed Max. "Sure, but when you're planning on being the next Salvador Dali . . ."

"Not nudes, actually," Blake burst in hastily, his cheeks flushing. "And Dali's not my thing."

"What is?" asked Ellie.

"Well, to be honest . . ."

"Excuse me," interjected Pandora, walking toward the French doors and gesturing to everyone to follow. "We're supposed to be taking photographs, not discussing your little hobbies. Now, then, aren't the views wonderful?" She gazed out over the rooftops to the River Thames, where a couple of barges were chugging slowly upstream past the ranks of cargo ships moored on the wharves. "Now, if you just take a shot of me pointing to the horizon, with everyone crowding around me. . . ."

Georgie had an overwhelming desire to push Pandora

over the edge and watch her plummet to the street below. Instead, she kicked the plate of revolting cake under the sofa, and grinned with satisfaction as a smear of chocolate icing stained the pristine leather. Blake gave her the thumbs-up sign as he headed for the door, which Georgie considered fairly decent, considering he'd probably end up getting the blame for the mess.

Georgie stomped out onto the balcony. Abby was glowering at her, tapping her hand on the balcony rail, and sighing; Ellie was gazing into space, smiling the sort of sickly smile that covers up a distinct desire to scream obscenities.

"No, no," Pandora shrieked as Georgie took the shot. "My profile's better this way—take one more."

She turned and smiled up at Max, puckering her lips in a silly, girly fashion.

"I want one of my Dad on his . . ." Georgie began again, shoving her father back into the sitting room and blocking Pandora's way. At that moment Abby's phone shrilled and she grabbed it like a drowning man seizing a life belt.

"Hello, yes? Oh, my God, no!" Her sister clamped a hand to her mouth and dropped into the nearest chair. "Is it bad? I can't bear it."

Her bottom lip quivered and she bit it.

"Abby, what is it? What's happened?" Ellie demanded anxiously. "What's wrong?"

Abby ignored her, her eyes wide with horror.

"He did? He does? I'm coming—I'm coming right now, okay? Bye!"

She stuffed her phone back in her pocket and leaped to her feet.

"I've got to go," she gasped, clamping her hand to her mouth and stifling a sob. "You all stay—I'll get a cab—I . . ."

"Darling, what on earth is it?" Max asked, an arm around Abby's shoulder. "What's happened?"

"It's Marcus." Abby stifled a sob. "There's been an accident. He's in the hospital, and his mum and dad are abroad on holiday, and he keeps asking for me, and I've got to go because . . ."

{ 43 }

"Of course you must go!" Her father was already scooping Georgie's skateboard into a carrier bag. "Pandora angel, phone for a mini cab, will you?"

He paused and turned to Georgie.

"Who is Marcus?" he mouthed at her. "Boyfriend?"

"Mmm," Georgie murmured noncommittally. After all, it didn't seem the right time to tell him that Abby had broken up with Marcus—her boyfriend of precisely nine weeks—over a month ago under less than friendly circumstances.

"Don't cry, Abby," Ellie was saying, hugging her sister and scooping up all their shopping bags. "I'll come with you. You don't have to do this on your own."

Abby looked at her sister in alarm.

"No, I don't want you to. I mean, we can't both desert Georgie on her birthday, can we? I'll get a taxi from the station, you tell Mum what's happened."

"We'll talk about it on the train," Ellie said, patting her hand.

"There's nothing to talk about!" For a moment, Abby's eyes flashed with anger. "I mean, honestly, I'll be fine."

"I want to take a picture of Dad before we go," Georgie half-whined. "Dad, stand over by the . . ."

"Georgie, not now," her dad insisted. "Abby's upset—we must get going. You can take my picture anytime."

"Yes, but . . ."

"I've got a meeting in Hove a week on Friday. I thought I'd pop along and take you out to supper afterward." He smiled at his three daughters. "We'll combine it with a photo shoot, okay?"

"Okay," Georgie grinned. "I'll be an expert by then."

"When you've quite finished," Abby butted in. "I've got to get the train, or I'll be late—I mean, Marcus will think I'm not coming."

That's when it clicked. How could she be late? Georgie thought. People lying prone on hospital beds weren't about to whiz off into the night. Abby was plotting something—Georgie was certain.

She didn't know just what her sister was up to as yet,

but with a bit of luck, and a bit of gentle blackmail, there just might be something in it for her.

"Ellie, wake up, we're nearly there."

Ellie's eyes flew open as Georgie nudged her in the ribs.

"You've been asleep all the way from London," Abby said accusingly, grabbing her bag from the overhead rack.

Ellie rubbed her hand over her aching temples. She hadn't slept, she had simply closed her eyes in order to think. About Dad, and Pandora, and the new flat.

And that guy Blake.

Dad had never invited them to stay with him—not at the old flat or the new one. But then, Blake had problems and, judging by the look on Pandora's face, pretty awful ones at that. After all, thought Ellie, they must be bad if he's willing to spend days on end with Pandora. Root canal work would be preferable.

"Frankly, I don't know how you could just nod off after everything that's happened," Abby persisted.

Immediately Ellie felt a pang of guilt.

"Oh, you mean, Marcus? I'm sorry, Abby, you must be feeling . . ."

"Marcus? No—well, I mean, yes, of course, Marcus," Abby stammered, slipping her arms into her jacket. "But what about Dad and . . . ?"

"So you noticed it too?" Ellie felt a wave of relief wash over her. "Didn't he look dreadful?"

"Slightly deficient on the fashion front, I admit," Abby grinned. "That shirt . . ."

"No, not that. I mean, he was so jumpy. I reckon . . ."

She stopped. No, it was too crazy. She was just letting her imagination run away with her. Dad just seemed off because of the weight loss. Nothing more.

"You reckon what?" Abby asked.

"Oh, just that he seemed a bit stressed, that's all," Ellie improvised hastily. After all, he *had* seemed stressed. For some reason Ellie couldn't get the scene in the restaurant where Dad's card was rejected out of her mind, and she wasn't certain that Dad had seemed as though he was joking about Abby's mobile phone, at all. Then again, Ellie was known as a worrywart.

"Huh," muttered Abby. "I'd be flipping stressed if I were living in that flat, too. Wall-to-wall bland. How could he bear to swap Holly House for that soulless box?"

She's right, thought Ellie. Holly House had meant the world to Dad. His parents, his grandparents, and even his great-grandparents had lived there; there were stories and memories in every corner of the eighteenth-century house that years ago had stood alone on a hilltop overlooking Brighton, its front windows gazing over the rooftops all the way to the English channel, and its rear ones looking out over the rolling sweep of the South Downs. Over the years the expanding town had encroached on the house, but even now, almost overtaken as it was by a mishmash of redbrick Victorian villas, mock Tudor semis, and squat postwar bungalows, it retained its spacious, set-apart atmosphere.

"No one's going to get their hands on Dashwood land, that's what your Grandpops used to say," Dad would tell them, recalling the story of how their grandfather had refused to sell off the land to property developers. "We've got it all—sea air, space, and the sound of birds to wake us in the morning."

Of course, Ellie and her sisters used to raise their eyebrows, tap their foreheads, and mutter about galloping senility and gross sentimentalism—but Dad would just smile and tell them that there were some things in life that were sacrosanct, and Holly House was one of them.

Well, he doesn't think that anymore, does he? Ellie thought bitterly, as the train lurched forward and crawled into the station. One come-hither giggle from Pandora and he just upped and walked away from the house—and from them. How could he endure being cooped up in a high-rise without a blade of grass in sight and pretend to love every minute of it?

"I've just had a thought," Ellie burst out as the train juddered to a halt in the station. "Maybe Dad . . ."

Stop it, she admonished herself fiercely. Okay, so she'd spotted a few letters on his desk with the words "Final demand" in red letters, but that didn't mean anything. Dad's memory was never good at the best of times.

"Hurry up," Abby was urging her, jumping from the train, grabbing her arm, and pulling her down the crowded platform. "I've got to grab a cab."

"There's no need to get a taxi," Ellie insisted, fishing her mobile phone out of her bag. "Mum's coming to pick us up as soon as we've phoned her—she'll drop you off."

"No!" Abby burst out, hitching her bag over her shoulder. "I mean, I just need to get there, you know what I mean? That train journey seemed to take forever. . . ."

Ellie nodded. She guessed that despite all her protestations to the contrary, Abby still had a bit of a thing going for Marcus.

"Okay, but before you go, ring Mum will you? My reception's terrible here."

"I haven't got time." Abby quickened her pace as they crossed the concourse toward the taxi rank.

"Give me your phone, I'll do it," Georgie offered, falling in step beside her. "I left mine at home."

Abby tossed the phone at her sister and joined the queue, tapping her foot impatiently as the row of taxis edged forward. Georgie flipped back the cover and began scrolling through the menu.

"Hurry up!" Abby urged, as an empty taxi pulled up beside them. "Just speed dial. It's number two!"

Ellie touched Abby's arm as Georgie punched the numbers.

"You're sure you don't want me to come with you? I mean, what if he's really badly hurt—you're not that good with blood and stuff."

"I'll be fine," Abby assured her. "I mean, the hospital said it wasn't critical."

She clambered into the taxi.

"Where to, love?" the driver asked, pausing to slurp coffee from a paper cup.

"The Sussex County Hospital," Ellie told him. "Which wing, Abby?"

"Wing? Oh, North, I think," she gabbled.

"There isn't a North wing," Georgie cut in. "It's East, West, and New."

"New, that's it," stammered Abby. "I knew it began with N."

The taxi driver quaffed the last of his coffee, tossed the cup into the nearby litter bin, and clicked the switch on the fare meter.

"You'll ring us when you need picking up, won't you, Abby?" Ellie called to her sister as the taxi began edging away from the curb.

Abby nodded as the cab inched forward. "But it might

be quite late," she called back at them. "You know, if Marcus is . . ." Her voice was drowned out by the sound of the taxi's engine.

Ellie waved and turned to Georgie. "Poor thing," she sighed. "I reckon she's in for a tough evening, don't you?"

Georgie muttered under her breath, something that sounded like "Hardly."

"What did you say?" Ellie demanded.

"Hard," Georgie replied, nodding gravely. "Very, very hard."

But even Ellie could see that Georgie knew something

she didn't.

⚜ SECRET NO. 4 ⚜

Very few things are worth taking a risk for—
love, family, and the prospect of a first kiss

She'd done it! Abby was here, at Club XS—the newest, trendiest club in town. And she was on the dance floor with Fergus. Okay, so it had taken nearly two hours before he'd asked her to dance but that was only because Melissa Peck, who was in the year above Abby and who everyone knew was a total slag, kept dragging him off, and he was too nice to tell her where to go. But Abby had seen him glance in her direction every few minutes, and the more great shapes she'd thrown on the dance floor the more he'd watched. The best bit had been the look on Melissa's face when Abby had shimmied past them, and Fergus had grabbed Abby's arm and sidled up next to her.

That one moment made it all worthwhile—bribing Phoebe to phone her at Dad's place and pretend to be the hospital receptionist; the battle to get past the bouncers by pretending she'd left her ID in her mate's pocket and he was inside; the pangs of conscience about inventing Marcus's accident, and the gnawing worry that Mum would find out the truth and she'd be grounded for eternity. None of that mattered now—she and Fergus were really connecting, and Abby knew full well that besides the fact that he was unbelievably hot, hooking up with an older guy from Bishop Radford was going to make her more popular than ever. When Abby glanced over Fergus's shoulder to see her friend Phoebe (who had legs up to her armpits and was no stranger herself to snagging hot older guys) watching her with envy, it confirmed how worth it this whole episode had been.

When she'd called Phoebe that afternoon to beg her to call and give the fake news about Marcus, Phoebe had insisted on coming along.

"What are you going to tell your Mum?" Abby had asked.

"The truth, of course," Phoebe had replied. "She doesn't care what I do these days—as long as she's got the house to herself and that nerd Vernon."

Abby sighed. Sometimes she thought life would be a lot easier if she had a laid-back, passion-seeking mother who cultivated men the way her mum cultivated freesias and hollyhocks.

Remembering Phoebe's words, Abby felt a pang of conscience. If Mum knew what she was doing, she would go ballistic. But she didn't, Abby reminded herself. And in a little while, she would kiss Fergus good-bye, grab a cab, go home, and give them the good news that Marcus wasn't half as badly injured as she'd thought, and that would be that.

"Cool club," she sighed into Fergus's neck as a slow song ended, and she tried to ignore the blisters on her feet from walking around London in her silver wedges. She ran her tongue over her top lip, the way that *J17* magazine said was a dead sexy turn-on.

"Are you thirsty?" Fergus asked, slipping his arm round her shoulder and guiding her toward the bar, which had tropical fish swimming under the glass-topped counter and stools in the shape of giant seashells. "What can I get you?"

"You can get me a fruit punch!" Melissa appeared at Fergus's left elbow, thrusting her chest in his direction. "The *passion* fruit variety."

The way she put all the stress on the word "passion" made Abby want to claw her eyes out. Or vomit. Either one, really.

"And then we'd better make tracks, yeah?" Melissa asked.

Abby's stomach lurched as Melissa nuzzled up to Fergus and gazed at him with her round, irritatingly pretty eyes.

"You're not leaving, surely?" Abby gasped. "I mean, it's only—oh cripes, it's nearly ten-thirty!"

"Bit late for you, is it, little one?" Melissa smirked at her condescendingly. "Time you were tucked up in bed?"

"Now, *there's* a good idea . . ." Fergus's witty innuendo was cut short when Melissa's kitten heel engaged with his left foot.

"To make tracks, I mean," he laughed hastily. "Coming, Abby? We're going to The Lighthouse—you know, over at Shoreham Harbour. They've got a dusk-till-dawn rave going on!"

Abby's heart sank. There was no way she could go. It was one thing to pull the wool over Mum's eyes for a couple of hours, but to dash ten miles down the coast for an all-nighter was out of the question. But then again, if she didn't go, Melissa would get her claws well and truly into Fergus, and she wouldn't stand a chance. She had to think of something, some way to keep Mum in the dark and get a few more hours to make Fergus fall hopelessly in love with her. . . .

And she had to do it in about ten seconds flat.

"Mum, you can't do this—Abby will kill me!" Georgie jumped in front of her mother and attempted to block her way to the front door. "Please, Mum!"

"What do you expect me to do?" Julia Dashwood demanded, slipping her arms into her cashmere jacket and grabbing her car keys. "Sit around here while my daughter is prancing around in that dreadful, seedy club?"

"Mum, it's not that bad," Ellie interrupted half-heartedly. "I mean, she is sixteen, after all."

"And if Abby finds out that it was me who told you about everything, I'll be dead meat," Georgie pleaded.

"By the time I've dealt with her, she won't be in any position to criticize anyone!" Julia stormed. "It's not just the club—although heaven knows, that's bad enough—it's the lies. And when I think of Marcus's poor mother . . ." She shook her head as words failed her.

"But—" Georgie started.

"Georgina, leave it!" Her mother pushed her out of the way and wrenched open the front door. A rush of cool night air sent a shiver down Georgie's spine. "Ellie, you come with me. Georgie, stay here, get ready for bed, and if Abby gets back, phone me, got it?"

The front door slammed and Georgie heard the car engine firing up and the scrunch of gravel as Julia and Ellie roared off down the drive.

She ambled through to the sitting room and began idly flicking through the pile of birthday cards still lying on the walnut coffee table. Why hadn't she kept her mouth shut? Come to think of it, why had she grabbed Abby's phone in the first place and offered to ring Mum? If she hadn't done that, she would never have scrolled through the CALLS RECEIVED menu and seen that it wasn't the hospital who had phoned Abby, but Phoebe Spicer.

Not that she had had any intention of dropping Abby in it—not at first. She'd reckoned that keeping quiet about those two being together deserved a ticket to the movies or enough cash for at least one session at the Snow Dome. But within minutes of getting home, things had gotten out of hand.

"What sort of accident? How bad is he? When did it happen?" Julia's questions came thick and fast.

Georgie shrugged.

"I don't know," she said. "Abby didn't say."

"She just said," Ellie interrupted, "that his parents were abroad, and he was asking for her."

That's when things got a bit sticky.

"Abroad?" Julia queried. "Nonsense. I saw Madeleine only yesterday at the hairdresser's. That woman is so gray, it's untrue. And the wrinkles!"

She patted her own immaculate golden-blond bob, and sighed.

"You must have misheard. I must phone her at once to see if we can help in any way."

"No!" Georgie blurted out. "I mean, she's probably at the hospital, and besides, maybe she was having her hair done to get ready for going on holiday and . . ."

"You could be right," her mother mused and for a second, Georgie thought the moment had passed. "Then again, if they're not there, they won't answer the phone, will they? And at least if I leave a message, they will know we're all thinking of them."

Georgie winced, remembering what had happened next—the phone call to Marcus's mother who had screamed into the phone and nearly fainted from shock until, by some stroke of good fortune Marcus had sauntered through the front door, large as life and without a scratch on him. The Spanish Inquisition that followed as soon as Julia hung up the phone had left Georgie with no option but to come clean about the call from Phoebe Spicer.

After calling Phoebe's mum and giving her an earful about responsible parenting, Julia slammed the phone down and stormed into the sitting room, her normally pale skin flushed.

"She's at Club XS!" She had made it sound as if Abby were at that very moment drinking cocktails with the leader of the local Mafia. And with that, she and Ellie had taken off in the car, leaving Georgie to sit and imagine how angry Abby would be when she found out.

The music was pumping through the club when Abby first noticed the crowd parting. Fergus was standing just in front of her, waiting for her to say whether or not she could come to the rave and Melissa was staring at him with her big stupid eyes. Abby was about to tell him, that yes, of course she'd join him—no way was she about to let Melissa get her slimy paws on Fergus without a fight—when she heard it. When she heard *her*.

"Abigail! Out! Now!"

It can't be, thought Abby. She closed her eyes for a second, willing her mother's crystal tones to fade alongside the music. Instead, they got louder.

"I mean it, Abigal!"

For a moment, Abby stood rooted to her spot on the dance floor, her mind racing as she stared disbelieving at her mother, who was standing, arms akimbo, in the middle of the crowd, the flashes from the strobe lighting making her look like a resurrected ghost.

How did she know where to come? Who told her? Abby's thoughts were spinning around her, in rhythm to the music.

"I said it was past your bedtime, didn't I?" Melissa jeered, nestling up to Fergus. "Anyway, we're off. Ciao!"

As she dragged Fergus toward the door, Abby prayed that he would turn and at least give her a wave, or grin at her, or acknowledge her presence somehow.

But he didn't. Melissa pulled him through the door, and if Abby was going to be completely honest about the whole thing, it didn't really look like he minded.

Please, God, Abby murmured silently in her head, let me die right now, okay? She could feel her face burning with the shame of it all as her mother grabbed her arm, and Abby caught Phoebe's eye.

"Bad luck!" Phoebe mouthed, and put her hand to her ear, mimicking a phone before ducking behind one of the gaping onlookers.

Julia dragged Abby toward the exit, pulling her through a sea of mocking faces. That's when she spotted Ellie lurking in the doorway.

"What are you grinning at?" Abby snapped at her sister, although in truth Ellie wasn't even smiling. "Enjoying the role of little Miss Perfect yet again, are you?"

The moment she'd said the words, she felt guilty. It wasn't Ellie's fault that they shared a mother who was still locked in the Stone Age.

"I tried to get her to stay in the car," Ellie whispered apologetically, as their mother stomped out onto the pavement, pushing a couple of people lighting up cigarettes out of the way in her frustration. "I tried to come in and get you alone, but she wouldn't have it."

"How did she find out?" Abby began, only to find herself being shoved unceremoniously into the back of the car with a curt "Seat belt! Now!"

"I found out," her mother interjected, "by phoning Marcus's mother to commiserate over his supposed accident."

She spat the words out and released the clutch with

such ferocity that the car lurched forward like a kangaroo on speed.

"Oh, no—was she—did she . . .?" Abby stammered.

"Have a heart attack? Collapse with fright? Almost—till Marcus showed up. That's when Georgie told me the truth."

"Georgie?" Abby glanced at Ellie. "How did she know anything?"

"Phone," muttered Ellie. "She scrolled through and . . ."

"The devious brat!" Abby sputtered, but she knew full well that faced with Mum in overdrive, anyone would have come clean.

"She didn't mean—" Ellie started.

"Never mind, it doesn't matter now," Abby said dejectedly.

"Oh, doesn't it?" her mother snapped. "I think it matters a great deal. You are grounded. For a month."

Ellie gasped. Surely her mum couldn't be that harsh?

"It doesn't matter," Abby shrugged. "After tonight no one will ever ask me out again. I'm a laughingstock, an outcast, a social pariah; and Fergus . . ."

She'd been doing so well. But the thought of Fergus, who by now was probably speeding to Shoreham with Melissa's head on his shoulder, finished her. She did what she'd been fighting against for the last ten minutes.

She burst into tears.

❦ SECRET NO. 5 ❦

Even mums have hearts

"I'll just take this up to Abby."

Ellie looked up from the *Sunday Times* the following { 61 } morning and smiled to herself as her mother piled hot crois-sants and fruit onto a breakfast tray.

"She's forgiven, then, is she?" Ellie asked, opening a kitchen drawer to find a pen for the crossword.

"No—yes—oh, I don't know!" Julia sounded exasper-ated and defeated at one and the same time. "Maybe I was a bit over the top . . ."

Just a tad, Ellie thought, but decided that silence was the best option.

"It's just that, it's so hard, being a single parent. . . ."

Ellie bit her tongue and counted silently to ten. Then she repeated the exercise, in German. It was all very well for her mum to moan about Abby being a drama queen, but it was pretty clear where she got it from. Her mother talked as if she were living in a high-rise on social security, rather than enjoying a five-bedroom house on an acre of beautiful gardens, with an ex-husband who paid all the bills.

Ellie swallowed. With all the drama of the previous evening, her worries about Dad had been pushed aside. But now an image of him swam before her eyes, as clear as if he were standing in front of her, leaning against the oven like he used to—bum warming, he'd called it.

"Dad looked really tired yesterday," she ventured, as her mother poured a glass of apple juice and balanced it on the tray.

"Really?" her mother replied curtly, pulling off her Laura Ashley apron and flinging it over the back of a chair. "I guess keeping up with someone just out of diapers would do that to you."

"What's for lunch?" Ellie cut in, determined not to let her mother move toward the self-pitying spiral that she could feel sneaking up on them.

"Roast chicken. Did you say tired, though?" Julia added anxiously.

"Pardon?"

"Dad—you said he was tired—I mean, not ill or anything?"

"No, he's fine," she reassured her mother, sorry now that she had brought it up. "Although, I did think . . ."

"Right, well, it's eleven o'clock," Julia interrupted Ellie. Perhaps she wasn't much in the mood for self-pity today either. "Surely that girl can't still be asleep? Mind you, all that throwing up last night must have worn her out. I hope she hasn't caught a bug at that awful XS place."

Ellie raised her eyebrows. "Mum, you know full well that Abby throws up the moment she doesn't get her own way," she snapped. "She's done it all her life."

"Right, well, I'm going up." Julia pushed past Ellie, kicking open the kitchen door with her foot.

Ellie shut the drawer she was searching in for a pen and opened another. As she scrabbled among the chaos for something to write with, she found a letter. And even though it wasn't in Ellie's nature to read what wasn't hers (except for an occasional peek in Abby's scarlet diary to see if she was still just blubbering on about dentist appointments and homework assignments), something about the note caught her eye.

Ellie began reading out loud, which was something she always did when she was nervous.

" 'Dear Mrs. Dashwood,

" 'Since we have received no reply to our several items of correspondence with yourself, and since the balance outstanding on your Visa card is now well in excess of your credit limit . . .' "

"Mum!" Ellie turned, but her mother was already

halfway up the stairs. She took a deep breath and read on.

"'. . . we must ask you to return your card immediately and to settle your account within seven days. In the event that you do not cooperate, we will have no option but to issue a court order for reclamation of outstanding . . .'"

"Oh, my God, Mum!" Ellie shouted. "Mum, come here!"

There was no reply. Ellie ran up the stairs two at a time, the letter clutched in her hand, and sped along the landing toward Abby's room.

The low murmur of voices stopped her in her tracks. Abby's bedroom door was closed, but Ellie could tell that Abby was crying, and Mum was making the sort of soothing noises that she used when they were tiny and fell over and got gravel in their knees. Ellie slumped down on the top stair to wait and began chewing her thumbnail.

A court order! It made Mum sound like some sort of criminal. What was Mum thinking about? Ellie had seen that the outstanding balance was over £9000. Sums like that didn't accumulate overnight, not even with Mum's spending ability. Besides, her mother said she sent all the bills to Dad and he paid them.

But clearly he wasn't paying them anymore.

Ellie wheeled around as Abby's door opened, and her mum came out, looking slightly flushed.

"Mum, I need to talk to you," Ellie began and then hesitated when her mother held up a hand.

"No more talking until I've had a strong cup of tea," she declared.

Ellie followed her mother down the stairs and into the kitchen.

"Is Abby okay?" she asked.

Her mother turned the tap and filled the kettle.

"I guess," she sighed. "We've declared a truce, put it that way. She will never, ever go anywhere without telling me, and I'll try to loosen up a bit about curfews and clubs." She shuddered on the final word as if the mere thought of such places was more than she could bear. "And she will spend every evening between now and exams studying—heaven knows she needs to. Those mock results were dire, and if she doesn't pull her socks up before the real thing . . ."

"Mum," Ellie ventured, before her mother could get carried away over Abby's lack of academic prowess. "I found this."

"What's that, dear?" Her mother flicked the switch on the kettle and threw a couple of tea bags into the teapot.

"It's from the credit card company," Ellie replied. "It says that you owe them a load of money and . . ."

"Elinor! Since when has it been appropriate for you to read my private correspondence?"

Ellie tried to bite her tongue but it didn't work.

"Since you started filing it in the kitchen cutlery drawer," she retorted. "Mum, this is important."

Her mother frowned.

"Give it to me," she demanded, snatching the letter and scanning her eyes across it. "Oh, I've dealt with that."

She tossed the letter onto the table, and Ellie sighed with relief.

"Thank goodness," she murmured. "So, you paid it?"

"Well, of course *I* didn't pay it," she laughed. "Your father did. You know he looks after all that sort of stuff."

Ellie took a deep breath. "And he's really cleared it? All of it?"

"Of course, darling," her mother assured her, but Ellie didn't feel so reassured.

꧁ SECRET NO. 6 ꧂

*There's nothing like a bit of competition to make you want something
(or someone) more than you probably should*

St. Ethelreda's School had stood high on the cliffs overlooking the English Channel for nearly 300 years, its redbrick
façade and octagonal bell tower visible for miles along the
coast. Surrounded by rolling sports fields, all-weather tennis
courts, and two lacrosse pitches, the exterior still bore the air
of the stately home it had once been—although Mrs.
Eveline Passmore, the headmistress (a woman of large but-
tocks and little humor whose upper lip had never seen the
effects of depilatory cream) was apt to comment that the
behavior of some of her girls must cause the ghosts of past
Lords of the Manor to turn in their graves.

All three Dashwood sisters loved St. Ethelreda's,
although for totally different reasons. For Ellie, it was the
vast library with its floor-to-ceiling shelves, oak-paneled
recesses, and huge bay windows—a place where she
could lose herself in books without anyone interrupting; for

Georgie, it was the sports hall, the swimming pool, the play-ing fields—anything, in fact, that gave her a break from studying—and outdoors smelling the sea air; for Abby, the best thing about St. Ethelreda's, apart from the purpose-built theatre and dramatic arts center, was its proximity to Bishop Radford College. She had chosen computer design as one of her GCSE options for the simple reason that the com-puter room windows overlooked the college playing fields, where the neighboring boys' school practiced rugby.

Sadly, drooling and swooning had not, Abby reflected the following Friday, featured very highly in her week. For one thing, it hadn't stop raining for the last three days and all outdoor sports had been canceled. For another, Melissa had arrived at school on Monday morning, arm in arm with two of her snooty mates, and made a beeline for Abby.

"Abigail! Out! Now!" Melissa had jeered in a voice which, had Abby not felt so totally humiliated, she would have had to admit was an exact replica of her mother's stri-dent tones in the nightclub.

"Like Fergus said, little girls shouldn't play big girls' games," Melissa added, as the bell rang for registration.

"Fergus said that?" The words were out before Abby could stop herself.

"Along with other things," Melissa reported. "Oh, and just one other thing. Fergus and me—we're an item. So just back off, baby face."

While Abby had howled her eyes out, Phoebe had reasoned that she should be looking on the bright side.

"I mean, look at it this way," Phoebe had pleaded, stuffing paper tissues into Abby's hand. "If Melissa didn't see you as a threat, she wouldn't have bothered warning you to back off. Stands to reason—Fergus fancies you, and Melissa's dead worried."

Abby had clung on to that hope all week, even on Tuesday when Melissa flashed a friendship bracelet under her nose ("at least it's not a ring," Phoebe reasoned), and Wednesday when she saw Fergus dropping Melissa off at the school gates in his MG Midget ("not just Melissa," Phoebe reminded her. "Chrissie and Justine as well"). She bombarded Ellie, who was in Melissa's class, with questions about what she was saying, how she was looking, whether Fergus rang her on her mobile phone in the lunch hour, but as usual Ellie was useless.

On Thursday, Melissa was not at school. Abby's mood swung from joyful anticipation of dire tragedy ("Maybe she's got some terrible illness and will be housebound for weeks!") to sheer dread ("Perhaps she and Fergus have eloped"). When Abby ate, she felt sick; when she slept, she dreamed of Fergus jeering at her, one arm around Melissa. She couldn't concentrate in class and already had a detention for failing to hand in homework on time.

Then, in the school dining hall, just at the very moment

Abby pushed her plate of vegetable lasagna toward Phoebe, Ellie came over to their table.

"Why are you looking so miserable?" Ellie asked, slinging her purple-and-gold blazer over her shoulder and grinning at her sister. "The sun's out, the afternoon lacrosse game is on. . . ."

"It's pretty bloody obvious why I'm miserable," Abby retorted. "Not that you'd understand since the only thing to turn you on is some boring old Day Car book. . . ."

"Descartes," Ellie corrected her, making a big show of inspecting her fingernails. "I just thought that you'd be pretty chuffed—you know, with all that's happened with Melissa and . . ."

"What? What's happened?" Abby jumped to her feet. "Tell me."

"I don't know all the details, of course. . . ."

"Never mind details, just talk! Talk!" Abby demanded.

"Melissa was crying in French class and I asked why, and she said—well, I don't remember exactly what she said, but it was something like—"

"Get on with it, Ellie!"

"Well, Melissa told me to get lost, and according to Verity, Fergus dumped her last night. Something about her being self-centered and always wanting her own way. . . ."

"Yes! Yes!" Abby punched the air in delight. "Did she say anything else?"

"No—oh, just that apparently Fergus is rugby mad, and the rumor is that Melissa refuses to do the girlfriend-on-the-touchline bit because she hates getting cold."

"That's it! Oh, my God, that's it!" Abby flung her arms around her sister's neck and hugged her. "Ellie, you're a star! You've just given me my life back."

"Abby, you can't do this," Phoebe urged her at the end of the afternoon as they headed for the locker room to change out of their outfits. "You've got detention, remember?"

"I know, and I'll do the detention," Abby assured her. "All you have to do is buy some time for me."

"Why me?"

"Because you're my friend, because you love me, and because this is one of those crucial, life-changing moments when my whole destiny hangs in the balance. . . ."

"Okay, okay, I get the message," sighed Phoebe, opening her locker and stuffing her lacrosse cleats inside. "What do I have to do?"

"You just go and tell Mrs. Gourlay that I've gone to the nurse's office. Say I've got period pains. . . ."

"You used that one last week and the week before," Phoebe reminded her. "There's only so many periods you can have in one month."

"Fine, say I look really pale and faint, and you're worried that I've got mental burnout, okay?"

"Like she's really going to swallow that one," teased Phoebe, slamming the locker door shut. "And what if she comes looking for you? It's not worth the risk."

"Of course it's worth the risk," Abby told her, glancing at her watch. "Fergus has got rugby training, right?"

"So?"

"So, all I have to do is be there, look enthusiastic, clap when he gets a goal . . ."

"They don't *get goals*," laughed Phoebe. "They *score a try*."

"Whatever," snapped Abby. "I'll stay just long enough for him to see that I'm the sort of girlfriend he needs and then I'll scoot back to the detention room, apologize, clutch my stomach pitifully, and do detention. Simple!"

Abby grabbed her blazer, threw it around her shoulders, and fumbled in the pocket for her lip gloss.

"How do I look? Is my hair okay? Should I put eyeliner on?"

Phoebe gave her a friendly shove.

"Just go," she ordered. "Before I change my mind."

Abby grinned, and pushed her way through the clusters of girls thronging around the students' exit. She ran across the quadrangle toward the playing fields, her heart pounding in anticipation of seeing Fergus. But as she reached the school driveway, she saw something that almost sent her into immediate cardiac arrest.

Her mother's silver BMW was swinging through the school gates and screeching to a halt outside the main entrance, sending showers of gravel in all directions.

"I don't believe this." Abby swore under her breath. What on earth was her mother doing here? Ellie couldn't be in trouble and Georgie . . .

Of course—Georgie. She was going off with Tom and his mum that evening, down to Dorset for the Zorbing day tomorrow. They were going to spend the night at Tom's grandmother's, and Mum had arranged to fetch her and drop her over at Tom's after school.

The coast was clear. Over the fence she could see the Bishop Radford rugby squad doing their warm-up exercises at the far side of the games field. Any minute now, they'd run around the perimeter of the field to warm up, and she'd be there, and Fergus would see the look of enthusiasm and devotion on her face.

Abby smoothed her shirt down as she prepared to climb over the fence. She knew that as soon as Fergus saw her, he would know that she was the one.

"Mum? Couldn't you have waited in the car park like every other parent?" Georgie charged up to her mother, who was sitting in one of the high-backed oak chairs outside the headmistress's study. "It's dead embarrassing when you hover around like I'm some eight-year-old kid. . . ."

She stopped dead as Julia turned to face her. Her mum looked as if she had seen a ghost, and her hand, clutching a sheaf of papers, was shaking.

"Georgie, go and get in the car," she told her. "I have to see Mrs. Passmore."

"Why?" Georgie gasped. "You haven't seen my report card yet, and if it's about that acid burn on the lab floor, I can explain."

A faint smile crossed her mum's face and faded as fast as it had come.

"It's not about you," she sighed. "It's just business."

"What business?" Georgie asked.

"It's got nothing to do with you," her mother snapped. "I just intend to tell that woman precisely what I think. . . ." But Julia's tirade was interrupted when the office door swung open and Mrs. Passmore was on the other side. "Oh, Mrs. Passmore! There you are."

Mrs. Dashwood leaped to her feet and the head-mistress, clad from head to foot in black velveteen and looking a tad less friendly than the Ice Queen, boomed, "Come in, come in. So glad you finally saw fit to drop by."

The door closed firmly behind them. Georgie looked quickly over her shoulder and then edged toward the door, straining to make sense of the low murmurs inside.

". . . a silly mistake . . . ?"

". . . hardly, there has been no check for nearly five months. . . ."

". . . perhaps lost in the system . . . ?"

". . . my staff never loses anything. . . . Mr. Dashwood is not answering calls. . . ."

". . . running multinational conglomerates takes time, Mrs. Passmore. . . ."

Georgie was just beginning to make a bit of sense of the conversation when a hand landed on her shoulder. Georgie wheeled around, halfhearted excuses already forming in her head.

"Oh, it's you," she sighed with relief, as Ellie pulled her away from the door. "Mum's in there with Mrs. P. I was trying to listen, till you came along."

"What have you done this time?" Ellie asked with a grin. "Not skateboarding in the staff car park again, surely?"

"No," she retorted. "And the scratch on Mrs. P's car wasn't even visible to the naked eye. Anyway, they're not talking about me—for once."

Ellie frowned. "So what's going on?"

"Couldn't hear much—something about checks. I hope they hurry up, though—I'm supposed to leave for Dorset any minute. Hang on, I think they're coming. Scoot!"

They flew along the corridor and were halfway down the stairs to the students' exit by the time the study door opened.

"I will see that this is sorted by Monday, Mrs. Passmore," Georgie heard her mother trill. "And please, in the future, just remember that my ex-husband is a force to be reckoned with in the city."

"Go, girl!" Georgie whispered. "It's time someone put that old cow in her place."

Ellie simply sighed and said nothing.

"I feel pretty, oh so pretty, I feel pretty and witty and . . ."

"Oh, Abby," Ellie said as her sister flew into the kitchen and perched on one of the huge milk churns that served as stools.

". . . and I pity any girl who isn't me tonight. He saw me!"

"Who saw you?" Ellie sighed, ripping the top off a container of yogurt.

"Fergus. He looked at me twice in the first five minutes of rugby practice, and I swear that when they all got into that huddle thing . . ."

"I assume you mean a scrum?"

"Yeah, that—well he kind of burst out of it, and stared at me straight in the face, kind of with yearning, you know? I think I've cracked it!"

"Cracked what?" Her mother burst into the room. "Don't tell me you've broken another lacrosse stick. You really are . . ."

"No, Mum—I was talking about my math homework."

She's a quick thinker, I'll give her that, thought Ellie, winking at Abby.

"Well, as you've cracked it," Julia murmured sweetly, taking a spoon of yogurt from Ellie's carton, "shouldn't you go and write it all down? Before you forget how to do it?"

"Sure!" Abby was clearly in an A-1 good mood. *"I feel pretty, oh so pretty . . ."*

She danced out of the kitchen, blowing kisses with both hands, movie-star style, as she kicked the door shut behind her.

As Abby hopped up the stairs, the phone in the hall shrilled.

"That might be your father," Julia gasped. "I left a message on his answer phone. Stir the sauce, Ellie."

Her mother dashed into the hall and grabbed the phone, and the image of Pandora's nephew Blake flashed in Ellie's mind. How could someone so interesting—never mind handsome—be related to that twit Pandora? Must be by marriage, Ellie decided.

"Hello? Oh, Georgie, it's you. No, darling, no of course I'm not disappointed, I'm thrilled—are you safely there? Lovely!"

"Now, do be careful. . . ." Ellie mouthed to their cat, Manderley, who was eyeing the half-empty yogurt container hopefully. "Make sure . . ."

"Now, do be careful," her mother's voice resounded

from the hall. "Make sure you follow all the safety instructions and if you change your mind . . . no, well I know you won't, but if you do . . ."

Ellie put the carton on the floor, and Manderley stuck a pink tongue gratefully into its depths. From upstairs came the thud-thud of Agro Rampant's latest hit, punctuated with Abby's slightly discordant singing.

"Georgie's arrived in Dorset," her mother said, coming back into the room and closing the door. "I'm not happy about this Zorbing, you know."

"She'll be fine, Mum," Ellie assured her. "At least she's not bungee jumping."

"Of course, it's all down to the divorce, you know," Julia muttered through gritted teeth. "She's going off the rails—kids from broken homes do that, it's a proven statistic."

"Mum! Georgie is not going off the rails, she's been a daredevil all her life. You can hardly blame Dad—I mean, I know you're worried about the school fees. . . ."

"I am not worried," her mother declared. "I just want your father to give that opinionated Mrs. Passmore a piece of his mind! Trying to say he hasn't paid the fees. As if."

"Yes, but what if she's right?"

"Don't be ridiculous, Ellie," her mother retorted. "You know full well your father's primary concern is for you three girls. He'd use his last penny to see you right."

"I know, Mum," Ellie nodded.

"Anyway," Julia continued, grabbing her wax jacket, "I'm going down to the garden to pick some mint. Chuck me the flashlight, will you? Does your sister have to have that racket blaring quite so loudly?" Julia flicked on the torch and stomped out of the back door, muttering under her breath.

The door had hardly slammed behind her, when the telephone in the hallway shrilled again.

"Mum . . ." Ellie began and then stopped. No point in calling her mother until she knew it was Dad, and besides, Ellie did hope to have a word with him. She ran to the hall and grabbed the phone.

"Hello? Ellie Dashwood speaking. . . . who? Blake!"

For some inexplicable reason, her heart lurched.

"Sorry, I can't hear . . . hang on."

She covered the mouthpiece and yelled up the stairs.

"Abby, turn it down—I'm on the phone!"

Realizing that it was pointless to try to make herself heard over the din, she grabbed the handset and darted through to the den. Sticking a finger in her left ear, she tried again.

"Sorry, I'm back. Total chaos over here—my sister . . ." She knew she was babbling, but somehow her tongue appeared to have taken on a life of its own. "Anyway, how's things your end? How's the painting . . ."

But Blake interrupted her before she could go on.

"Ellie," he said quietly, "are you sitting down?"

That was the last thing she'd hear before her life changed forever.

She'd read in books about people's blood running cold, but she had always thought it was just poetic license. Perching on the arm of the old armchair that had been her father's favorite, she knew it actually happened.

"When? Where? But . . . Oh, God. You mean . . . yes, at once. Okay. Bye."

She let the phone fall from her hand, her heart racing and nausea rising in her throat. Her hands were shaking, and when she stood up, her legs felt as if they were about to buckle underneath her.

Keep calm, she told herself firmly, taking a deep breath. *Tell Mum. Get Abby. You've got to keep calm. It'll be okay—it's going to be fine.*

She repeated the words, mantralike, as she ran down the hall, through the kitchen and out the back door into the garden.

"Mum!" she yelled. "Mum, come here!"

Through the dusk, she could make out the pinpoint of light as her mother emerged from the herb garden, waving the torch. Ellie ran across the lawn toward her.

"It's Dad. . . ." Ellie began.

"About time, too," Julia said. "Thank heaven for that—I'll just take my boots off and . . ."

"No, Mum," Ellie cried, grabbing her arm. "Dad's not on the phone. He's in the hospital. He's had a heart attack."

Even in the dark, Ellie could see the color drain from her mother's face. "Mum, Blake rang. The hospital asked him to. They say we've got to go. Now. They say . . ."

Her voice shook and she could feel the bile rising in her throat.

". . . they say it's critical. Mum, I think Dad's dying."

⚜ SECRET NO. 7 ⚜

Nothing hurts more than a heart broken without warning

"I'm scared." Abby closed her eyes and tried to breathe deeply as her mother maneuvered the car through the barriers of the Chelsea and Westminster Hospital parking lot.

"It'll be okay, though, won't it?" she said for the fifth time in as many minutes. "I mean, they can do heaps for heart problems these days, can't they? Pacemakers and bypass surgery and stuff."

"Of course they can," her mother replied confidently, ramming the stick shift into park and switching off the engine.

The knots in Abby's stomach tightened, and the palms of her hands felt cold and sweaty at the same time. She hated hospitals at the best of times. Everything about them scared her: the awful smell of disinfectant mixed with unspeakable secretions, the sight of people lying on trolleys groaning in pain, and the way those wretched fluorescent lights made even the healthiest visitor look like the walking dead. Once, when Georgie had taken a tumble—

"Georgie!" Abby gasped. "We haven't told Georgie."

"Until we know more, there's no point," her mother reasoned. "She'd be asleep now anyway, and she's got this treat tomorrow. Ellie and I agreed she can come up and see Dad on Sunday."

A familiar stab of jealousy pierced through Abby's anxiety.

"Oh, Ellie and you agreed, did you? Well, I don't agree. What if Sunday's too late—what if Dad's . . . ?" She stopped. What was she saying? Dad would be fine. He *had* to be fine. "I didn't mean—it's just that . . ."

Ellie reached out and touched her hand.

"It's okay," she whispered. "We'll call Georgie in the morning."

Abby clutched Ellie's hand. Her sister could be an awful pain and a goody-goody, but she was brilliant in a crisis.

"You two better get going." Julia released her seat belt and switched on the courtesy light.

"But, Mum, you're coming too, surely?" Abby gasped.

"I can't come." Her mother's voice was calm but firm. "Pandora . . ."

"To hell with Pandora!" Abby burst out. "This isn't about Pandora—it's about Dad. We're his family, not that slag."

"She's his wife, Abby—she's the one he chose to be with."

Abby saw her mother's lip tremble as she turned away.

"Oh, Mum, don't feel like that," she pleaded. "He's ill, he'll be scared, he'll want you, I know he will."

"You have to be there, Mum," Ellie pleaded. "For all our sakes."

To the girls' relief, Julia nodded slowly, sighed, and opened the car door.

"I'll come as far as the ward," she said, putting an arm around both of them for a quick hug. "Tell you what, we'll find a hotel, and then you'll be able to visit him again in the morning. What do you say to that?"

Abby's heart lifted slightly. "The Gore? Can we stay there? That is such a cool place!"

She caught her sister's eye and guilt washed over her.

"Sorry," she whispered. "Sorry."

None of them spoke as they walked down the corridor, the clatter of their heels breaking the late evening silence.

"Please, God, let him be okay," Ellie prayed quietly, fingering the cross and chain around her neck, the one her dad had given her when she was confirmed. "I'll do anything as long as you make Dad well. Please. Please."

"This is it." Her mum pointed to double doors marked *CCU*. She read, "'Press green button for admittance.'"

Ellie pressed.

"Yes?" A voice echoed through the speaker unit at the side of the door.

"We've come to see our father, Max Dashwood," Ellie stammered, moving closer to the speaker.

"Ah. Right. Just a minute."

They waited, the silence broken only by the sound of Abby gnawing at her fingernails. The door opened and the staff nurse smiled at them.

"Come in," she said. "I'm Roxanne—now, if you'd just like to wait in here. . . ."

She pointed to a door marked RELATIVES' ROOM.

"We'd really like to see our dad," Ellie said. "We've driven all the way from Sussex."

"I'll only keep you a moment," Roxanne said, opening the door and ushering them in. "Can I get you a tea? Coffee? No?"

She turned to go, just as a tall, broad-shouldered guy in a white coat stepped quietly into the room.

"I'm Dr. Nisbet, and I'm looking after Max." His voice was soft, with a pronounced Scottish lilt.

"How is he?" Ellie demanded.

"You're his daughters?" the doctor queried, looking from Ellie to Abby and back again.

Ellie nodded.

"And you are . . . ?" He turned to Julia.

"She's his wife," Abby said. "Come on . . ."

"I'm his ex-wife. I'm here because the girls need me."

Ellie's heart went out to her mum. She knew that Julia was here because there was nowhere else on earth she would be; she had never stopped loving Max, and Ellie could see it on her brave face more now than even the days after he'd left, when she'd cried and sputtered on about how they'd first met.

"Of course, if Pandora . . . if the new Mrs. Dashwood doesn't want . . ." Julia began edging toward the door.

"Mrs. Dashwood is taking a bit of time out—having a meal downstairs in the cafeteria," the doctor said.

"Cow! How could she eat at a time like this?" Abby protested.

The doctor raised his left eyebrow a fraction of a millimeter.

"I do have to warn you that your father is a very sick man," he went on gently. "Very sick indeed. You'll see a lot of wires, and machines, and we have had to catheterize him, so . . ."

"It's okay," Ellie burst in. "We understand."

She didn't want explanations. She wanted to see her dad.

Dr. Nisbet nodded and stood back to let them through the door. Ellie snatched Abby's hand and held on to it tightly, the way she used to when they rode roller coasters.

"In here," he said, gesturing with his arm.

Ellie took a deep breath, and they followed him into the room, past a couple of old men wheezing on daybeds, and over to a curtained cubicle. The doctor pulled back the curtains, and nothing, not all the words he had said, not all the episodes of *ER* or *Hospital Alert*, could have prepared them for what they saw.

Their father lay on his back, his face gray, his lips tinged with blue. He looked somehow much smaller without his clothes. The skin of his neck lay in folds against the pristine white of the hospital gown, his mouth was half-open, a thin tube resting between his lips. Behind his head, a monitor bleeped.

"Oh, Max, my love . . ." Julia burst.

The lump in Ellie's throat doubled as her mother moved from behind them to the bedside and tenderly took one of Max's limp hands. Beside her, Abby was stifling sobs.

"He will be okay, won't he?" Ellie murmured as the doctor moved to one side.

"We will do everything in our power," the doctor reassured her. Raising his voice, he moved toward Max.

"Not giving up yet, are we, old chap?" he said, smiling at Ellie. "He's not conscious, but he can probably hear everything at some level. Just chat to him normally. And sound positive, okay?"

Ellie nodded, swallowing hard.

"Now, you stay with him and I'll just send a nurse along to check his obs. Observation, blood pressure . . ."

"I know." Ellie smiled. "I watch *Casualty*."

She squeezed Abby's hand.

"Come on, Abby, you heard what the doctor said. We've got to talk to Dad, be normal."

"Hi, Dad," Abby muttered. "Are you okay? Well, no obviously you're not, but . . ." She faltered. "I can't do this. I'm going to be sick."

She clamped a hand to her mouth and flew out of the room.

Julia went to follow Abby, but first she leaned over Max and brushed her lips briefly against his forehead.

Ellie noticed that tiny beads of perspiration dotted his brow like dew on grass in the early morning. Was that right? Was that meant to happen?

"Mum, is he . . . ?"

"I'll be back in a minute, Ellie," Julia said, closing the door behind her. "Just keep talking to him."

Ellie pulled a canvas chair up to the side of the bed and gingerly touched her dad's hand.

"Hi, Dad, it's Ellie," she began. "Georgie's gone Zorbing with Tom, otherwise she'd be here too. She'll come on Sunday, though, tell you all about it. . . ."

She faltered. She'd never talked to an inert body before.

". . . she's dead excited about it—not that I'd want to roll down some vertical hill in a big plastic ball, but you know Georgie—never happy unless she's risking life and limb on some death-defying stunt!"

Was that a movement? Did his eyelids flicker?

"Dad?"

Her eyes strayed to the monitor above the bed, the wavy lines going up and down, up and down, up and . . .

Then they stopped.

A straight line on the screen. No wavy bits.

An alarm blared.

"No! Help, someone help!"

She heard a voice screaming. Footsteps running.

Then the doctor's strident tones, "He's in VF! Call the CRASH team!"

"Dad, Dad! No, Dad!" someone was shouting. They shouldn't shout, Ellie thought. Not in a hospital.

An arm around her shoulder, a voice in her ear. "Best you wait outside. . . . Doing all we can. . . ."

And then the doctor's voice, urgent and demanding: "Quickly, everyone, we're losing him."

Ellie sat motionless, staring at the wall in front of her. A picture of a pond with ducks and a windmill; a few notices about "Bring-and-Buy Sales in aid of the Nurses' Home Refurbishment and the Kidney Dialysis Unit"; a phone number for bereavement counseling . . . She snapped her eyes away as the door opened.

"Mum?" She jumped to her feet and then sank back in the chair. "Oh, it's you, Pandora."

Pandora burst into the room, threw her bag onto the nearest chair, and began pacing the room.

"You're here? How come . . . ? I was going to phone later but . . ."

"Blake phoned," Ellie mumbled. "He said . . ." Before she could finish, Pandora gabbled on.

"God, this place is so incompetent!" She began drumming her long, French-manicured fingernails on the window ledge. "Of course, I'm having Max moved—we'll go private . . ."

"Pandora, have they told you what's happening?" Ellie burst in, her voice wavering.

"What's happening is that some trumped-up nurse—probably not even fully qualified for all I know—tells me I can't go in and see him because, well, I don't know why! Why they can't talk in plain English and . . ." She stopped in midflow as the door opened and Ellie's mum burst in, closely followed by a pale-faced Abby, clutching a plastic tumbler of water.

"What's going on?" Julia demanded before seeing Pandora. "They wouldn't let us back in—oh, Pandora. How are you?"

"How do you bloody think I am?" Pandora stormed. "I haven't had any sleep, the cafeteria serves a load of junk food—do you know, they didn't even have chamomile tea, and they call themselves a hospital. I've had to send Blake home for some proper food and . . ."

"I hardly think that matters right now," Julia retorted, looking more baffled than angry.

"No, you're right, of course." Pandora looked abashed. "I'm so worried, I can't think straight. Sorry."

"So what happened, exactly?" Julia asked gently.

"He just collapsed. I mean, it all happened so fast. We were out jogging and he sort of keeled over and . . ."

"Jogging? And that was your idea, I suppose?" Abby stormed, chucking the plastic cup into the waste bin. "You stupid . . ."

"Abby, enough!" Julia said, as Roxanne the staff nurse, came into the room.

Julia turned to face her. "Can you throw some light on just what is going on?"

The nurse touched her arm gently.

"The thing is," she began, "your husband's had . . ."

"He is *my* husband, not hers!" Pandora snapped. "Can't you even get that right?"

"Sorry, I wasn't told." Roxanne let her gaze go around to each of them. "The thing is, Mr. Dashwood's had a bit of a setback. The doctor will come by in a minute to talk to you."

"What do you mean, *setback*?" gasped Julia, but the nurse had already scuttled off. Ellie thought how odd it was that nurse's shoes always squeaked; you wouldn't think that would be allowed in a place like a hospital, would you? So irritating. Then again, she was beginning to realize that the voice screaming earlier had been her own.

"Ellie, what happened?" Her mother shook her arm.

Ellie broke her gaze from the wall.

"I was just sitting there, trying to talk normally, and then the machine just stopped. Those wavy lines, they all went straight."

"You don't mean . . . ?" Julia grabbed the back of the chair to support herself just as the door opened yet again and Dr. Nisbet stepped into the room.

And before he spoke, Ellie knew. Before he had said a word, her blood was turning to ice in her veins.

". . . did all we could. . . . heart simply gave out. . . . so very sorry." The doctor's words washed over her, seeming to come from a long way away.

"You mean—you don't mean . . . he's dead?" Her mum's words ended in a sob.

"Dead? Max? He can't be. . . ." Pandora clamped her hand to her mouth and turned away. "Maxi—no, no, no."

"I'm afraid he died despite all our efforts," the doctor said. "His heart really was in a very bad way."

"NOOOOO!" Abby let out an ear-piercing wail, flew

across the room and began beating her fists against Pandora's shaking shoulders. "You killed him! You killed my dad! I hate you, I hate . . ."

Pandora staggered, a look of genuine fear on her face. "It wasn't my fault—I didn't do anything. . . ."

Ellie leaped to her feet and in an instant had grabbed Abby by the arms and pulled her away. "Abby, stop it," she shouted. "It's not Pandora's fault. . . ."

It's mine, she thought. Mine for telling him about Georgie rolling down a hill in a Zorb. Ellie was suddenly sure the shock had tipped him over the edge.

"It is!" Abby wailed, tossing her head from side to side and fighting Ellie off with her elbows. "She made him go jogging! If she hadn't made him, he'd be alive now and . . ." Abby's knees crumpled, and she sagged to the floor, rocking backward and forward, tears streaming down her face.

Julia put her arms around Abby and helped her to a chair. For one awful, fleeting moment, Ellie wanted to shake her sister. As usual, she was taking center stage—didn't she realize that they were all in this? That they all loved him? Pandora standing there, running her fingers endlessly through her hair; Mum, hands shaking, trying so hard to be strong; and Ellie herself, feeling numb, dead inside, as if she were playing a part in some far-fetched, third-rate TV drama with the sort of plot that everyone knows just can't be real.

"He said he enjoyed the jogging." Pandora's voice was flat as she turned to face Ellie. "He said that he wanted to get fit so that we'd have years and years together to . . ." Her voice broke and her shoulders heaved.

Julia went over and touched her hand. "I'm sure it was nothing to do with jogging," she said gently. "You shouldn't blame yourself. . . ."

"I don't!" Pandora spun around and faced Julia, her moment of weakness clearly over. "I blame you, actually. All those years when you stuffed him full of red meat and cheese and . . ."

"It's not Mum's fault," Abby screeched. "You killed his spirit—you made him give up everything he ever loved—you murdered him!"

"How dare you!" Pandora countered, her face dark red. "He was happier in the one year we were together than he'd ever been with . . ."

"Now, now this isn't going to help any of you, is it?" Dr. Nesbit intervened. "Mr. Dashwood was a grown man—what he ate, and how he lived was up to him. His heart was diseased, his arteries all furred up. None of you are to blame."

"I want to see him." Ellie was surprised at the strength of her own voice.

"Darling, no, I don't think that's a good idea," Julia began.

"I want to see him." She repeated the words slowly and firmly and turned to the doctor. "Can I do that?"

"Of course," he said. "I'll just make sure he's ready."

He slipped out of the room, closing the door quietly behind him.

"He makes it sound like Dad's gone upstairs to change for a dinner party," Abby said, and burst out laughing. The laughter got louder, more shrill, more uncontrolled until she was wailing and hitting her head with her bunched-up fists, her whole body shaking.

And suddenly, Ellie couldn't take any more.

She walked out of the room.

{ 95 }

But even then, standing in the corridor, with no one watching, she couldn't cry.

"Miss Dashwood," Dr. Nesbit tapped her, "you can come in now."

Ellie entered, but inside it wasn't Dad. Just a look-alike body, the closed eyelids pale and waxy, the long fingers splayed still and rigid against the white sheet. Dad—the vibrant, bouncy, fun-loving Dad she had known her whole life was gone.

"I love you, Dad," she whispered. "I love you so much."

And still the tears wouldn't come.

When she finally left the room, after holding the hand that she couldn't imagine had ever been her dad's, she bumped directly into Blake.

"I'm so sorry. Really. I just don't know what to say," Blake said, clutching a Marks and Spencer shopping bag. He touched Ellie's arm as she stood, eyes half closed, in the hospital corridor.

"Thanks," she said, thinking as she said it how utterly stupid the word sounded.

"Are you okay? I mean, can I do anything?"

Ellie shook her head.

"I guess you need to see to Pandora," she whispered. Get her off our backs, she thought silently. Take her away.

"I'll get her home," Blake assured her. "She's the last thing you need to cope with right now."

As he disappeared toward the Relatives' Room, it occurred to Ellie that he was the first guy she'd met besides her dad who didn't need to have things spelled out in words of one syllable.

Abby's head throbbed. Her face ached. Her eyeballs were burning in their sockets, and her guts were heaving. Dead. Dead. Dad is dead.

Abby lay in the hotel bed as the shriek of ambulances from the nearby hospital rang through the room, and whispered the words under her breath. How could it be? Only last weekend, he'd been laughing and joking and spoiling them rotten at the shops.

"I love to give my girls a good time!" His words rang in her head.

"No, no, no!" She bolted upright in the bed, bunching her fists and rubbing them violently against her eyes. "Dad, dad, dad. . . ."

"Abby, it's okay! Abby, wake up, it's me, it's Ellie—you're dreaming. . . ."

"I'm not dreaming. . . . I just want him—I just want him back."

Ellie held her sister tight, trying to make the comforting noises that their mother had raised them with.

"I hope Pandora drops dead," Abby sobbed. "Murderer!"

"I know," Ellie nodded, tears beginning to trickle down her cheeks.

Abby looked at her sister, a little shocked at her tears. Ellie could read it on her face.

"He was my dad, too, you know," Ellie said, the anger rising in her stomach and her voice at the same time. "Just because you were his favorite, even though I worked my tail off—"

"Ellie, no, stop," Abby said. "It was never like that."

"Well, it was to me," Ellie said, stifling a sob.

"Come," was all Abby said. She opened her arms and folded them around her sister. And then, for the first time in as long as she could remember, Ellie wept and wept as though her heart would break.

❦ SECRET NO. 8 ❦

*There is nothing you should be gentler with than love—
except possibly newborn kittens*

"Okay, Zorbanauts! Are you ready?" The Sportsextreme attendant grinned and gave Georgie and Tom a friendly shove into the Zorb.

For an instant, Georgie's stomach lurched as she asked herself just what she was doing inside a gigantic, clear plastic inflatable ball poised at the top of a steep ramp on a windy Saturday morning.

"You okay? I mean, you can get out if you don't want to do it," Tom began.

"Get out? Who do you think I am?" Georgie protested. *Get a grip*, she told herself firmly.

"Okay, here we go now, folks!"

With a jolt, the huge ball launched itself off the ramp and began rolling down the steep hill. One minute Georgie was staring at the grass, scattered with dandelions and the odd cowslip, the next she was staring up at the sky, the next spinning, seemingly out of control, Tom's grinning face flashing past hers.

"You okay?" Tom shouted above the vibration of the ball.

"Yeah!" she yelled back.

Just then the ball lurched over a ridge, picked up speed, and hurtled at breakneck speed toward the bushes at the bottom of the hill. Georgie opened her mouth to speak but the words wouldn't come—a huge rush of air went spiraling down her throat.

And then as suddenly as it had started, the ball came to rest, Georgie hanging upside down, Tom lying next to her, laughing his head off.

"That was totally surreal!" Georgie cried, as the cone-like hole at the side of the ball was opened by a guy wearing a sweatshirt that said *Adrenalin Junkies, Inc.* "Thank you so much, Tom."

Tom grinned and gestured to the attendant.

"This is the guy you have to thank," he told her. "Josh, meet Georgie."

"Glad to meet you, Georgie. Of course, that was pretty tame, really." He winked at Tom. "But I guess that was about as much as you could take, being a girl and all."

"What?" Georgie exploded, all thoughts of growing up shoved to one side. "I'll have you know I went rappelling down the Seven Sisters cliffs, I've done paragliding and scuba diving and I would have gone caving, only my mother . . ."

"Go on, Josh," urged Tom, stifling a giggle. "Tell her before she bursts a blood vessel."

He glanced up the hill, where his mother was running toward them, her hand clutching her chest.

"Quickly! Before my mother gets here!"

Josh laughed.

"How would you like to HydroZorb?" he asked. "Same as before, only we fill the ball with a couple of buckets of water. It's ace—bit like a cross between a roller coaster and a waterfall."

"Cool!" Georgie burst out. "But actually, I don't think . . . I mean, how much does it cost?" No way was she going to land Tom's mum with paying out loads of money.

"Free," Josh laughed. "We want to take some pictures for our new brochure, and the boss thought you two guys would give just the right image."

"Image of what?" Tom's mother panted up to them. "Sheer unmitigated stupidity? Total recklessness? Never, ever put me through something like that again!" she gasped.

"It was ace, Mrs. Eastment," Georgie assured her. "You should try it."

"I would rather face a den of starving lions," Tom's mother assured her dryly. "Here's your camera, Georgie. I took a few great shots, although I don't think you'd better show them to your poor mother. She'd have heart failure."

"I'm going to e-mail them to Dad," she said. "He wants me to keep him updated on everything I do."

"Brave man," murmured Tom's mum. "Now, then, how about lunch? There's a nice pizza place just a few miles down the road."

"We're doing it again," Tom interjected firmly. "With water this time."

Mrs. Eastment closed her eyes and groaned.

"Tom, no, my nerves won't stand it."

"But you're not going to be the one doing it," Tom protested. "Come on, Mum, it's not like you to be a wimp. It's usually Georgie's mum who worries."

{ 101 }

Georgie saw the color flood his face as he realized what he was saying.

"Precisely!" Mrs. Eastment responded triumphantly. "What would Mrs. Dashwood say? I can't let her daughter . . ."

"I'll call her," Georgie said. "It'll be fine—trust me."

She scooted a few meters up the hill, made a big show of punching numbers on her mobile phone, mouthed a few words, and then gave the thumbs-up sign to Tom. She had learned something from her sister Abby over the years, that was for sure.

"She's cool about it," she declared, crossing her fingers behind her back and grinning at Tom's mum. "So let's go!"

Mrs. Eastment sighed, "Well, if you're sure your mother's comfortable with the idea."

Georgie nodded furiously, trying to quell the rising guilt of her fake phone call.

"This is just the best day ever," she declared. "I'll never forget it!"

"I can't go in." Abby stood on the threshold of Max's apartment, tears streaming down her face. "It'll just remind me of when we were here last week with Dad."

"Darling, this isn't about us. It's about what Dad would have wanted. Now, trust me." She pressed the bell and almost at once the door was opened by a white-faced Pandora, who took one look at them and burst into tears.

"I can't cope with all this," she sobbed, sinking into the nearest chair. "My psyche is all over the place and my aura is fragmenting."

"Really? Dear me, how painful," murmured Julia, looking around the flat in obvious amazement. "Now, can we help in some way? Phone someone?"

"My sister's coming down," she sniffed. "And Blake's here, of course. He's just gone out for some herbal tranquilizers."

"That's good!" Abby could tell that her mother was highly relieved at not having to cope with Pandora for long.

"It's so unfair," Pandora went on, "that I should be robbed of him after such a short time. . . ."

"Oh, and you don't think you were unfair to Mum, snatching Dad away from her and treating him like some tame puppy. . . ."

"Enough, Abby," Julia interrupted. "This is not the time or the place."

Pandora sniffed.

"I'm sorry," she mumbled. "He was your dad. I'm sorry. I know it's been hard for you all. It's just that I don't know where to begin. There's the funeral to be arranged . . ."

"That's up to us," Julia said firmly.

"No," Pandora retorted. "He was my husband."

"Indeed he was." Julia smiled sweetly. "But in his will he specified that he wanted his funeral at St. Peter's in Brighton, and his ashes to be scattered over the South Downs."

"Oh. Well, he was about to make a new will—we were discussing it only a week ago," Pandora stammered.

"Well, as he didn't, the old one stands, doesn't it?" Julia smiled. "I'll phone the funeral directors tomorrow. Don't you worry about a thing."

Abby saw that Ellie was as gobsmacked as she was at her mother's assertiveness. If only Dad could see her now, Abby was sure he'd have a change of heart about her.

Julia picked up her bag and ushered the girls to the door.

"I'll be in touch about the arrangements," she said. "Oh, and do take care of your aura, won't you, my dear?"

They were almost back at Holly House when Julia's mobile phone rang from the depths of her handbag.

"Get that, Ellie—oh, no, leave it—I can't face talking to anyone yet."

Ellie swallowed hard and slid her hand into her mother's bag, pulling out the phone.

"It's a text message," she told her. "From Georgie. Tom's mum will be dropping her off in ten minutes."

Her mother bit her lip and turned toward Ellie. "When they get here . . . I mean, would you—could you tell her, Ellie? You're better at these things."

"Mum, I can't." Ellie protested. "What could I say? Oh, hi, Georgie, how was your weekend? Oh, and by the way, Dad died."

"No, you're right. It's my job," Julia sighed. "I'm her mother, after all. And the poor mite's fatherless and . . ."

"You'll be fine at it," Ellie assured her. "Abby and I will disappear, and then . . ."

"No!" her mother gasped. "You must be there—we've got to support one another through all this. There's so much to think about—choosing the coffin, the hymns . . ."

"You were dead cool, the way you dealt with Pandora, Mum." Abby broke the silence that she'd maintained for almost the entire journey from London. "About the arrangements and everything."

Her mother sighed as she drove the car through the gates and up the drive toward the house.

"I was a bit hard, I suppose," she admitted. "She did love him, after all. I'll make it up to her, though—let her choose the music or something."

Abby frowned. "So we can't stop her from coming, then?"

"Don't be ridiculous, Abby," Ellie protested. "She has every right to be there."

"I didn't know murderers were free to roam the countryside at will," Abby muttered.

Ellie reached into the backseat and squeezed her hand. As her mother maneuvered the car toward the front door, she stared out the window. Suddenly, everything she looked at reminded her of her father. The cracked birdbath that he had made when he started sculpting; the leaded light window by the front door with "Maximilian Dashwood 1959" scratched onto it by the young, rebellious Max who had grown up here; the sonic mole traps that he'd insisted would expel wildlife at twenty paces, but never did.

Julia switched off the car engine, but none of them moved. It was as if they all knew that the moment they went inside the house, they would have to face the enormity of it all. It reminded Ellie of the days after Bridie died; none of them could face looking at her empty basket, scattered with her rubber toys, yet none of them had the heart to get rid of it. Facing the house was going to be like one giant Bridie basket.

The drone of a car engine broke their silence.

"Georgie. It's Georgie," Ellie murmured, as Mrs. Eastment's battered Volvo came up the drive. "What do we do? How do we tell her?"

The car pulled up next to them, the door opened and Georgie leaped out, closely followed by Tom. Julia, Ellie, and Abby stumbled out of the car as Georgie came running toward them.

"Mum, it was awesome! Honestly, you've never seen anything like it—there was this huge ball—and it went so fast, and I've got some wicked photos to send to Dad, and Tom and me are getting our pictures in a brochure and . . . Mum? Mum?"

Julia, tears streaming down her face, enveloped Georgie in a hug.

"Julia, dear?" Margie Eastment pressed the lock button on her key chain until the car beeped, and came anxiously toward Julia. "Is something wrong? It wasn't that dangerous, I promise you."

Ellie stepped forward and touched Georgie's shoulder. "Georgie, listen. There's something we have to tell you. It's about Dad. He . . ." She closed her eyes, as if not seeing Georgie's face might help.

"What about Dad?"

"He had a heart attack on Friday," Ellie began.

Her mother squatted down and cupped Georgie's face in her hands.

"Georgie, darling, Dad died early this morning. I'm so, so sorry."

It was, thought Ellie, as if the entire universe were holding its breath. Like the freeze-frame when you zap the video button to go and get more chocolate. Like those stills they sell you at Disney World, when a moment on a roller coaster is captured forever—everyone's mouths open or eyes closed, hair flying wildly about.

Then, slowly, the picture moved on. Georgie's eyes widened, her mouth became a wide, round, gaping hole. Tom's mother clamped her hands to her mouth; Tom took two steps backward, gripping his mum's arm.

And then Georgie screamed.

Georgie didn't know how long it had been since she had run away from the house, or how long she had been up here on the path to the old windmill. The sun was low in the sky, and she had a stitch in her side, and her cheeks burned from the constant flow of salty tears. It was as if a dam had burst inside her and everything—tears, memories, guilt—were all spilling out onto the chalky path.

She had run and run for as long as her body would

keep going, trying not to think about what her mum and Ellie had said. But it didn't work. Their words kept echoing through Georgie's mind.

"I was there, by the bed, when it happened," Ellie had told her. "We'd all been there—talking to him and holding his hand, so he knew he wasn't alone."

That was the worst bit. They'd all been there and she hadn't.

Even Pandora had been there.

"I hate you, I hate you, I hate you!" Georgie's shouts echoed across the cliffs, as she hammered her heels up and down on the scrubby grass, causing a flock of screeching gulls to fly into the air in alarm.

"Hate who?"

A shadow fell across her outstretched legs.

Tom jumped off his bike and let it fall to the ground.

"Get away! Get lost!" The words came out as broken sobs. She couldn't let Tom see her like this; one of the main reasons he was her mate was because he said she wasn't a wet fart like most girls he knew. "I said leave me alone!"

She turned away, desperate to hide her tears from him. Tom didn't move an inch, which didn't really surprise her, because he never did anything unless he really wanted to— and that was one of the main reasons that he was her mate, as well.

"Want some gum?" he said, pulling a somewhat mangled strip from the pocket of his jeans. "I bought chocolate as well, but I dropped it and now it's covered with grass."

Georgie sniffed.

"Dad did that once with an ice lolly and Bridie ate it, stick and all."

"I'm sorry," Tom said. "About your dad. Bloody bad luck."

"Bad luck? It's not luck, you stupid moron," she yelled. "She did it. She killed him—that Pandora cow!"

"I doubt it." Tom sounded totally unfazed. "Come on, we're going home."

{ 109 }

He bent to pick up his bike.

"What do you mean, you doubt it?" Georgie snapped, wiping her eyes with the back of her hand and staring at him in disbelief. "And I'm not going anywhere."

"I doubt that even Pandora would murder her husband in broad daylight on a jogging path in the middle of London," he reasoned. "And you are coming home, because your sister said that if I found you, she'd give me five pounds. I've found you and now I want paying."

To her astonishment, Georgie found herself smiling.

"I'll come if you split it fifty–fifty with me," she decided.

"Seventy-five–twenty-five," Tom parried. "I did the finding, after all."

"Sixty-forty and that's my final offer," she said, repeating their long-standing game.

Suddenly she gasped and turned to Tom, her eyes filling with tears again.

"How could I do that?" she gasped. "How could I be so awful? Dad's dead, and I'm playing dumb games with you?"

For a moment Tom didn't say a word. He kicked at a clod of earth lying on the path and then bit his thumbnail.

"I guess he'd be pleased, in a funny kind of way," he mumbled after a moment, avoiding Georgie's eye.

"Remember what he used to say?"

"What?" Georgie frowned.

"He said that Ellie is his clever kid, Abby is the feisty one, but you—Georgie—are the tough nut that no one can crack."

"I don't feel tough," whispered Georgie. "I feel small and tired and angry and . . ." She hesitated.

"And what?" Tom asked.

"Nothing," she said.

"Go on," he urged. "You feel small, tired, angry, and what?"

"Hungry," sighed Georgie. "Have you still got that chocolate?

⚜ SECRET NO. 9 ⚜

Your heart is the one thing no one can take from you—
at least not until you decide to give it away

DASHWOOD: Suddenly, in London, MAXIMILIAN
FREDERICK, adored husband of Pandora and father of
Elinor, Abigail, and Georgina. Funeral service will be
held at St. Peter's Church, Brighton on April 7th at 12
noon followed by cremation at Downs Crematorium,
Bear Road, Brighton. All enquiries to T. L. Marchant,
Funeral Directors, 33 Montpelier Road, Brighton

"How dare she! The cow!"

Abby slammed *The Daily Telegraph* down on the
kitchen table and stabbed at the death announcement with
her finger.

"No way is she getting away with that," she stormed.

Her mother looked up from the pile of mail in front
of her.

"She already has," she sighed. "Besides, what's wrong
with it?"

"What's wrong with it?" Abby thundered. "*Adored hus-band of Pandora?* And what about you?"

"I'm nothing now. . . ."

"And then she just puts *father of Elinor, Abigail, and Georgina,* like we don't adore or love him at all. Well, I'm not having it!"

"Not having what?" Ellie ambled through the back door with an armful of daffodils, her skin still blotchy from a night of crying. "Where do you want these, Mum?"

Julia motioned toward the table weakly, and Ellie settled into a chair. All the days seemed to be merging into one for Ellie. In the daytime, she felt dead inside, like a robot pro-grammed to do the tasks her mother couldn't face. At night, she dreamed. Always the same dream: Dad lying on that bed, white and still, and then dissolving until there was noth-ing left but a tiny damp patch. She would wake to find the pillow wet with tears, and she'd sob and sob until her head throbbed too much to sleep.

"Mr. Diplock will be here any minute," Julia said, break-ing Ellie's trance.

"Why is he coming anyway?" Ellie asked. "I know he's Dad's lawyer, but surely he could wait till after the funeral?"

"I don't know," Julia said. She shrugged. "Said he had something important to discuss that wouldn't keep."

"Ellie, read this!" Abby thrust the paper under her sister's nose, and Ellie scanned the announcement. "Isn't that just the pits?"

Ellie glanced at the notice and sighed.

"It's awful seeing it in black and white, I guess," she murmured.

"Not that—what she's put." She wheeled around to face her mother. "You said she couldn't do all this stuff."

"I said she couldn't alter the funeral arrangements," her mother corrected her. "What else she does is up to her. She's his wife—widow—whatever."

"Well, anyway, the wording on this is all wrong and I'm going to make sure . . ."

At that moment, the front doorbell rang.

"Oh, my goodness, he's here already!" Julia leaped to her feet and scooped up the pile of condolence cards in her arms. "Abby, let him in. Ellie, do those flowers. Georgie—where's Georgie?"

"With Tom," Ellie said. "He's being brilliant—getting her to help him build a skateboard ramp to take her mind off things. Should I get her?"

"No, let her be." Julia shook her head, slipped off her apron and ran her hands through her hair. "I'll get rid of Mr. Diplock as quickly as I can. There's so much to do and besides, Pandora can deal with all the legal stuff. Get off her backside for once."

Abby shot a glance at Ellie and gave her a quick

thumbs-up sign. It was always easier to cope with Mum when she was in a feisty mood. She just hoped it would last.

"Don't go, Elinor." Mr. Diplock, her father's longtime lawyer, motioned for Ellie to stay in the room. "I—er—I think it would be a good idea if the whole family were together to hear what I have to say," he suggested. "Just to make sure that you all understand the implications."

"The implications of what?" Julia sounded distracted. "I have quite a lot to get through before the funeral on Friday."

"Exactly," said the solicitor in a soothing tone. "So perhaps we could call the other two girls? Make a start."

As Ellie went in search of Abby and Georgie, it occurred to her that James Diplock looked as drawn and strained as any of them.

By the time she found Abby, who was scribbling away frantically in her diary (which looked, Ellie noted, a bit different from the journal Ellie had peeked in before), and Georgie, who was halfheartedly watching Tom knock nails into a piece of wood, her mother and James Diplock had pulled chairs up to the mahogany dining table. There were sheaves of paper spread out its entire length.

"Right," he began nervously after the girls had sat down. Abby and Ellie perched on the sagging sofa and Georgie, as usual, knelt on the floor. "As you know, I've been Max's solicitor for some years now, and for most of that time, he was happy to follow my directive."

What does he mean—most of the time? Ellie thought.

"You've been wonderful," Julia assured him. "The divorce settlement that you drew up has been a godsend."

"Yes, well," coughed James. "There was, however, one thing over which I failed totally to influence him."

Ellie frowned. "What is it?"

"A few months ago, business went badly for Max. He'd sunk hundreds of thousands into a couple of new ventures that went base over apex. Moreover, the stock market was plunging and his personal expenses were soaring. His new wife . . ."

". . . is a total cow!" interjected Georgie.

"Georgina!" Julia snapped.

James hurried on, "Anyway, he was getting into fairly deep financial difficulties." He took a deep breath. "So he did something drastic—I begged him not to, but . . ."

"What did he do?" Ellie demanded. "Can you get to the point, please?"

"Elinor, your manners," her mother snapped. Clearly, thought Ellie, her mother was more taken up with the niceties of etiquette than with the drama unfolding in front of them.

"He put Holly House into his new wife's name," James blurted out. "He'd already borrowed a couple of hundred thousand by putting the London apartment up as credit, and he must have known he'd lose that if things failed to get better."

Ellie's mind was racing. She wasn't going to be a lawyer for nothing. "And that means . . ." Ellie began, but the words wouldn't come out.

"It means," continued James gently, "that Pandora now owns this house, lock, stock, and barrel."

"Dear God, no!" Julia turned pale and clutched her throat. "But how—I mean, this house has been in the family for generations."

Abby gasped.

"You must have got it wrong—Dad would never give Holly House to anyone," she stammered.

"I'm sure he thought he was putting it into safe hands for you four," James assured them. "Keeping it safe and out of the way of his creditors, until things began to look up."

"But if Mum and Dad owned the house together, surely it reverts to her?" Ellie began, but James held up his hand.

"That's the problem, Elinor dear," he sighed. "They didn't. Max owned it outright, which meant that creditors could have seized it, but it also meant that he could sign it over to the new Mrs. Dashwood without much fuss, as well."

Ellie's heart ached as her mother visibly cringed at the term "the new Mrs. Dashwood."

"You may recall that many times over the years, long

before your—well, your difficulties—I met with you both and suggested it go into joint names."

"You did?" Julia sounded vague, and Ellie had a great desire to shake her.

"Of course, Max kept saying he'd get round to it, but you know what his memory was like. He never did put your name on the property title, and that meant he could do whatever he liked with the property without consulting you. I'm sure he meant it only to be a temporary measure, until he got back on his feet."

Images of the final demands on Max's desk, his outburst about the cost of Abby's phone, and the look on his face when his card was rejected at the restaurant flashed through Ellie's brain as the solicitor turned to Julia.

"Well, exactly!" Julia stood up, color returning to her cheeks. "Pandora will realize that. I mean, what would she want with a great barn of a place like this? She's got the apartment, after all."

James paused and ran a finger around his collar.

"Actually, no. She hasn't. She heard yesterday—it's being repossessed to pay your ex-husband's debts. Max had known that for several weeks, but hadn't plucked up the courage to tell Pandora." He sighed. "It's as much of a shock to her as it is to you."

So that was why Dad had been in such a state, Ellie thought. He knew that everything was on the line.

"Of course, originally Max left you all a great deal of money in his will."

"Oh, well that's all right, then," sighed Julia. "We can buy the place back."

"No, it's not all right," James stressed. "He may have expressed a wish for you to have his money. But there is no money left, none at all. Just a pile of debts and a dozen or so very angry creditors."

"We've got nothing?" The hollowness in Abby's voice shook Ellie as much as the news. "Nothing at all?"

"There are a few things, books, pictures—oh and three pieces of sculpture," James said brightly. "I've got them in the car."

"But the bottom line is that we're broke." Ellie didn't bother phrasing it as a question; she knew it was the truth.

"Yes, I'm afraid so," James said softly. "Of course, I'm sure that, in any other circumstances, the new Mrs. Dashwood would want you to remain here at Holly House."

"You mean, she actually . . . ?" The words stuck in Ellie's throat.

Georgie sprang up from the floor, wild-eyed and cheeks flushed.

"She can't throw us out!"

"Of course she can't, Georgie," Julia interjected. "Don't be so silly."

"I'm afraid she can," he said firmly, shuffling some

papers. "In view of her strained circumstances, and the imminent repossession of the flat, she is anxious to take possession of the property at the earliest possible convenience."

He flushed and cleared his throat. "Well, on Thursday, to be precise."

Julia gasped.

"But that's the day before the funeral," she whispered. "She can't . . ."

"She won't expect you to leave just yet, of course," James reported apologetically. "She's said that you can stay as long as you need to in order to set other arrangements, but she will arrive on Thursday, by dinnertime. She asked that I let you know."

{ 119 }

"But we'll have to leave?" Julia asked, the shock in her eyes visible.

"Yes." James nodded. "I am so very, very sorry."

"Can I have this one?" Abby gestured to the largest of the three sculptures that had been blocking the hallway ever since James left the house the day before. "It speaks to me."

"It does?" Georgie eyed it with bemusement. "What is it?"

"A bird," Abby said. "See, its beak's open, and its wings are spread and it's about to take off, into the blue yonder, in search of its destiny. . . ."

"Okay, okay," Georgie said hastily. "I'll have the little, fat cherub thing—it's kind of cute. Even though it hasn't got any legs."

Ellie sighed. Ever since the solicitor had left and Mum had told them she had a small sum tucked away for a rainy day—though she wasn't sure how much—Ellie had tried to stay hopeful, even though the feeling in the pit of her stomach told her otherwise.

"That leaves the round thing with the hole for me," she murmured. "Looks like a giant Polo mint."

"You've got no soul," Abby declared, raising her eyebrows. "Can't you see it represents life? The hole is the abyss into which we all fall unless we follow our destiny."

Ellie frowned at her sister. Between Abby's dreamy antics and her mother's unwillingness to deal with the fact that they might very well soon be homeless (with three very odd sculptures in tow, mind you), Ellie felt as though she and Georgie might be the only ones with their heads screwed on properly. Too bad a straight head couldn't get them back their dad, or the rights to their home.

Ellie looked up at Abby then, noticing that she was no longer smiling at her odd sculpture. "Abby, what's wrong?"

"What the hell do you think is wrong?" her voice broke.

"Sorry, that was dumb of me," Ellie agreed. "Do you want a tissue?"

"I feel so guilty." Abby ran her hand over a rough patch on the sculpture. "All that time—I didn't know—if I had, I wouldn't have . . . but I didn't so I couldn't . . ."

"Abby," Georgie laughed softly, "We can't understand a word you're saying. You didn't know what?"

"That Dad was broke," Abby sniffed. "I just said yes to everything he offered to buy, and he paid our bills, and all the time he couldn't afford it."

She paused and gazed up at her sisters with red-rimmed eyes.

"And it killed him." She choked on the words.

"Abby, listen," Ellie ordered. "Dad chose to spend that money. No one made him. He did it because he loved us so much, and he hated to say no to us."

Georgie took a deep breath, and grabbed both her sisters into a hug.

"What's this?" Julia demanded the following morning, picking up the local weekly paper.

DASHWOOD: Tragically and without warning, **MAXIMILIAN FREDERICK**, for 20 years the cherished and loving husband of Julia, and adored father of Ellie, Abby, and Georgie. A man of enterprise, humor, and passion, his loss will leave emptiness in the lives of many. Funeral to be held tomorrow at St. Peter's Church.

"Who put this in the paper?"

"I did." Abby stuck her chin out defiantly. "And it's no good you telling me to apologize, because I won't. I'm not sorry because it was the right thing to do."

"Yes, I know."

"And just because you . . . Wait, what did you say?"

Her mother smiled.

"I said, Yes, it was the right thing to do," Julia repeated. "Thank you, darling. It means more than I can say."

She gave Abby a hug.

"Oh—and there is one more thing you could do for me?"

"Anything, Mum," Abby assured her eagerly. "What is it?"

"Make sure Pandora gets a copy, will you? Without fail?"

Abby grinned.

"Consider it done," she promised, picking up the paper.

✤ SECRET NO. 10 ✤

Apparently even wretched cows fall in love

"Please, can we eat?" Georgie pleaded the following evening. "It's nearly eight-thirty, and my stomach thinks my throat's been cut."

Her mother sighed, opening the door of the oven and peering in for the tenth time in as many minutes. "If they're not here in ten minutes, we'll eat," she agreed.

"They?" Ellie looked up from her attempts at German translation. Even Georgie stopped fiddling with her iPod for a minute.

"Oh, didn't I tell you?" Julia looked sheepish and began clattering dishes. "Pandora phoned a couple of hours ago. She's bringing her nephew Blake—I think you said you met him at Dad's? I'm putting him in Nanny's old room."

"Blake? He's coming here? To live? With Pandora?" Ellie gasped.

It occurred to Georgie that she didn't look as upset by the idea as she should.

"Oh, I don't imagine he'll live here," Julia said. "He's just coming down for a while to give Pandora moral support."

A screech of brakes followed by the sound of barking stopped the conversation and the Dashwoods all looked at each other.

"This is it," said Ellie. "I'll go and let them in."

"I'm coming too," Julia said. "Abby, pour the wine. Georgie, take that snarl off your face, if you can manage."

"I'm not sure I can," muttered Georgie as she listened to her mum usher Pandora and Blake through the front door.

"You know my girls, of course," Julia was saying as Pandora, dressed from head to foot in sugar-pink leather, entered the kitchen with a sheepish-looking Blake in tow.

"You've got a dog!" Georgie gasped, as what appeared to be a badly woven rug on legs hurled itself against her.

"Yes, sorry," Blake said nervously. "I mean, is it okay? I can put him in a kennel, only I haven't had time to organize it." He grabbed the dog by its collar. "Down, boy! Behave!"

"He's fine," Georgie said decisively. "We love dogs—Dad had . . ." The words caught in her throat.

"What's his name?" Ellie put an arm around her sister.

"Morris," said Blake, trying to restrain the enthusiastic animal. "He's a cross between an Old English sheepdog, a Newfoundland, and something ugly that we haven't yet identified! Are you sure you don't mind him being here, Mrs. Dashwood?"

Julia smiled and shook her head. "Not at all," she said. "He can sleep in the boot room."

"Great." Blake smiled. "He's usually with my parents, but they left for a holiday in Barbados this morning, so I'm in charge." Morris promptly lay down on Pandora's suede boots and panted pathetically. "Or not, as the case may be," grinned Blake.

"Just keep that awful hound away from me, that's all I ask!" Pandora wrinkled her nose. "Ghastly creature."

"Takes one to know one," muttered Georgie to Abby, as Morris licked her left foot appreciatively.

"This is the kitchen," Julia butted in unnecessarily, throwing Georgie a warning glance. "I thought we'd eat in here because it's so cozy. Pandora, do sit down. Supper's ready." She gestured toward the most comfortable chair. "Would you like a glass of wine?"

"Terrific," cried Blake, clearly embarrassed by his aunt. "Let me help. Pandora—white or red?"

"Neither, thank you," Pandora shuddered. "Do you know what alcohol does to the liver?"

"Probably rather less," muttered Julia as she began placing plates in front of the guests, "than I'm about to do to you."

"What was that, Mum?" Georgie asked with a smirk.

"Nothing, nothing at all," said Julia as she plopped dinner onto Pandora's plate.

"What is this?" Pandora poked at the food in front of her.

"Game pie," Julia said. "Locally shot pheasant and partridge with onions and bacon and . . ."

"I can't eat that!" Pandora shrilled. "I'm vegetarian. Didn't the girls tell you?"

She eyed Ellie, Abby, and Georgie as if they had committed a terrible social gaffe.

"We forgot," Ellie said sharply. "We were too busy mourning our dad and arranging a funeral."

To her credit, Pandora blushed and nodded.

"Yes, well, that's understandable," she conceded. "Still, you know now. Oh—and I only drink soya milk, I don't eat anything from a cow. . . ."

"Right, makes sense." Georgie said, and everyone cocked their heads in wonder at Georgie's change in attitude. "Well, you wouldn't want to eat your own relatives, would you?" added Georgie before Ellie kicked her under the table.

". . . and I like my tea made with bottled water, not tap water. Too many nasty things get into our homes these days."

"Tell me about it," murmured Abby.

Dinner finished up in relative silence, punctuated

only by Blake's admirable attempts at small talk and an occasional giggle from Georgie as Morris stuck his wet nose against her leg, looking for table scraps.

"I'm sorry to be a pain," Blake said as they cleared away the supper dishes, "but I think I should pop out and take Morris for a walk."

"But it's dark," Pandora protested. "And you won't know where to go."

"I'll come with you if you like," Ellie butted in. "I mean, that is, if you don't want to be alone."

"That would be great," grinned Blake. "Only, don't you have loads to do for tomorrow?"

Ellie shook her head, "Nah. The one thing I want to do about tomorrow is forget it's going to happen. A walk is just what I need."

"Terrific, then," Blake said, and then asked Morris if he wanted to go for a walk a few times, much to the big dog's excitement.

Ellie opened the door and showed them the way toward the front pathway, where they stood in silence for a moment, looking out on the town below them.

"It's an amazing view." Blake gazed out at the moon-lit sea, the floodlit Brighton Pier, and thousands of tiny lights twinkling along the seafront. "And it smells so different from London." He gulped in deep breaths of the salty air.

"Wait till you see it in daylight," Ellie enthused. "There's a wonderful view right across the bay to Worthing."

"How will you bear to leave? Oh gosh, I'm sorry, that was so tactless."

"It's fine. I mean, it's something we've all got to get used to," she said, pausing under a streetlamp and pulling her jacket tighter around her body.

"So where will you go?" Blake asked, yanking Morris's lead as the dog attempted to lie down in the middle of a puddle.

"I don't know," Ellie said shortly. "I'm afraid we won't be able to stay in Brighton—my mom won't tell me what's what on the money front, and houses here go for a bomb. I don't even know how we're going to pay for school anymore, and there are my A levels next year, and . . ." She turned away in embarrassment. What possessed her to talk to a total stranger about such personal stuff? "I'd better get back," she said quickly, turning around. "If you want to walk on . . ."

"No, I'll come too," Blake said, stopping in the gravel drive for a moment. "You must hate us."

"Not you, just Pan—" Ellie stopped herself. "Sorry, I didn't mean . . ."

"It's okay," Blake said, stuffing his hands in his pockets. "She can be a bit much at times, I guess. All her fads about food and stuff."

"Bizarre," agreed Ellie.

"The thing is, her parents—that's my grandparents—they died out in Africa when she was ten. Her mum was ill with some waterborne disease, and there was a car crash while her dad was trying to rush her to hospital."

"That's awful," gasped Ellie.

"Ever since then she's been paranoid about hygiene and food and that kind of stuff," Blake went on, pulling Morris away from his close inspection of a banana skin in the gutter. "My mum was nineteen at the time and became a kind of proxy mum to Pandora, but I don't think she ever got over it."

"I didn't know," murmured Ellie, feeling a wave of guilt about all the evil thoughts she'd spent the last year thinking.

"I think she married your dad because she needed a father figure—or at least, that's what Mum says," he went on. "So you see . . . oh, look, I'm sorry, this is crazy. You don't want to hear all this."

"I do," Ellie insisted, because as long as Blake kept talking she didn't have to think about Dad or the future. "It helps. I don't know why, but it does. So you two get on well, then?"

It struck her that you would have to be a saint to get on with Pandora.

"Not really," Blake admitted. "She lived with us after my mum got married and had me, so in some ways she's more like a big sister than an aunt. A very irritating big sister most of the time," he added.

"So how come you agreed to come down here with her?" Ellie asked.

"Because she persuaded your dad to let me stay with them for a few weeks, and I owe her one," he admitted. "If it hadn't been for Max and Pandora, my father and I would have come to serious blows."

Ellie started. Blake seemed too soft to come to blows with anyone.

"Why?"

"Oh, it's a long story," he mumbled as they turned into the drive of Holly House. "You've got enough on your plate without me going on and on."

"I told you—anything's better than thinking about tomorrow and Dad in that coffin and . . ." Her voice broke and she turned away.

"Well," said Blake in a matter-of-fact voice, "the bottom line is that my father wants me to do law . . ."

"That's cool," she began, and then stopped since it was clear from the expression on Blake's face that he wasn't keen on the idea.

"He's an international lawyer, Grandpa was a barrister, and the whole family expects me to follow suit."

"So tell him no," Ellie replied. "If that's not what you want."

Blake gave a short laugh.

"That's what everyone says—everyone who doesn't know my father," he said. "*No* is not a word that my father responds well to."

"But surely . . ." Ellie stopped as Blake started to shake his head and kick at the gravel driveway.

"Dad's motto is always the same: *He who pays the piper calls the tune.* He holds the purse strings, so he always wins." Blake itched at his forehead. "Sorry—I always babble on when I'm uptight. Anyway, what are you going to do with your life?"

"Go to university, study . . ." For some reason that she couldn't quite explain, the words stuck in her throat. ". . . not sure what yet—plenty of time to think about careers later. . . ." *Ellie Dashwood, you are a wimp,* she told herself angrily—Ellie knew full well that law school was in her future. She fished in the pocket of her jeans for the back door key. "Anyway, what do you really want to do?" she asked, eager to divert attention away from her future. "Really, if you could choose?"

"You really want to know?"

"Of course I do."

"I want to be an artist. Or an illustrator. Oh, anything as long as it involves painting and drawing." He eyed her closely. "Go on, laugh."

But Ellie didn't laugh. To her horror she began to

{ 131 }

sob. All she could think about was her dad and his wonky sculptures, and that no matter how much her mum wanted to pretend otherwise, nothing was ever going to be the same again.

🐚 SECRET NO. 11 🐚

Love does not die easily—it often grows while no one is watching

"What time do we have to get changed, Mum?" Georgie asked, pushing her cereal around her bowl on the morning of the funeral, looking from her mum to her two sisters, who were all gathered around the table.

Her mother didn't reply. She was staring, spoon halfway to her mouth, at a letter that she had just opened.

"No," her mother breathed. "No, no, NO!"

The final word was a scream as the spoon clattered to the table, splashing milk and cornflakes over the table as Julia leaped to her feet.

"I can't take any more!" she sobbed, tears streaming down her face. "What's the point—you try to be brave and hold things together, but there's always someone wanting to pull the rug from under you! First Pandora, now this hateful woman . . ."

"Who, Mum? What's happened?" Abby pleaded, her heart thudding.

"Now this!" Julia flung the letter onto the table.

Abby snatched it up and scanned it hastily. "It's from the Headmistress," Abby gasped.

"Read it out," Ellie ordered, taking a seat.

"'Dear Mrs. Dashwood,'" Abby read in a quavering voice. "'Firstly, please accept the sincere condolences of the Board of Governors, myself, and the Senior Management Team on the death of your husband.

"'Further to our recent conversations, and while sensitive to your loss, I have to write to inform you that, following a meeting of the Governors, I must ask you to settle all outstanding school fees within fourteen days of today's date.

"'Failure to do so will necessitate the school requesting the removal of Elinor, Abigail, and Georgina.

"'Yours truly, Eveline Passmore.'"

"She can't do that!" Georgie gasped.

"She can," Ellie said, putting an arm around her mother's shoulders and squelching the desire to point out that she'd seen this coming. "Don't cry, Mum. It'll be okay, we'll work something out."

"Like what?" her mother sobbed. "First the house, now the school—what have we got left?"

Ellie clenched her jaw to stop herself from crying. Even though she'd expected it, Ellie realized that being enrolled at St. Etheldra's was perhaps the only thing left to tie them to Brighton after losing Holly House. And now it looked like they weren't even going to have that.

"We've got each other," Ellie said resolutely. "Dad wouldn't want us to go to pieces."

"You're right, of course." Julia sniffed and nodded. "And besides, if I write to Mrs. Passmore, reason with her . . ."

"Passmore and reason don't go together," muttered Abby. "Trust me. Don't waste your breath."

"What's going on?" Pandora wafted into the kitchen, dressed in black chiffon and knee-high boots. "I can't have people falling apart now, I need support. . . ."

"We've got to leave school because there's no money," Abby said, glaring at her. "Doesn't that make you feel awful?"

{ 135 }

"I left school at sixteen, and it didn't do me any harm," Pandora declared.

"When you've only got two brain cells, there's not much harm to be done, is there?" muttered Abby.

At the funeral, the girls wept when they saw Pandora sitting in the front row where their mum should have been. It was practically the only thing any of them could concentrate on—everything else was simply too much.

Georgie sat stoic, tears running down her cheeks, unconsciously picking at her cuticles until they bled. Abby pretended she was Katharine Hepburn in *On Golden Pond*, as she walked slowly and steadily behind the coffin as they left the church—if she'd let herself think of anything else, she was sure she'd crumble to the ground.

And Ellie watched as the family she had always known changed forever, right in front of her eyes. There would be no more Dad, and the rest of them would be changed forever without him.

Just keep handing around the canapés and don't think about it, Georgie told herself firmly. *Don't think about Dad locked up in that coffin, don't remember the velvet curtains opening, and the coffin sliding through, and Dad tumbling into flames and being burnt. Don't think about leaving Holly House and school and . . .*

"Come on, I've got something to show you." Tom firmly removed the plate from her hand, dumped it on the sideboard, and grabbed her arm.

"I can't, Mum said I had to be a good hostess and talk to everyone."

"It was your mum's idea," Tom assured her. "You look like you've seen a ghost. . . . Oh, gosh, sorry, that . . ."

"It's okay." Georgie tried a watery smile as Tom pulled her through the throng of murmuring guests. "It's just that I can't imagine Dad gone. I mean, really gone—cinders, ashes . . ."

"So remember him like he was," Tom told her, taking his

jacket from the hat stand in the hall and pulling an envelope out from the pocket. "Go on, look! It's your photos—remember you wanted me to print them off on my Photo Suite on the computer? Well, this is them!"

Georgie began flipping through the images—Dad and Pandora grinning at the camera; Dad and Pandora on the balcony with Ellie and Abby; Pandora, lips puckered, fawning all over Dad. Pandora—man stealer, home wrecker, who even now wasn't talking to the mourners but lying down in a darkened room because she said she needed to be alone with her agony. Alone with her guilt, more like, thought Georgie.

"Georgie, where are you going?" Tom shouted as she pounded up the stairs two at a time and into her bedroom.

She wrenched open drawer after drawer until she found her nail scissors. Then she began. She plunged them into Pandora's grinning face, photo after photo, wishing that she could actually make blood flow from those pallid cheeks. Then she cut the pictures in half, ripping Pandora into tiny fragments till only her dad's face smiled up at her.

"Georgie, I'm sorry, I didn't mean to upset you." Her bedroom door flew open and Tom, red faced, burst in. "Only, your mum thought the pictures would be good for you to have. Hey, what are you doing?"

"Getting rid of every trace of that cow," Georgie panted. "I may not be able to get her out of my house, but no way do I want her in a photo with my Dad. Ever."

Downstairs, Ellie knew she should be circulating, making polite conversation to all the black-suited business friends of her father and the wrinkled great aunts from Portsmouth with their loud voices and voracious appetites, but she couldn't bring herself to smile or be polite. For now, she just wanted to sit here in the conservatory, with Manderley asleep at her feet, and try to make sense of what was happening to their lives.

The latest blow had come just after they'd left the funeral to come back to Holly House for the reception and Julia had taken Ellie aside and confessed that their savings amounted to only £30,000. Fine for living on for a bit, but not nearly enough to buy a house, or pay for even a year of the girls' tuition.

"You could get a job, Mum," Ellie had ventured. "Raise a mortgage?"

"A job? Darling, I couldn't," her mother had said. "I can't do anything."

Ellie had bitten her tongue, but hours later she was still stewing. Her mum was such a defeatist—heaven knows there were jobs that anyone could do, no matter what experience they had.

"There you are, precious lambkin!"

A bejeweled hand landed with a thud on her left shoulder, and Ellie looked up to see Davina Stretton, her godmother, and her mum's oldest friend.

"You came!" Ellie jumped up and gave her a hug. "We thought you wouldn't make it."

"Angel, the traffic! Solid jams all the way from Burnham. I nearly cried—well, I did cry, thinking of you poor lambs going to hell and back at the funeral, and me not on hand to succor and support."

Ellie laughed and then promptly burst into tears. Big, wet drops fell from her eyes and Ellie wiped at her thick eyelashes with the heel of her hand. "I'm so glad you're here," she said, flinging her arms around Davina's ample chest. "Everything's so awful."

"You poor love, I know what losing a father is like," Davina murmured.

"It's not just Dad," Ellie sobbed. "Although of course that's the worst, but her taking the house, and us being homeless, and there's no money because—"

"Darling, wait," Davina interrupted. "I'm all confused. Now, sit down."

Davina pushed Ellie back down into the wicker chair and produced a packet of lime-green tissues from her enormous handbag.

"Blow!" she ordered. Ellie blew.

"Now," Davina instructed her. "Deep breath and tell all."

Ten minutes later, after Ellie had told her the whole story, Davina stood up, pulled back her shoulders, and slipped her handbag over her arm.

"Right," she said. "This needs sorting once and for all. Leave it to me."

"There's nothing you can do, Davina. She's got the law on her side," Ellie sniffed.

"And you," snorted Davina, "have got me. I'll think of something, I promise. Now, lead me to the food, angel, will you? And is there alcohol? Your darling father always kept a rather palatable claret, I seem to recall."

After a drink and a pep talk from Davina, Julia seemed to brighten a bit. She was still at the funeral of the man she loved, of course, but Davina seemed to convince her that she had to take action—that it would make her feel better. So together Davina, Julia, and Ellie all slipped into the study, and Julia took out a piece of stationery and a pen and began writing.

"Okay, listen to this." Julia sucked the end of her roller pen and began reading the letter she had been scribbling for the past several minutes.

"'Dear Mrs. Passmore,

"'With regard to your letter, which I must confess showed an innate lack of tact and good taste on your part,

I am unable at this point to settle the outstanding bill for fees, owing to . . .'"

"Go on," urged Ellie.

"That's all I've put," Julia confessed. "What should I say—owing to what? Owing to what?" Julia tapped her pen on the table and bit her lip.

"Owing to there being no money, perhaps?" Ellie suggested. "You've got to tell her the truth, Mum. I mean—they'll understand. There might be some kind of charity fund for cases like ours."

"Ellie, you're a genius." Davina said. "Of course, that's the answer. I mean, a school like St. Ethelreda's is bound to have contingency plans."

{ 141 }

"'Owing to my late ex-husband having died insolvent,'" Julia read out loud as she wrote. "It does sound very disloyal, written in black-and-white like that," Julia murmured, taking a sip of tea.

"Put the bit about scholarships and stuff," Ellie urged, wishing she could just snatch the notepaper from her mother and do the thing herself.

"'I wonder whether there might be some bursaries, scholarships, or distress fund money available since the girls have been with you since the age of five and are, as I am sure you will agree, a great attribute to the school.'"

"That should do it," Julia exclaimed triumphantly,

signing her name with a flourish. "They can't say no to that, now, can they?"

"Surely not!" said Davina.

Ellie smiled, but she well knew they could say whatever they wanted. "C'mon back to the guests."

Julia and Ellie spent the next couple of hours being polite to the remaining guests while Abby and Georgie sat huddled together on a nearby couch. Finally, the last of the guests left.

"I'm so tired I could sleep standing up," sighed Julia, shutting the door on the last of the mourners. "Just look at all this mess."

"We'll all help, Mum," Georgie said. "Pandora, you vacuum, I'll clear the tables, and Abby can load the dishwasher."

"Vacuum?" Pandora stared at them as if someone had suggested that she should lead them all in a chorus of "Rule Brittania." "I'm bereaved. I'm going back to bed."

"*I'm bereaved*," mimicked Georgie. "So are we all, but it hasn't caused us to lose the use of our arms and legs."

And with that Pandora sniffed off down the hall. It was the only fitting end to the worst day of their lives.

☙ SECRET NO. 12 ☙

You don't often get to choose the people that come into your life,
but sometimes you get awfully lucky

Before the weekend was over, Pandora had driven everyone to screaming pitch. For one thing, she had decided that
Brighton was the pits.

"I'm so used to the London life, you see," she simpered
on Saturday morning. "Always something on, something
new to do . . ."

"They call Brighton 'London-by-the-Sea,'" Julia pointed
out. "It's very lively—and full of history. There's the Royal
Pavilion and the Laine and, of course, the Theatre Royal has
all the London productions."

"And it's dead trendy," Abby added. "Although of
course at your age I guess that doesn't count for much."

By lunchtime her moans had switched to the house
itself.

"Are you telling me you don't have a single bidet in the
entire house?" she demanded

"Be who?" asked Georgie.

"Do you realize that carpets harbor formaldehyde?" she cried that evening. "They give off toxic emissions."

"Rather like you, then," Abby muttered out of earshot.

"This kitchen is like something out of a costume drama," Pandora shuddered on Sunday. "All this wood is scratched."

"It's distressed pine," Ellie explained.

"Not half as distressed as us," Julia murmured into her left ear.

But it was the plant-filled conservatory that was
Pandora's real bugbear.

"It's such a health hazard," she declared, touching the Swiss Cheese plant with the tip of her finger. "Surely you get insects and things."

"Oh, dozens," Georgie said airily. "But it's only the tarantulas and the cockroaches that cause any real bother." Georgie waited for her mother to shush her, but all she got from Julia was a broad grin and a wink.

A couple of hours later, with Pandora holed up in her room, and Julia in her garden with Abby and Georgie—all attempting to stay as far away from the house as possible—the phone rang.

"Ellie, darling, is that you?"

"Davina!" Ellie beamed as the familiar voice boomed

down the telephone a couple of days later. "Yes, it's me. Shall I call Mum?"

"No, dear, just answer me this. What are you doing for A level?"

Ellie frowned.

"French, German, Psychology, General Studies. Why?"

"And what examining board?"

"Oxford. Davina, what are you on about?"

"Talk soon, dearest one. Got an idea. Must dash. Chin up!"

Ellie set the receiver down, watching it for a moment as though it might reveal Davina's secret. When it didn't, she decided to head outside to track down her mother and sisters in the garden by the old summerhouse.

At first Ellie was annoyed to find Blake there instead. She had planned to take time out to talk with Abby and Georgie, cry a bit, and then get herself together for another online search for their new home. But as she walked closer, she saw what he was doing.

"That's amazing!" Ellie's mouth dropped open as she stared at the sketch pad on Blake's lap. "How do you make it look so real? It's practically like a photo!"

Blake was drawing Holly House—every leaf of the Virginia creeper that clung to its walls, the crack in the leaded light window halfway up the stairs, the old bird's nest that still perched precariously on top of the rickety drainpipe.

"It's not finished," Blake said hastily, smudging a corner of the roof tiling with his thumb. "I can't get the light right—see, the way that shaft of sun hits the window?"

"Well, it looks pretty good to me," she said.

And so do you, she thought, and then immediately despised herself for even thinking such a thing at a time like this.

"Mum, will you take me driving this evening?" Ellie pleaded later that night. "My test is only two weeks off and I still can't parallel park properly."

"Oh, Ellie, you'll have to cancel and reschedule," Julia sighed. "I've got far too much to worry about right now without all that."

Ellie bit her lip and counted to ten. Was sitting in a car for half an hour that demanding? After all the hours Ellie had spent house hunting online, couldn't Mum do this one thing for her?

"I could take you," Blake said, scraping the last of the apricot crumble off his plate. "I mean, if that's okay with you."

Ellie felt her insides turn over—so much so she placed a hand on her belly.

"Really? That would be great," she replied. "I might not be that good, though."

"Which translates as hang on tight and pray," Georgie chipped in.

As long as it's me he hangs on to, Ellie thought, and then blushed.

Ellie and Blake shuffled out to the car and took off for some of the side streets. Ellie did well, although she was more nervous than usual with Blake there next to her, and she couldn't help but glance at him out of the corner of her eye from time to time. Occasionally, he looked like he was looking at her, rather than at the road, as well.

"Okay," Blake said after an hour of driving around the streets of Brighton and Hove. "Pull into that lay-by for a minute."

Ellie steered the car into the pull-in and switched off the engine.

"How did I do?" she asked.

"Okay," he said hesitantly. "But I think we should practice some more. Like every day? Just to be on the safe side."

"Am I that bad?" Ellie sighed.

"Your driving is great," he said. "But I need to find out how good you are at other things."

"Oh, like the Highway Code, you mean," said Ellie, her mouth for some inexplicable reason going completely dry.

"Not exactly," he murmured, leaning toward her and touching her hand as it rested on the gear lever.

For one moment, Ellie thought he was going to kiss her. She closed her eyes, but when she didn't feel his lips on hers, she opened them and saw that he was sitting clear on the other side of the car, staring ahead.

"Okay," he said. "Pull away. Carefully now, watch that cyclist."

So that's that, then, thought Ellie.

"We need to do this every day for a week," Blake said. "After school—two hours. Okay?"

"Sure," she said, trying to sound dead cool. "Good idea."

After that initial lesson, the next week was a blur for Ellie— she was still mourning her dad, but her driving lessons were proving a terrific distraction. She and Blake began to do other things together, too, and her sisters were plenty quick to notice.

"You've got paint on the back of your neck," Georgie told Ellie over supper one evening.

"Art homework," gabbled Ellie.

"You don't do art," retorted Georgie.

"And grass stains on your jeans," chirped Abby.

"Helped Mum garden," muttered Ellie.

"And I'm the pope," retorted Abby with a smirk.

The Dashwood sisters knew each other all too well.

Ellie peered in the mirror and frowned at her reflection.

Okay, so she wasn't stunning, but she wasn't ugly either. She cupped her hands to her mouth, blew, and then sniffed. Her breath was okay, so it wasn't that.

So why hadn't he kissed her? It had been two weeks, and not even when Ellie had leaned toward him, her eyes closed, pretending to be enjoying the sunshine that was actually making her skin itch, had he kissed her. Nor had she enjoyed a lip-lock when she'd leaned over him to unlock his door, or when she touched his hand, or when he showed her one of his sketches of her lying in the grass.

Never mind that on three occasions now, when they had pulled over in the car up some country lane, he had taken her hand, leaned toward her, breathed her name—and then pulled back and talked about something totally banal, or suddenly got all businesslike and made her practice her three-point turns.

He'd put his arm around her, he'd played with her hair, he'd held her hand as they walked down country lanes. But he hadn't kissed her.

"Ellie, can I borrow your history notes from last . . . what are you doing?"

"Nothing!" Ellie sprang back from the mirror where she had moved on to practicing puckered kisses. "Don't you ever knock?"

"You've got it bad, haven't you?" Abby demanded, ignoring her question. "You've taken to wearing lip gloss and mascara and blusher, even for breakfast, and now you're kissing yourself in the mirror. Has he kissed you yet?"

Ellie gave up pretending and shook her head.

"No," she said. "He clearly doesn't fancy me—one minute he's coming on strong . . ."

"Is he, now?" exclaimed Abby, flopping down on the bed. "Tell me, then—I want all the details."

For some reason that she couldn't quite work out, Ellie found herself telling Abby everything—how she liked talking to Blake because he was so easy to be with, how she had tried to be really alluring and feminine, about the almost-kisses, and about how she worried that she was doing something wrong.

"If you ask me," said Abby, "you're onto a loser with that one."

"So, it is me," Ellie sighed. "Go on, give it to me straight."

Abby giggled.

"That's the point—you can't have it straight," she smirked. "Get it?"

"What are you on about?"

"If you ask me," Abby pronounced, "Blake likes you a lot."

"Really? You're sure?" Ellie's heart lifted.

"Certain," said Abby. "Not that it will do you much good."

"Why? Oh, I get it—oh, thanks, Abby. Of course—he's holding back out of respect for my grief. That is so sensitive, so caring, but I really wish he wouldn't."

"You just don't get it, do you? He's not taking things further, because Blake Goodman is, unless I'm very much mistaken, gay."

Ellie gasped. *Gay?* He couldn't be. I mean, not that it mattered, but Blake? Not Blake, surely?

All Ellie could think was, *But it would be such a waste.*

♚ SECRET NO. 13 ♚

Sometimes things really are too good to be true

"Blake! Telephone!"

Georgie yelled across the hall as Ellie and Blake were shuffling out the door, about to go for another drive.

"I'll wait in the den," Ellie whispered as Blake grabbed the handset. She began to close the door and then stopped as she heard Blake's gravelly tones.

"Blake here—oh, Lucy, it's you."

Lucy? Who the hell is Lucy?

"What? Oh, I had the mobile phone switched off. Sorry. No, love, of course I wasn't trying to . . ."

Ellie froze. *"Love"?* He'd never called her "love."

"What? Of course I miss you—yes, yes. How are things?"

Ellie found herself holding her breath as she tried to stop her heart pounding.

"Oh, you poor thing! Well, look, don't worry. I'll pop down soon, okay? What? No, I can't. Not here."

Ellie strained to catch his words as his voice dropped.

"What? Okay then. Yes, yes—of course I love you." It was the faintest whisper.

He had a girlfriend. Abby was wrong. Blake wasn't gay at all. He was in love with someone else.

Right then, Ellie would have preferred the first option.

As Blake hung up the phone, Ellie slipped outside before she could be caught with her ear to the door. He came outside, and although Ellie couldn't be sure if she was mistaken, he appeared a bit low.

"Actually," Ellie said, hesitating by the car, "I think I'll give the driving a miss today. Loads to do!" Like kicking myself for being such a fool or alternatively howling my eyes out.

"No way," Blake interjected, opening the passenger door. "You're almost there, and the test's next week."

He's right, she thought. I need to pass if only to get some freedom. So he's got a girlfriend? So what? Better to find out now. I haven't got time to get mixed up with a guy anyway. Ellie was willing to tell herself almost anything to thwart off the hurt she could feel inching toward her chest.

"Where shall we go?" Blake asked as Ellie fired the engine. "Town center for traffic practice or dual carriageway for overtaking?"

"Who was that on the phone?" Ellie ignored his

question, slammed the car into gear, and accelerated down the drive.

She felt Blake stiffen beside her.

"Phone? Oh—no one."

"C'mon, Blake!" she retorted, swinging the car out into the road. "Of course it was someone—Lucy, didn't I hear you say?"

Blake blushed. Bad sign.

"Yeah—I just meant—well, no one important."

Ellie's heart lifted a millimeter.

"She's an old friend—of the family, you know? Her mum and my mum are old friends. We practically grew up together."

As Ellie turned to catch his eye and saw the flush spreading from his neck to his forehead, she had a very nasty feeling that this Lucy was not just a mate.

That night, after they returned from the world's most awkward driving date, Ellie closed the door to her room and sobbed. She'd never liked a boy before—not really, anyway—and now she felt stupid and angry and disappointed all at once. *But enough is enough*, Ellie told herself, as she opened her door to go to the bathroom to splash water on her face.

"Why are you crying?" Georgie demanded of Ellie as they bumped into one another in the hall.

"I'm not," Ellie mumbled.

"Oh, cut the crap," said Georgie.

"Georgie, your language!" Ellie snapped

"Stop being a prude and stop fibbing," replied Georgie cheerfully. "You've been crying—is it Dad?"

Ellie shook her head.

"No—I mean, yes," she muttered.

"Which means, no, it isn't, but yes, you think it ought to be," sighed Georgie. "It's Blake, isn't it?"

"What on earth makes you think that?"

"You want a list?" Georgie began ticking off reasons on her fingers. "One—you, Miss Workaholic, have taken to leaving your homework and going out driving. Two—every time he comes into the room you run your hands through your hair like this." She put her hands to her head and fluffed up her already unruly locks. "And three—well, he is rather dishy, isn't he?"

"Yes, I guess he is," Ellie sighed. "Not that you normally notice such things."

Georgie shrugged.

"I like him," she said. "He's normal. Which round here is quite a bonus, if you ask me."

Later that night, when Blake appeared at the front door with Morris, Ellie decided to let the whole thing go. Sure he was the kindest, sweetest, most interesting guy she had ever met, but so what? Clearly, he was in love with someone else, and Ellie should never have let her feelings get so out of control—at least that was what Ellie told herself.

"Look, Blake, I'm sorry I was off with you," Ellie said as he unhooked Morris's leash. "It's none of my business whether you have a girlfriend or not."

Blake swallowed hard.

"Look, about me and Lucy," he began. "I think I should explain. . . ."

"Got to dash," Ellie butted in. "Loads to do. . . . See you at supper."

A couple of hours later, Julia tapped a glass with her fork to get everyone's attention. "I have an e-mail!" she announced.

"How do you know?" Abby asked, shoveling lasagna onto her plate. "You can't even switch the computer on, never mind print anything."

"Enough of your cheek!" Julia grinned. "It's from Davina. Ellie loaded down it."

"Downloaded," giggled Georgie.

"Whatever," Julia said. "Anyway, I think you should all read it."

Blake jumped up.

"I'll leave you in peace, then," he said.

"No, stay, Blake," Julia said. "We need all the advice we can get."

She unfolded a sheet of paper and began reading.

"'Dearest Julia,

"'In light of all that's happened, I've come up with a solution! And this is it; you remember Ma had that little cottage on our farm? Well, she's in the rest home now, bless her—the stairs were just too much for her and her memory's gone AWOL—but she refuses to sell the place, and I thought, why not offer it to you and the girls?

"'It's not what you're used to, of course—only three bedrooms and a boiler with a mind of its own, but it would be lovely to have it lived in again. And North Norfolk's got a lot going for it as well—sandy beaches, plenty of space, the odd nice little fish restaurant. I'm on the board of governors of Cromwell Community School; I've checked that all Ellie's subjects are available there, and of course, being a state school, there are no fees to pay. What's more, they use the same examining board, so it has to be destiny, darling!

"'Anyway, angel, let me know what you think. Pop over and see the place at the weekend, why don't you? Oh—and if you agree to slap a bit of paint about the place and mow the lawn, I won't charge rent.

"'Must dash off now—Mother's Union tea at The Grange and I'm on kettle duty!

"'Love to the girls, and keep your chin up. Love, Davina.'"

"So, what do you think?" Julia eyed her three daughters anxiously.

"Think? I think it's totally dumb," Abby shouted. "Norfolk, for heaven's sake? That's the boonies—all sand dunes and farmers with straw hanging out of their mouths."

"That's so not true!" Blake laughed. "I go there a lot with—well, with friends, you know. Sailing and stuff."

"You do?" Ellie said. "So do you know this school? What's it like?"

"What does the school matter?" Abby butted in. "Are there clubs? No! Are there huge department stores? No. Is life in Norfolk worth living? No, I don't think so!"

"Abby, if you haven't got anything constructive to say, don't speak," ordered her mother. "Georgie, what do you think?"

"Do we really have to leave here?" Georgie's voice was small and filled with emotion, and for a moment she didn't look a day over six years old.

"Yes, darling, I'm afraid we do."

"What about the letter to Mrs. Passmore about the scholarships?" Ellie asked.

"I'm afraid she won't offer them to us," Julia said. "I heard last week, but I haven't been able to bring myself to tell you girls."

"Well," ventured Georgie, "I'll go if I can have a horse."

"The answer is no," said Julia. "Could someone please offer something useful to this discussion?"

Blake cleared his throat.

"This friend of yours, Davina? It wouldn't be Davina Stretton, would it? Lives at Marsh Farm?"

"That's right," Julia said in surprise. "Why? Do you know her?"

"Not know her, exactly—but I've met her a couple of times because she's Lucy's—she's the friend of a friend of mine," Blake told her, a frown puckering his forehead. "Her farm is near Burnham Market. . . ."

"Never heard of it," Abby cut in, wondering why Ellie suddenly looked as if she could murder someone.

"It's an okay place," Blake told her. "Just down the road from Sandringham—the Queen's country house, you know? It's got some cool pubs, sailing club . . ."

"Discos? Nightclubs? Open air raves?" demanded Abby.

"Well, no," said Blake.

"I rest my case," Abby said.

"I suppose if none of you are happy about it, we'll have to think again," her mother sighed. "But this is rent free, and I'll have a ready-made friend, and I'm sure Blake would take you girls out and about a bit."

"Of course—well, no, actually, I mean, I am not up there that often, come to think of it," Blake stammered. "But of course, when I am, I'd be delighted."

I knew it, Abby thought, noting the crestfallen expression on Ellie's face. He's gay, and he doesn't want us to know. It's obvious. Poor Ellie.

"I just don't know what to do," Julia whimpered, tears welling in her eyes.

"Let's take it!" Ellie said decisively. "It'll be fun."

Fun like a terrible rash in summer, thought Abby, though she didn't say a word.

"But what would Dad say?" her mother began. "I mean, the Dashwoods have lived here for generations and . . ."

"So perhaps it's time we blazed a new trail," Ellie declared, taking a deep breath. "Dad would understand. We've got to move on, Mum. We're going to Norfolk."

🎔 SECRET NO. 14 🎔

No matter what anyone else says, it really is the thought that counts

Ellie ran her finger lightly over the picture in her hand and blinked away the tears that it had brought on.

"It's not very good, and I can do better," Blake told her as he shoved it into her hand, pink with embarrassment. "But what with you leaving and everything, I thought you might like to have it."

It was the picture she had seen him struggling with a few weeks before—Holly House in the late afternoon sun. Holding it now, and standing for the last time in front of the home she loved so much, she marveled at the detail— the robin on the birdbath, the crack in the leaded light by the front door where Abby had hit her rounders ball years before, the straggly ivy, and the flowering honeysuckle.

"'For Ellie from Blake with love,'" she read the words scrawled in charcoal in the corner of the picture and bit her lip. Leaving Holly House was so hard. And leaving Blake wasn't exactly easy either. Ellie had passed her driver's test, and they'd only have a few weeks of their new school to wrap up before summer vacation began, but none of that was making Ellie feel much better.

"Right, everyone! Ready?" Julia's voice was bright but her shoulders were tense with the pain of leaving as she stepped onto the lawn and looked back at the house.

Ellie rolled up the drawing, slid it into a protective tube, and picked up the bag at her feet. "Thank you, Blake," Ellie said, her voice wavering a bit. "It means so much."

Blake didn't say anything, but he did put his arms around her. Still no kiss, but the hug felt wonderful.

"Bye, house," Abby said softly, tears streaming down her face. "We're sorry—we never meant to leave you."

"Come on, Abby. Let's go." Ellie touched her sister's arm and opened the car door. *Concentrate on the good bits,* she told herself firmly—*like driving your own car without L plates. Think about being independent and having a new life. Don't think about what you're leaving or where you're going. Just do it.*

And with that, the Dashwood sisters all hugged Blake, and along with their mother, they piled into their two cars filled with their belongings—Ellie driving one, Julia driving the other—and left Holly House behind for the last time.

* * *

"This can't be it," Abby gasped as her mother pulled up outside a small, flint-built cottage. "It's in the middle of nowhere."

"Nonsense," Julia replied briskly, waving to Ellie as she pulled up behind them. "We've just come through the village, with that lovely church . . ."

"You call that a village?" Abby retorted. "More an accident at the side of the road, if you ask me."

Julia got out of the car and stretched, taking gulps of sea air. From the direction of the sand dunes came the smell of salt and seaweed, mixed with the less appealing odor of manure from a nearby farm.

"Ellie darling, look at that view," she said encouragingly, pointing across the marshes to the distant inlet where the white and red sails of dinghies and yachts bobbed in the light breeze. "Imagine waking up to the sight of the ocean every day."

"We could see the water before, too," Georgie interjected sulkily.

Suddenly, the door of the cottage burst open, and Davina, dressed in cord trousers, a baggy sweater, and an extraordinary porkpie hat, came down the path and enveloped Julia in a bearlike hug.

"Welcome to Marsh Cottage," she cried. "I just know you are going to love it here!"

"No brain as well as no dress sense," Abby muttered under her breath. "It's going to be hell."

They grabbed some things—a few boxes, the picture of Holly House, and one of Max's sculptures—and headed inside. They did all the polite things. Admired the inglenook fireplace and tried to ignore the flowery wallpaper and hideous carpet. They thanked Davina for the pie and cake that was waiting on the chipped Formica-topped table in the tiny kitchen, murmured appreciatively as Davina described the delights of the local sailing club and nearby nature reserve, and agreed that within a few weeks they would have made the place really homey.

They made up the beds, unpacked their clothes, and drank tea. Georgie sent a text message to Tom, Abby hid her diary under the mattress in the bedroom that she had to share with Ellie, and Ellie vowed silently to work like fury in order to escape to university as soon as she could.

Ellie hung her picture of Holly House in the tiny hallway so that it would be the first thing they saw every time they walked into their new home. And that was when they all gave up trying to be brave and wept in the strange, musty-smelling place that they were supposed to call home.

"I can't believe that wretched Pan—" Abby started, tears streaming down her face.

Georgie interrupted her. "I think . . ." she paused. "I rather think we should just forget about her now. Let's never mention her again—she's taken up too much time already."

Ellie nodded, and after a moment, Abby did too. Mum

was the last to agree, but when she did, they all felt a bit stronger for the promise.

By the end of the first week in the house, they were all but unpacked. Only a few boxes remained untouched, and with the way Julia was turning over the house, Ellie had no doubt they'd be stored soon enough as well.

"Red, definitely red," declared Abby as she and Ellie pored over a paint chart.

"No way," retorted Ellie. "It's bad enough having to share a bedroom with all your mess and junk, without having to take on board your bizarre tastes in décor."

Ellie stabbed a finger at the chart.

"Blue Serenity," she read. "That's much more like it."

"Oh puh-leese!" Abby retorted. "It's cold enough in this place without decorating it to look like the inside of an igloo."

Ellie flung the paint chart to the floor. "We might as well stick with this awful biscuit-mixed-with-vomit color, then," she groaned. "I think . . ."

Abby held up a finger for Ellie to hold on as her mobile phone rang. "Who? Oh, Chloe—hi!"

She waved a hand in Ellie's direction and pointed to the door.

"Okay, I'm going," Ellie sighed. "I still say blue is best."

Ellie trotted down the rickety stairs, and sat down at the

kitchen table, her chin resting in her hands, and gazed out of the window.

What's wrong with me? There was Abby upstairs, nattering away to her new friend Chloe, who it had taken her precisely one hour to meet at the local shops. Georgie was out with a guy from her school, who she'd apparently met in the first five minutes of her first day, who owned his own dinghy and was teaching her to sail it in the harbor. Even her mother seemed to have got a life overnight—if you could call the local Women's Institute and a flower-arranging class a life.

"Hi, there!" She jumped as the back door opened and Davina burst in. "Is Mum around?"

"She's gone to WI," Ellie shook her head.

"That's where I'm off to," Davina chortled. "Running late as usual—the blasted bicycle had a puncture, and I hoped Mum would give me a lift."

"I'll take you," Ellie said, jumping up. "I've nothing else to do."

Davina eyed Ellie closely as she grabbed her car keys and headed for the door.

"What's wrong?"

"Nothing," Ellie said automatically, slamming the front door behind them and unlocking the car.

"Oh, come off it, this is me you're talking to," said Davina, heaving her ample frame into the passenger seat. "Homesick, are you?"

The word hit Ellie's brain like a laser beam.

"Yes," she said, firing the engine. "That's it—I miss Brighton, I miss my friends, the school here is horrible. . . . Oh, I didn't mean to be rude—it's really kind of you to fix me up and . . ."

"Darling, stop apologizing," laughed Davina. "It was bound to be hard going to a new place. So come on, let off steam—what's the worst part?"

"Well, I know it's only been a day, and I'm sure I'll get used to it, but it's just so huge, and so noisy. The building is the pits, all that concrete and muddy-brown paint," complained Ellie, pulling away from the curb. "And they don't have enough computers, and I haven't made a real friend."

Ellie stopped. She knew she sounded like a petulant child.

"It'll get better, sweetheart," Davina said. "I promise."

"I know." Ellie smiled. She didn't believe a word of it, but it seemed the polite thing to say.

They drove along and Ellie took in the sights—the view of the ocean and overgrown grass. It was the type of place that would make a lovely vacation, Ellie realized, so long as you got to leave at some point. She dropped Davina off at the village hall, and was about to pull back out into the road when her mobile phone bleeped that she had a text message. Ellie punched the READ button.

HI! HOW'S THINGS? HOPE TO BE UP IN NORFOLK VERY SOON—CAN WE MEET? BYE4NOW. B.

She grinned to herself, even though she didn't know what to make of it. It was the third time he'd texted her since she left Brighton, and it hadn't even been forty-eight hours. Her stomach flipped all over again.

⚜ SECRET NO. 15 ⚜

*Planning love is like trying to control the weather—
impossible, frustrating, and unnatural*

"What are you doing tonight?" Chloe asked Abby at Friday
lunchtime, spooning spaghetti down her throat as if her life
depended on it.

"Amusing myself by breathing in and out, probably,"
Abby sighed, toying with her cheese roll. "There's nothing
else to do round here, unless bird-watching turns you on. On
a Friday, back in Brighton, I'd have been going out clubbing or hanging out at the Pier. There's this guy, Fergus—did
I tell you about Fergus? He . . ."

"You've told the world about Fergus." Chloe grinned,
her freckled cheeks dimpling. "The one you dumped, right?"

"Yes," agreed Abby carelessly. "He was okay, but I
had to cool it. He came on too strong. But it was fun while
it lasted."

Chloe looked at her admiringly, and Abby told her conscience that it was only a tiny lie.

"I guess," she added, raising her voice over the din in the cafeteria, "fun is a thing of the past."

Chloe pulled a face.

"Oh, don't start again," she said. "You talk as though nothing happens round here."

"Well, does it?" Abby stuck a fork into her food.

"There's the Young Farmers Club—that's neat, we did a raft-building competition last week, and next month we're having a 'hoedown' for charity. You should come along."

"I don't know," muttered Abby, ripping the ring pull off her can of cola.

"—and sometimes we go to Fakenham for a movie— or . . ."

She was clearly having trouble thinking of any other attractions within a ten-mile radius of the village.

"Anyway," Chloe said, brightening suddenly, "there's the disco on Saturday. That'll be ace—it always is."

Abby stopped fiddling with her lunch and looked up. "Disco? Where? I didn't know there were any clubs round here."

"Not at a club. Here, silly," laughed Chloe.

"Here?" Abby's heart sank. School-based discos were always a disaster.

"Sure—it's in aid of Save the Children, and Cat-a-clysmic is playing."

"Who the hell are they?" Abby asked.

"Just the best new sound around," Chloe said, pushing her plate to one side and fishing an apple out of her bag. "It's four guys from Year 12. . . ."

"Oh, Chloe—I thought for one glorious moment they were a proper band, not some dumb, amateur bunch. . . ."

Chloe's chubby face flushed.

"That is such an up-yourself remark!" she snapped. "You don't know them, you haven't heard them. . . . You know, I'm beginning to think Samantha was right—you're stuck up."

Abby touched her arm. "Okay, I'm sorry," she said. "I didn't mean it. Are they good?"

"They're amazing," Chloe enthused, apparently mollified by Abby's apology. "Ryan's got a sensational voice and Liam plays the keyboard—he's good, too. But of course, it's Nick Mayes that really brings the whole thing together—he's the drummer, and he's dead sexy and . . ."

"And you fancy him!" Abby grinned.

"How did you know?" Chloe asked, almost choking on her apple. "Did Amy let on? I'll kill her—or was it Sam—she's a real motormouth. . . ."

"The look on your face told me," Abby said, laughing. "I know about these things. So are you two an item?"

"I wish," she sighed. "Sometimes I wonder if he even knows I exist."

"So, make it so he has no choice," Abby replied.

"Oh, yeah. Like how?" Chloe demanded.

"Well, go to the disco and flaunt yourself, make him see you, dance funky, be a bit loud. . . ."

"I can't—I'm not like that," Chloe sighed.

"You can act, can't you? Pretend you're playing the vamp in a play," Abby suggested. "Works for me every time."

"I suppose I could try. If we got there early . . ." Chloe bit at her fingernail.

"Hang on," Abby butted in, "what's with the 'we'? I'm not going."

"I thought you were bored," Chloe challenged. "What, we're not cool enough for you?"

"It's not that," Abby cried hastily, desperate not to lose the first friend she'd made since moving. "It's just that—you know, with my dad just having died, going to a disco seems . . ." She paused, remembering how important timing was in moments of deep emotion. "It seems callous, somehow."

She saw at once that it had worked. Chloe reached across the table and grabbed her hand.

"Oh, sorry, Abby—I didn't think. But look, maybe coming to the disco would help you move on. I mean, when my mum died . . ."

"Your mum? I didn't know . . ."

"She died when I was thirteen," Chloe sighed. "Cancer. For ages I didn't go anywhere, do anything, except look at old photos and cry."

"Tell me about it," whispered Abby, a lump swelling in her throat. Even trying to act sassy never managed to totally take away the ache in her heart over her dad.

"But then my dad told me that Mum would hate to see me wasting my life and that I had to live it to the full for her."

Chloe held Abby's gaze until Abby had to look away from embarrassment at having lied to her new friend about something so awful.

"I guess your dad would feel the same, wouldn't he?"

Slowly Abby nodded. She could almost hear her dad's voice—*Life's for the living, kiddo,* he used to say.

"So come to the disco," Chloe urged. "Everyone else is. It's only £4 and half of that's for charity. And if you can't hack it, leave early."

"Okay, I'll come, but on one condition," Abby told her. "You do everything I say, right? I'm going to make sure that by the end of the evening, this Nick person is panting for you!"

COMING 2 NORFOLK 4 SAILING WEEKEND. CAN I C U? PICK U UP 8PM SAT? LOVE BLAKE

"Yes!" Ellie grinned to herself and punched the SAVE button on her phone.

Tina Gregory leaned across the Common Room table and peered at her.

"I haven't seen you look so cheerful since you arrived here." She grinned. "What's up—have you just won the lottery?"

"What? Oh, no, it's just a friend—he's coming up at the weekend," Ellie said, feeling the color flooding her cheeks as she realized her reactions had been noticed. She'd only just gotten to know Tina, who was in all the advanced placement classes with her, and while she seemed really genuine, Ellie wasn't about to loosen up too fast.

"He? You never said you had a boyfriend."

"It's not like that," Ellie protested, because to be honest she wasn't quite sure what it was like. "We're not—I mean, it's nothing."

"Ellie, when someone as buttoned up as you goes all pink around the gills and can't string two words together, it is clearly something," teased Tina. "I must say, it comes as a huge relief."

"What does?"

"The fact that you're human, after all," Tina declared. "I thought the only guys you were interested in were dead poets. Is he sexy?"

"Sexy? Well, I mean—it's not as if . . . and besides, he's got a . . ." Ellie stumbled uncharacteristically over her words.

"Ellie. Is he sexy? Yes or no?"

"I guess."

"You guess? Well, I suggest that come the weekend, you find out for sure! Tart yourself up, and give it all you've got, you hear me?"

Ellie took a deep breath and nodded.

"Okay," she said resolutely. "I think maybe I will."

This is so cool, thought Georgie, leaning back out of Adam's Topper and feeling the salt spray prick her cheeks. Adam was okay—not like most of the guys at her new school. At least he didn't do soppy chat-up lines or try to grope you in mixed football, and truth was, he reminded her a bit of Tom, who she missed a ton already.

The wind was freshening and the little boat cut through the waters of the sand flanked inlet like a knife through butter. She'd never realized that sailing was so easy—you just had to hook your feet under the strap, lean back, watch the boom and . . .

"Georgie, look out!" Adam's agonized shout broke in on her thoughts. "To starboard!"

"To what?" Georgie cried, as the wind carried his words away.

Then she saw the red-sailed dinghy bearing down on them, so close she could catch the mischievous grin on the skipper's face.

"Oh, help, what do I do?"

"He's taking our wind—heave to!"

She hadn't a clue what he meant, but it was too late anyway. She felt herself falling backward and saw the sail coming toward her like a shroud.

And then she was in the water. Cold, and very, very wet.

"If you tell a living soul, you're dead meat!" Georgie gasped, scrambling back into the Topper. For one thing, she hadn't mentioned Adam or the boat to her mother— she knew the kind of reaction she would get—and for another, falling off a bike or a horse or a boat wasn't in Georgie's nature, and she didn't want anyone thinking she couldn't handle herself. "And stop laughing!" she spluttered.

"I'm sorry," Adam teased. "But you looked so funny. It's just as well we were in the harbor. I didn't realize you were clueless about sailing."

"Watch it!" Georgie protested. "I've sailed Toppers before. Well, once before."

"It wasn't your fault, actually," Adam told her. "It was that other guy. He should have given way to us. Total moron."

He maneuvered the boat up against the jetty.

"But I have to tell—Dad said if I ever had an accident with someone else in the boat, I had to own up. Something about insurance."

"Come off it—I'm hardly going to sue you, am I?" Georgie reasoned. "And my mother will have apoplexy if she finds out—she thinks boats are dangerous at the best of times."

"Everyone round here has one, even if it's only an old rowing boat," Adam said, and pointed toward the nearby snack bar. "Are you getting something?"

Georgie shook her head.

"We're poor," she said. "I mean, seriously poverty-stricken. No home of our own, no allowances to speak of . . ."

"So get a job," Adam said, throwing a rope over the mooring post.

"A job? Don't be daft, I'm only thirteen."

"So? No one takes any notice of that. There are loads of Londoners who come up to sail for the weekend—they stick notices on the clubhouse board, asking juniors to get boats ready on a Friday night, and then clean them up on Sunday evenings. They pay £10 a session if you're lucky."

Georgie grinned.

"Great. So come on," she twittered, giving him her hand.

"Come on where?"

"To the boathouse—hanging about here is losing me money."

☙ SECRET NO. 16 ☙

No one is perfect, but sometimes people are perfect for each other, anyway

"That does it! This has got to stop!" Ellie slammed a drawer and glared at Abby.

"What now?" Abby sighed, wriggling into her black satin trousers. "Okay, so the room's a bit messy. . . ."

"Messy? It's an absolute sty," Ellie protested. "You've got clothes all over the floor, books on my bed, and you've been using my makeup."

"Only the tinted moisturizer," Abby insisted.

"You left the cap off and it's all dried out. How am I going to go out in half an hour looking halfway decent?"

"So that's what all this is about?" Abby asked, laughing. "Pre-date nerves—it's okay. Quite normal."

"It's not a date and I'm not nervous," Ellie protested.

"'Course not. He's gay. We've established this," Abby said, blotting her lipstick on a tissue.

"You always think you know everything, don't you?" Ellie snapped. "He's not gay—he's got a girlfriend!"

There. She'd said it.

"A girlfriend? Are you sure?" Abby looked away from the mirror.

Ellie sighed and told her the full story.

"Oh, well, that's a relief then, isn't it?" Abby beamed, squeezing Ellie's hand. "I'm so pleased for you, honestly I am."

"What? Pleased that he's got someone else? I'm all nervous about some date that's obviously not even a date, and you say you're happy for me? Thanks for nothing!"

"Think about it—it's easy to wean him off this Lucy person. Changing his whole sexual orientation would have been a tad harder," Abby explained. "Mind you, she could just be a token girl—you know, to put people off the scent about his sexuality."

"I don't think so, Abby," Ellie muttered.

"Well, at least you're better off than me. Being single is the pits, but I guess I will have to get used to it," Abby replied. "So what are you wearing on this hot date?"

"Whatever I can find that you haven't borrowed, creased, or sat on," Ellie said. "And it's not a date!"

"Hold your horses," Abby ordered, yanking open the wardrobe. "Here—you look good in these."

She threw a pair of pink satin hipsters at her sister and pulled open another drawer. ". . . and finish it all off with my Chinese jacket!"

Ellie frowned.

"Isn't that a bit over the top?" she hesitated.

"No, you'll look dead sassy," Abby declared. "It's all about first impressions—if you've got it, flaunt it."

"Thanks," Ellie said. "Sorry I yelled."

"Sorry I left the cap off," Abby countered. "I wish I were coming with you and Blake instead of going to this dumb . . ." She stopped in midsentence as the door flew open and Georgie burst in.

"You two have got to stand up for me, okay? You've got to make Mum see sense because if you don't, I swear I'll run away and—"

"Georgie, what's going on?" Ellie interupted. "I'm trying to get ready to go out."

"I'm not stopping you," Georgie retorted. "I'm just letting you know that Mum needs dragging into the twenty-first century—like now."

The door burst open again and Julia stomped into the room, eyes ablaze.

"Thanks so much for knocking, Mum," Abby remarked wryly.

"Georgina, you do not run off when I'm trying to have a conversation with you!" Julia stormed, ignoring Abby completely.

"It wasn't a conversation, it was a lecture," Georgie snapped. "You should be pleased I got a job."

"A job?" Abby gasped, stepping back and standing on a discarded shoe.

"You're too young," Ellie added, brushing her hair vigorously.

"Don't you start," Georgie retorted. "It's just a few hours at the weekend, cleaning boats and stuff."

"Oh, well that's okay," Ellie said.

"It is most certainly not okay," Julia snapped. "What about her schoolwork? And besides, who will you be working with?"

"Ada . . ." began Georgie. "Oh, Alice and Emma and a whole gang from school." She thought it best to keep her mother off the subject of boys.

"And how do I know that the people you'll be working for are suitable?"

"Oh, like we are really in a position to be choosy!" Georgie shouted. "I need cash, they need help. I like boats, they've got boats. What's the problem?"

"You're only thirteen. . . ."

"Yes, Mum, I'm thirteen. So don't treat me like a ten-year-old, okay? You said we all had to knuckle under and make things work here. You said we had to try to make friends, make a new life. That's what I'm doing. Now, if you don't mind, I've got to go." Georgie stormed out of the room and clattered down the stairs.

"Wow!" breathed Abby. "I think puberty and

Georgie Dashwood have finally met. Could be interesting."

And even though Ellie didn't often agree with her sister's sense of humor, she winked at her as their mum trotted down the stairs in hot pursuit of their younger sister.

A few minutes later, with Georgie off to goodness knows where, Abby and Ellie ventured down the stairs, their nerves preventing them from realizing how sassy they looked.

"Now, Abby, have you got your phone? Remember never to put a drink down—it can so easily get spiked. And Ellie, dear, are you sure you're going to be warm enough in that skimpy top?"

"Darlings, am I interrupting anything?" a voice crooned in from the doorway. To Ellie's relief, her mother's attention was diverted as Davina, who had taken to showing up unannounced whenever the mood took her, burst through the open back door, carrying a tray of bedding plants.

"These need planting out as soon as poss, Julia, dear," she gabbled. "My goodness—aren't you two glamorous?" She beamed at Abby and Ellie. "Off on the razzle, are you? Jolly good for you."

"Abby's off with her school friends and Blake's taking Ellie out, apparently," Julia told her. "He's such a nice boy, that Blake—shame the relation to Pandora."

"Blake—you mean Lucy's Blake? Blake Goodman?" Davina cried. "Must be! Heaven knows there can't be that many Blakes around here!"

Ellie swallowed hard, the words "Lucy's Blake" reverberating around and around in her brain.

"He'll be here to pick me up soon," she mumbled, avoiding Abby's glance.

"Lucy's Blake, Lucy's Blake," she repeated the words under her breath as the doorbell rang, and Davina and her mum went to greet him.

"That's him!" Chloe grabbed Abby's hand and jerked her toward the corner of the dimly lit hall. "Isn't he to die for?"

Abby followed her gaze and searched the gaggle of guys setting up the drum kit. She couldn't see anyone remotely worth sacrificing life and limb for.

"Which one?" she shouted, raising her voice over the throb of Busted's latest hit.

"There, the tall one with the fair, curly hair—don't you just yearn to run your fingers through it?"

"Personally, no, but you clearly do," she laughed, placing her can of Dr Pepper on a table and nudging Chloe's arm. "So go on—get in there."

"What do you mean—I can't just go up to him and . . ."

Abby sighed, grabbed Chloe's shoulders, and turned her around to face her.

"Watch my lips," she ordered as the music faded and the DJ left the stage. "You go over there, you chat for a moment, then just as you walk away, you give him a dead alluring look and say something provocative."

Chloe chewed her lip and then gasped.

"Oh, my God, he's coming this way! I can't look—has he seen me? Is he . . ."

"Oh, for heaven's sake!" Abby stepped in front of Nick as he ambled toward the soft drinks bar. "Hi! You must be Nick Mayes—Chloe's told me what an ace drummer you are." She gestured to her friend and parted her lips in what she hoped was a winning smile.

"What? Oh. Right. Nice. Thanks." Nick looked somewhere past her left shoulder.

This, thought Abby, is going to be harder than I'd thought.

"So what's your scene?" she asked. "Garage? Hip-hop?"

Nick stared at her, a small frown puckering his brow. Abby scanned his features.

"Sort of folk-punk-pop, I guess," he replied with a glimmer of a lopsided smile.

"Cool," Abby murmured. "That is just so Chloe's thing. Right, Chloe?"

Chloe was standing, cheeks flushed and mouth half open, looking rather like a goldfish who had just found itself outside the bowl.

"Oh, me? Yes. Lovely."

"And have you recorded anything?" Abby went on, trying frantically to recall the jargon from her *Funk Now* magazine.

"No. Hope to. Soon. Perhaps." Nick mumbled, grabbing a can of cola.

Hopefully, sighed Abby to herself, his musical capabilities are superior to his conversational ones.

"Got to go," he said, glancing at his watch. "We're on in five."

Abby kicked Chloe's shin. "Say something," she hissed.

"Bye, then," Chloe whispered.

Nick nodded and ambled off, slurping cola as he went.
{ 185 }

"I give up," Abby sighed. "Was that your best effort?"

Chloe looked offended.

"On the sparkle front, you scored about minus ten," Abby commented. "But don't worry, we'll give it another go after they've played."

She eyed the group, who were taking their positions on the stage. The guitarist had acne that could have won awards, and the keyboard player had a shaved head, which was so not her style; but Ryan, the vocalist, looked quite cute in a swarthy, Celtic kind of way. And she had to admit that Nick looked passably fit. Hardly a star, but fit enough.

It's going to be a long evening, she thought. But then the band started playing, and Abby surprised herself when she realized she was actually dancing to the music—she couldn't help herself.

"They're good," Abby breathed several minutes later. "Very good."

"I said so, didn't I?" Chloe looked as chuffed as if she'd done the drumming herself. "Perhaps now you'll stop moaning about Norfolk every five minutes?"

Abby ignored the dig.

"How come," she mused, "Nick is such a dweeb to talk to but as soon as he gets drumsticks in his hand, he's passionate and fired up and . . ."

"You don't fancy him, do you?" Chloe's tone changed instantly as she halted her routine mid hip-shake. "You said he wasn't . . ."

"Of course I don't fancy him," Abby protested. "He is so not my type. And anyway, he belongs to you, or at least he will in ten minutes. Come on—and this time give it your best shot."

After some more dancing and coaching, Abby dragged Chloe over to the corner of the room where the band was dismantling their instruments.

"That was mind-blowing!" Abby began, touching Nick's arm. "Sensational—you've got a great sound going there."

"Great sound," echoed Chloe. "Dead cool."

"Thanks." Nick glanced at her, half-smiling, and then looked away.

Abby tried again. "You know, you should try to get gigs in a few of the clubs round here," she urged. "Oh, I forgot, there aren't any clubs round here, are there?"

"Sure there are—well, bars, anyhow. You know, Winkles, The Rotten Whelker. . . ."

My God, Abby thought, he can do whole sentences.

"I didn't know, I've only just moved here." Abby smiled. "I'm Abby Dashwood, by the way and of course, you know Chloe, don't you?"

Nick glanced at Chloe and nodded. "Yes, I guess I've seen you around."

Abby sighed inwardly. Clearly Chloe hadn't been thrusting enough. She had a lot to learn.

{ 187 }

"Not a bad idea, doing a gig," Ryan, the vocalist, cut in, stuffing sheet music into a bag. "Get more publicity and stuff."

"It was Chloe's idea," Abby said quickly. "She is just so into the music scene, a real beat junkie. Right, Chloe?"

"What? Oh, yes, sure," Chloe gabbled. "You're ever so good—better than half the bands in the charts."

"You think so? Really?" Nick sounded enthusiastic, and Abby tried to ignore the fact that he was looking at her and not Chloe.

"Sure," Chloe said. "Definitely."

"So—let us know when you've got it set up," she said, running her tongue along her upper lip—she didn't even mean to do it—it was just habit for Abby. "And we'll be there whipping up the crowds!"

She paused, praying that Chloe would come in with the punch line, or at least mimic her lip-licking routine. But nothing. Prayer, she thought, was very overrated.

"And of course," Abby murmured, dropping her eyes, "you'll have to wait to find out what else we can whip up when roused, won't you?"

"Will we, now?" Nick began to look animated, winking at Ryan and actually meeting her gaze.

She twirled away, snatching Chloe's hand. Well, at least now he'd remember them.

"Okay," she told Chloe firmly. "I've done the groundwork. Now it's all down to you."

At half past eight, Ellie decided that Blake was just being kind, taking pity on her in a new place and doing the right thing by dragging her along to the sailing club to meet his mates. True, he had introduced her to lots of people, showed her the club lounge, taken her out on the balcony and pointed out which dinghies belonged to which of his friends; but as the evening wore on, he seemed edgy and distracted. Worse still, every few minutes someone would come up to him and say things like "Great to see you— where's Lucy?" or "Lucy still not back, then?" while giving Ellie a sidelong glance.

By nine o'clock she had had enough. Well, almost enough.

"I'm sweltering," Blake sighed, taking her hand. "How about we get some fresh air?"

A big part of her wanted to call it quits, but a bigger part wanted to be out on the jetty, hand in hand, and hopefully lip to lip with Blake. That was the part that won.

As they ambled out to the end of the dock, Ellie found herself holding her breath, watching the ripples in the water as they swam away from the boats, willing Blake to tell her something she wanted to her. And then, he did.

"I really like you, Ellie," Blake said softly as they stood {189} at the end of the jetty, listening to the jangling of the halyards and the soft cooing of roosting seagulls.

He leaned toward her, cupping her chin in his hand.

"No," she said, pulling away.

"But, Ellie . . ."

"What about Lucy? All evening I've heard nothing but your mates going on and on about Lucy and where she is and why she's not with you." She took a deep breath. "So come clean—just what is the score with you two?"

Blake's arms dropped to his side.

"It's complicated," he sighed.

That, thought Ellie, isn't the right answer. She'd hoped for something along the lines of *Lucy? Oh, she's history.* Or, *Lucy? Am I ever pleased to be rid of her!*

"So explain," Ellie urged.

"Well, we started going out together ages ago, when we were still at school," he began uncomfortably. "You know, just having a laugh, but then . . ." He hesitated.

"Then what?"

"Then it got more serious," he admitted, nervously shifting from one foot to the other. "But that was ages ago."

Her heart lifted, and she allowed herself to enjoy the fresh salty air and the perfect nighttime temperature for just a moment.

"And now it's over?" She held her breath.

"Yes—well, no, not exactly."

The fresh salty air suddenly smelled a bit more like stale fish than Ellie had noticed before.

"Oh, great! It's not over and you're trying to come on to me? C'mon Blake, I wouldn't have thought it your style." That's when she realized they were still holding hands, and she dropped his.

"It's not like that, Ellie," Blake protested. "Lucy's gone away because . . ."

"So she's on holiday and you want someone to fill the gaps till she gets back, is that it?"

"You've got it all wrong," Blake stammered, reaching for Ellie's hand.

"So is it on? Or off?" she was trying hard to keep her cool, but it clearly wasn't working.

"Well, on. Kind of. But . . ."

Ellie took a deep breath and forced a smile on her lips. "Fine. Now if you don't mind, I think I'd like to go home."

She waited for Blake to protest, but instead he turned toward the balcony steps and strode toward the car park.

❦ SECRET NO. 17 ❦

If love is blind, then friendship probably could use some glasses, too

"Annie? Have you got a moment?"

"It's Abby, actually, short for Abigail." Normally Abby would have totally dismissed a guy who couldn't even remember her name, but these were extenuating circumstances. Destiny had clearly instructed Nick to walk across the schoolyard at precisely the moment Abby was heading for the IT suite, and God knows after talking to Chloe that morning, and finding out that she had yet to utter more than a word to Nick, she certainly needed Abby's help.

"Sorry." He grinned, stuffing his hands in his pockets. "About that gig idea of yours."

"Not mine. Chloe's," Abby said brightly, sidestepping to avoid a gaggle of year nines in PE outfits.

"Whatever," Nick went on. "I wondered—I mean, not if you don't want to—but I'm going to suss a couple of bars on Friday, and I thought, well, maybe you might like to come."

"Me?" This was not the plan. He was meant to want Chloe, not her. She had to get out of this and fast.

"I've got this new car," he went on eagerly. "We could go for a meal first, if you like, and then check out the bars. See which one you think is best."

"That would be great." She smiled sweetly. "Only, it's not me you want—I'm a new girl round here. Besides, it's Chloe who's got her finger on the pulse of the music scene."

"Right. So you don't want to come. Fair enough."

If he hadn't looked so crestfallen, if his hair hadn't at the very second flopped into his left eye, and if he hadn't, for one fleeting second, brushed his hand against hers, she would have turned and walked away.

"Of course I want to come," she said, flicking her hair over her shoulder and briefly touching his arm. "Tell you what—how about me and Chloe and you and—who's the vocalist guy?"

"Ryan?"

"Yes, him. Team effort—two musicians and two fans— the perfect combination for choosing your launch venue!" She knew she sounded like a paragraph from a badly written teen magazine, but desperate situations called for drastic solutions. "Pick us up at seven, yes? I'll tell Chloe. It'll be a blast. What a clever idea of yours!"

On Friday, Nick and Ryan picked up Abby and Chloe, and they began their night about town. Abby was fairly certain it was the dullest date she'd ever been on, though she was beginning to see what Chloe saw in Nick.

"I just need the loo," Abby said, stifling a yawn.

"Again?" Chloe gasped. "Are you ill?"

"No, dimbo," Abby hissed. "I'm leaving you two alone. It's called tact."

Honestly, she thought, pushing her way through the clusters of drinkers in the Rotten Whelker, I give up. Chloe had no technique at all. She sat there drooling at Nick, but she never took the initiative.

Abby pushed open the door of the Ladies and joined the queue. Nick was quite sweet, really, and if Chloe didn't act more assertively, someone else would come along at school and snap him up. She really should get on with it.

Abby yawned. I'm exhausted, she thought, what with moving seats every time Nick sits beside me and following Ryan to the bar in order to leave the lovebirds alone. And what does Chloe do? Nothing.

After forcing herself to pee for the tenth time that night, and readjusting her ponytail, she exited the ladies' room and hoped that she'd find Nick and Chloe deep in conversation. No such luck.

"Want a drink?" Nick caught Abby's arm as she headed back from the loo. "I'm leaving those two alone!"

He grinned, oblivious to Abby's expression of alarm.

"Ryan really fancies your friend," he said.

"He does?" Abby gasped.

Nick nodded. "Cool, isn't it?" he murmured. "Gives us more time to get to know one another."

"Um, huh, right," Abby said, glancing at Chloe and Ryan. "But—" Then, for some reason Abby stopped herself. Maybe it was the way Nick was smiling at her, or the warmth of his hand on the small of her back, but whatever it was, she didn't protest anymore.

After checking out the next bar, Abby became more and more certain that perhaps Chloe and Ryan really were the better match, anyway. They certainly weren't having any trouble with conversation, and goodness knows she and Nick had hardly shared a word all night.

{ 195 }

"This place has a better feel than the other bar, hasn't it?" Nick shouted over the beat of the band in McGinty's Cavern. "More upbeat."

"I don't like it," Ryan interrupted.

"I do," Chloe said. "You're so right, Nick."

"Well, yes, actually, it is quite good," Ryan burst out. "What I meant was, I don't like to make a decision on just one evening."

He edged closer to Chloe.

"So how about we do this again?" he asked eagerly.

"We?" queried Chloe, throwing him a withering look.

"I'm dead busy next week," Nick said.

"Me, too," Abby lied.

"That's fine," Ryan said enthusiastically. "Chloe and me could suss out some of the places in Cley or Holt and report back. Okay, Clo?"

Bad move, Ryan, thought Abby. Chloe hated having her name shortened.

"Actually, no," retorted Chloe. "It's got to be Nick's decision. He's the glue that holds this band together."

Okay, maybe she does still like Nick, then, thought Abby. I can work with that.

"Without him," Chloe went on, "the rest of you would be nothing."

Hang on, Abby cringed. That's a bit hard.

"Okay, so how about next Friday?" Nick said hastily.

"I can't do Friday," said Ryan.

"I can," Chloe said. "Abby can't though, can you?" She shot a warning glance across the table.

"No way," Abby agreed. "Worst possible night for me."

"In that case," Nick began.

"Actually, I could do Friday," Ryan interrupted suddenly.

"Great," Abby cut in, anxious to get the whole thing over with and go home. "You don't need me—you two and Chloe give it your best shot and update me afterward. Okay?"

"Cool!" Chloe's grin was as broad as a Cheshire cat's.

"I guess," muttered Nick.

"Fantastic," said Abby. "Can we go now?"

Abby was halfway up the stairs to bed when her mobile phone bleeped that it had a message: WILL U COME OUT WITH ME ON THURSDAY? JUST THE 2 OF US? CU 2MORROW. NICK

The only thing worse than knowing your guy has a girlfriend is hearing about her. The only thing worse than that is seeing her

"So come along, people—tell all!"

Davina, faithful to her self-established Sunday-morning after-church ritual, settled herself into one of the sagging armchairs in the sitting room of Marsh Cottage and put her feet up on the coffee table.

"The garden's looking so much better, Julia darling— you are clever. Love those blue things," she went on.

"Delphiniums," Julia smiled, offering her a plate of flap-jacks. "They were here already, just buried under a mass of bindweed. What I plan to do is make a path and then plant aquilegias and cranesbill, and maybe some kniphofias and sedums for the autumn, or perhaps . . ."

"And have you made friends, girls?" Davina rushed on, clearly anxious to avoid a horticultural dissertation. "I heard all about you falling out of Adam's boat, Georgie—sounds hilarious!"

Ellie grinned to herself as Georgie dropped her copy of *Dinghy Sailing for Beginners* and pulled a frantic face at Davina.

"Boat? Falling out? Adam?" Julia almost spilled her coffee in alarm. "Georgie, what's going on?"

"Uh, I didn't mean falling out as in falling out," Davina replied hastily, mouthing the word "sorry" to Georgie. "I meant leaning out, you know, sailing like a real pro! And how about Abby?"

"She's still in bed," Julia sighed.

"Well, not surprising, really," Davina commented, taking another bite of flapjack. "I saw her coming out of the Rotten Whelker bar last night and thought she looked a bit . . ."

"Bar?" Julia's coffee was destined to end up all over the carpet. "I specifically told her . . ."

"Coffee bar," Davina said hastily, causing Ellie to wince visibly. "Type thing, sort of," Davina ended lamely. "And you, Ellie darling—how's school? Have you made any friends?"

"Afraid not," her mother intervened. "I can't think why because—"

"Mum?" Ellie squashed the urge to throttle her mother.

"Well, we will have to do something about that," declared Davina. "I know—Lucy!"

Every nerve ending in Ellie's body went on red alert. "Lucy?" she gulped.

"That's right," Davina went on, biting enthusiastically into one of the biscuits Julia was offering. "Well, of course, you know Blake, so you're bound to meet Lucy soon enough—they come together like ham and eggs, bless them. Anyway, I've got a rather spectacular plan."

Ellie didn't realize that she had groaned out loud until she got a withering look from her mother and heard Georgie stifle a giggle.

"Lucy will be back soon," Davina said. "I'll bring her over and introduce you, and then she can take you under her wing—lovely girl—known her since she was a baby. Such a popular little thing. Her mother runs Head Cases, that wonderful hat shop in Burnham Market, father's something rather high up in—"

"Honestly, I'd love to, but . . ." Ellie butted in.

"That's settled then," Davina carried on. "She's a pet. You'll just love her."

Somehow, Ellie thought, I very much doubt it.

"See, I won't be around that much from now on," Ellie smiled sweetly. "I've got a job."

"Job?" Julia's coffee finally connected with the carpet. "You never said."

"I only heard yesterday," Ellie explained, leaping up and grabbing a box of paper tissues from the mantelpiece.

"It's at the sailing club—behind the bar, serving food, that sort of stuff."

She caught sight of her mother's alarmed expression.

"It's okay—it won't affect my schoolwork," she assured her. "Just Wednesday evenings, the odd Friday and Sunday . . ." And every other shift I can get, she added silently.

"Oh, Ellie, I don't know that that's altogether suitable," Julia began. "Bar work—it sounds so—well, rather lower class, somehow."

"Oh, Julia, don't be so old-fashioned," Davina retorted briskly. "The sailing club is the trendiest place around. What's the word you young people use? Buzzy. That's it, buzzy." She winked at Ellie. "And work's work, when all is said and done. Besides, it's the perfect place for Ellie to meet some more young people. And she's sure to hook up with Lucy because she hangs out there all the time in the summer."

Oh, terrific, thought Ellie. Just terrific.

Just then the phone rang and Georgie dashed into the kitchen to get it. A moment later she called for her sister. "It's Blake!"

Ellie sighed and excused herself from Davina and Mum's chitchat.

"Hello? Oh, Blake. What? No, we discussed this—you've got . . ." She dropped her voice as she caught sight of Georgie peering over the banisters with a grin on her face. ". . . someone else and . . . Really?"

She gestured to Georgie to go away. Georgie merely grinned.

"Just a chat? As a mate? Yes, okay—well, that's fine. When? Thursday? See you then." She replaced the handset.

"Ellie's going out with *Blaaa-ake*! Ellie's going out with . . ." Georgie chanted, running down stairs.

"Georgie," said Ellie.

"Yes?"

"Shut up."

The next day, back at school, Abby had a different type of run-in to deal with. As she crossed the main lawn, she caught sight of Nick's floppy hair, and strangely, she felt her stomach lurch.

"Nick, wait!" Abby belted across the school forecourt. "Thanks for the text message, but . . ."

"Yeah, sure," he said. "Oh, and by the way. I'm real sorry about your dad. Ellie told me in French today."

"Thanks. Look, I can't see you on Thursday," she said.

"Wednesday, then?"

Abby shook her head.

"Well, I guess I could do Tuesday if it was . . ."

"No."

"Is it because of your dad? I mean, we could always go somewhere really quiet—walk along Holkham beach or go over to Brancaster or something."

"No—I just can't come, okay?" Abby pulled at her own ponytail.

"Oh I get it—you're not interested," he muttered, his mood changing. "Why can't you just come out and say so?"

"Because it's not like that." Abby found herself chewing her lip. "Look, Chloe really, really fancies you. Surely you know that?"

Nick shrugged.

"And," Abby went on, "she's my friend. I can't start going out with the one guy in the entire universe that's she's asked me to help her get her hands on."

"But I don't want my hands on her," Nick said. "I want them—"

"Must dash," Abby butted in hastily. "Things to do."

Abby hurried off, positive she'd done the right thing and that would be that. Of course, three hours, four text messages, and two phone calls later, she was feeling a bit differently again. After all, she couldn't very well get Nick to go for Chloe if they didn't spend any time together, and if going out on another double date was the ticket, she was willing to take one for the team.

"I'll come, Nick, but it has to be a foursome again. Promise?"

Nick grunted down the phone.

"If that's the only way I get to see you, then I suppose I

have to go along with it," he sighed. "But don't think I like it, because I don't."

"He's here!"

Ellie jumped and smudged her mascara as Georgie burst into the bedroom and flopped down on Abby's bed on Thursday evening.

"Blake? Here? Now?" Ellie gasped.

"You sound just like Mum," Georgie giggled. "Of course, Blake—"

"Get off my bed," Abby butted in, shutting off her hair dryer and running her fingers through her hair. "You stink."

"Yacht varnish," said Georgie happily. "Me and the gang are helping Mr. Dutton do up his boat. Anyway, Ellie, they're in the sitting room and Mum's . . ."

"They?" Ellie swung round. "What do you mean, they?"

"Him and this other guy," Georgie said. "Piers someone or other—looks really up himself, if you ask me. Wears shades inside the house—I mean, how naff is that?"

Ellie grinned, both relieved that Lucy wasn't there and that her little tomboy sister had noticed what a guy was wearing.

"They're in the sitting room and Mum's just got to the *You will take care of Ellie, won't you?* bit . . ."

"Oh, no!" Ellie blotted her lip gloss on a paper tissue as the ancient bell pull in the porch clanged.

"It's okay, I'll get it," Georgie said. "It'll be Emma—she's taking me to Young Farmers. It's a rafting evening, but don't tell Mum. She thinks we're bottle-feeding lambs!"

She clattered down the still uncarpeted stairs.

"Do I look okay?" Ellie pleaded, throwing her makeup bag onto the bed. "I mean, not too dressed up and in your face?"

"Quite the opposite," Abby assured her.

"What? You mean I look a scruff? You could have said—oh, whatever, I don't have time to change right now."

"No, I don't mean that at all," Abby sighed. "You look classily casual, okay?"

Ellie was halfway through the door when Georgie charged back up the stairs.

"It's a guy for you, Abby," she panted, pushing Ellie out of the way to see Abby. "Nick Mayes?"

"Nick? From school?" Ellie asked. "Is this—well, you know . . ."

"No, it is not!" asserted Abby. "Nick's a mate of Chloe's—he's only picking me up because he's the one with the wheels."

"Well, he's in the sitting room now, along with Blake and Piers," Georgie went on, "and now Mum's moved on to the *You don't know the hell we've been through in the last six months* bit. You'd better get down there before she scares them all off forever."

* * *

"What's wrong?" Abby demanded as Nick drove through the village. "You haven't said a word since I got into the car."

He rammed the gears and accelerated.

"I didn't realize all your mates were so flippin' posh."

"What? Don't be dumb. . . ."

"Me? I'm not the dumb one—what about those two with their plummy accents, and their designer label gear? They looked at me like I was a right scruff."

"Don't be silly," Abby said. "Blake's not like that—he's hardly Mr. Sophisticated himself."

Nick sighed.

"And then when your mum asked where I lived, and what my dad did . . ."

"Oh, God, she didn't did she?" Abby sighed. "I'm sorry. She does tend to want a full CV from anyone I even look at."

"And just so as we get everything clear," he went on, pulling out to pass a woman on a bicycle. "My mum works in the supermarket in Burnham and my dad's been laid off, which is why I don't go around in Burberry and Hugo Boss, okay?"

"Will you shut up and listen?" Abby shouted. "I reckon you're a real nice guy, and I don't give a toss what you wear, okay?"

The moment she had said the words she realized her

mistake. She had wanted to make Nick feel good about himself, but suddenly he was gazing at her with wide-eyed adoration.

"You don't? I mean, you like me?"

"Of course I do," she murmured. What else could she say? "But Chloe—"

"Chloe nothing. So will you come to King's Lynn with me tomorrow? The Sunday market is great for old vinyl records—I collect them."

"Why don't you take Chloe?" Abby urged. "She'd be so into all that stuff."

"Oh, I get it—you don't want to be seen out with me. Well . . ." { 207 }

"I'll come," Abby said. "Of course, I'll come."

After all, they were mates. Just mates. And it would give her a great opportunity to point out all Chloe's good points.

"So, you're the famous Ellie!" The tall, lean guy with the Armani shades gave a mock bow before vaulting into Blake's MG Midget and perching on the folded soft top. "I've heard all about you—and I must say, Blake's usually a dark horse."

"Piers, for God's sake." Blake flushed scarlet as he climbed into the driving seat and started the engine. "You're embarrassing Ellie."

"No he's not." Ellie smiled.

"This," Blake went on, glancing over his shoulder, "is Piers Fordyce, who, when he's not playing the fool, is my best mate from school and soon-to-be America's Cup yachtsman."

"I wish." Piers laughed, as Blake accelerated down the lane. "Sorry to play gooseberry, but my car died this morning, and what with Lucy still away, I knew I could cadge a lift."

Lucy? Why couldn't everyone just stop saying that name all the time? Ellie was quite sure Lucy was the new four-letter word in her life. Her heart plummeted like a stone.

"I thought we'd drop Piers off at the sailing club and have a couple of drinks and decide what to do," Blake said, glancing at Ellie as he turned onto the coast road. "We could walk along the beach to Allie's Fish Bar or . . ."

"Come off it, Blake," Piers interrupted. "Don't tell me that's all you can think of doing with a gorgeous creature like Ellie? Where's your imagination, man?" He leaned forward and punched Blake on the shoulder. "While the cat's away and all that . . ." he chuckled.

Georgie was right—this guy is so up himself, Ellie thought.

"A walk would be lovely," she told Blake, glancing back at Piers. "Really good."

After they dropped Piers off at the club, Blake and Ellie

made their way toward the beach, taking their shoes off once they made their way over the dunes.

"I've found this course—Art with Photography, at Brighton College of Art." Blake stopped halfway along the sands. He turned to Ellie, a broad grin on his face.

"That's ace," Ellie murmured, her mind still mulling over the Lucy issue. "And have they got places?"

Blake picked up a seashell and tossed it back and forth in his hands.

"Yes, and what's more, I've got all the right A levels and stuff," he sighed. "I could live with Pandora rent free at Holly House—I mean, oh gosh . . ."

"It's okay," Ellie sighed, dragging her big toe in the wet sand. "I've gotten used to the idea."

"Well, it's just that it would be just so perfect."

"So, go for it," Ellie encouraged, trying to ignore the pang in her chest at the mention of her old home. "What did your parents say?"

Blake looked at her and raised his eyebrows.

"You want the shortened version, or the whole works? Mum said 'Oh Blake,' which is all she ever says if Dad is within earshot. . . ."

"And your father?"

"He told me I was wasting my education, failing the family, opting for an easy life, behaving like an idiot—and those were just the polite bits."

"Mmm." Ellie sighed sympathetically. "I guess you just have to go it alone, then."

Blake shook his head, his mood suddenly darkening. "How can I?" he argued. "College costs money. . . ."

"Get a job in the evenings, take out a student loan," Ellie began. "Anything's possible if you really want it enough."

"I guess," Blake murmured, sounding totally unconvinced. He glanced at Ellie. "I don't have to decide yet, I guess—not if I take a year off and start next autumn. Dad says I should take the next few weeks while I'm . . . well, I should think about the family reputation, among other things. That's when I texted you and said I was coming up. I just wanted to have a sane conversation with a rational human being." He smiled down at her. "Trouble is, it's not going to work."

Ellie frowned. "What do you mean?"

"I don't want to talk to you about it," he admitted. "I just want to kiss you."

Every cell in her body went on red alert. Remember Lucy, her conscience told her. He's Lucy's Blake—ham and eggs, bless them. She hated liking him so much despite being so angry about what he was doing, and she hated feeling like he liked her, too, even though there was someone else.

"Hey, I thought you said something about a fish bar," she gabbled, turning away just as his lips reached her cheek. She backed away and tried to laugh it off, picking up a seashell and tossing it into the dark water. She didn't want to make the moment any more awkward than it already was.

"What?" Blake pulled back. "I thought . . ."

"Come on," Ellie said, turning to him with as bright a smile as she could muster. "I'll race you along the beach."

She broke into a run, and it wasn't until she reached the disused slipway that she realized Blake hadn't joined in.

He was ambling toward her, hands stuffed in his jeans, and for a fleeting moment, she couldn't help wishing that she'd had the kiss before acting on her principles.

"Listen, Ellie," Blake pleaded, as they reached the door of the fish bar. "Give me five minutes to explain, okay? Just five minutes?"

"What's to explain?" asked Ellie, shaking him off. "You and Lucy are an item and . . ."

"Just shut up, will you?" Blake exploded.

Ellie was too taken aback by the outburst to answer.

"Yes, Lucy and I *were* an item. No, I haven't told her it's over yet. And you know why?"

"It's no concern of mine," Ellie lied, reaching back into her debate team lingo from St. Etheldra's.

"Because," Blake went on, ignoring her, "she's staying in Cornwall with her grandmother who happens to be dying."

Ellie swallowed. "Oh," was all she said because she couldn't think of anything else.

"Lucy's gone down to say her good-byes—and probably, knowing Lu, to check that's she's in the will!" He attempted a smile.

"I'm sorry," Ellie apologized. "I didn't realize."

"So, you see, I can't tell her it's over, can I? I can hardly dump her by phone. "

"I suppose that's true." Ellie nodded thoughtfully. "But when she phoned that time at Holly House, you said you loved her."

Blake's face turned red. "Well, she kept on asking me
if I did and it just seemed easier to go along with it until she got back, and I could explain to her face."

"So, when is she coming back?"

"Next weekend, all being well," Blake said. "I'll tell her then, I promise."

"Truly?" Ellie smiled. "I mean, only if you want to . . . I mean, if you think that you and I could . . ."

"We could," Blake assured her, leaning toward her and cupping her chin in his hands. "I'll show you how we could."

His lips were only a millimeter from hers.

"No, Blake!" She pulled away. "Not now. Not yet."

"For heaven's sake, I've said I'll tell her, haven't I? What's your problem?"

"The problem," Ellie retorted, "isn't mine. It's yours. And it's called Lucy."

"Fine," Blake looked at her, with a twinkle in his eye. "Then let's eat some chips, at the very least."

Ellie agreed, and after the waitress brought them over their fish-and-chips and pints, Blake made her an offer.

"Okay, so if I promise not to come on to you, can I see you tomorrow?" Blake smiled at her playfully. "I'll keep my hands in my pockets, I'll talk about the weather. . . ."

Ellie struggled not to laugh as she took a bite of fried halibut. Blake looked so appealing and pathetic.

"That would be great," she nodded. "And Blake?"

"Yes?"

"It's not that I don't like you," she insisted.

It's just, she added to herself, *that once I've kissed you I have a feeling there will be no going back.*

"Good." Blake smiled.

⚉ SECRET NO. 19 ⚉

Remember No.18? Um, yeah

Ellie grinned at Blake the following afternoon, as they walked barefoot through the sand dunes from Holkham beach.

"I never realized there were so many beautiful beaches round here," she told him, casting her eyes over the vast expense of seashore with its waving outcrops of sea grass and scattered piles of driftwood.

"They used this beach at the end of the movie *Shakespeare in Love*," Blake told her. "None of the locals were allowed on it for three days!"

He slipped a hand into hers.

"What shall we do now?" he asked. "Movie? There's a good one on in Hunstanton."

"I've got loads of homework," Ellie insisted, shaking her head. "I'm behind as it is."

"Just an ice cream and a coffee, then," Blake urged.

"Okay," Ellie grinned, turning down the path to the ice-cream kiosk. "What's another ten minutes?"

Blake and Ellie ordered their ice creams—pistachio and mud pie—and had just shoved one another's cones playfully in each other's faces when a shrill voice from behind made Ellie jump.

"Surprise, surprise!"

"Oh, my God!" The color drained from Blake's face and he lost his grip on his cone. It found the unfortunate landing place of Ellie's foot.

Ellie spun around to find herself staring into the face of a wafer-thin, pixie-faced girl with huge brown eyes, blemish-free skin, and the tightest-fitting leather miniskirt Ellie had ever seen. She knew instinctively who it was.

"Blakey, darling!" the girl cried, hurling herself at him. Blake looked at Ellie apologetically and hugged her awkwardly.

"Hi, Lucy," Blake stammered. "I thought you weren't coming up till next weekend."

"Couldn't stay away from you," Lucy piped up, her eyes scanning Ellie from top to toe. "And who's this?"

Ellie didn't need her psychology textbook to understand that Lucy was not exactly thrilled to see her.

"This is Ellie," Blake began. "She and I were just . . ."

"Oh, *Ellie Dashwood*," Lucy interjected, holding Blake's hand proprietarily. "Blake's told me all about you."

"He has?" Ellie was so taken aback that she struggled to get the words out. She wished she were dressed in something smarter than cutoff jeans and a sweatshirt.

"Oh, gosh, yes," enthused Lucy. "He told me all about your tragedy—you poor, poor, thing. It must be so hard for you, moving house, not knowing anyone, starting at a crap school . . ."

"How's your grandmother?" Blake cut in, as Ellie was wondering just how often Blake had been speaking to Lucy in order to impart all that information.

Lucy's eyes sparkled with unshed tears.

"She's gone into a hospice," she whispered. "They reckon she's only got a few more weeks at most."

Ellie's hard feelings softened. If Lucy was feeling one quarter as bad as she felt about her father . . .

"I'm so sorry, Lucy—Blake told me about it the other day at the sailing club," she said gently.

"So, you two have been out together?" Lucy's grief appeared to evaporate in an instant.

"Oh, no—just in a gang," Blake said quickly. "With Piers and some others, you know."

The look of relief on Lucy's face did not escape Ellie's notice. She also found it pretty hard to ignore the anger in the pit of her own stomach—if taking a romantic walk on the beach was hanging in a gang, then Ellie apparently had been confused about the English language for some time now.

"Piers? How is he? Bless him, he phoned me twice last week to see how Granny was getting on."

"He did?" Blake seemed annoyed. Which he shouldn't, thought Ellie, if he didn't care about Lucy anymore.

"I think he fancies me." Lucy giggled. "Now, don't look so worried, Blakey darling. . . ."

She leaned against him and puckered her lips. Blake pecked the top of her head.

"I must split," Ellie burst out. "Loads of homework to do. . . ."

"Homework?" Lucy cried. "Oh God, I keep forgetting, you're still a kid. I'm at college, but I guess Blake told you."

"No, actually," replied Ellie, fixing an oh-so-sweet smile on her face, "in fact, he hardly mentioned you."

She didn't bother to hang about to see the effect of her rebuff. There was only so long she could keep her cool.

Ellie had just finished her essay on the effects of aroma on supermarket sales, when the doorbell rang. Since everyone else was out, she had no choice but to answer it.

"Hi, it's me!" Lucy stepped over the threshold before Ellie could think up an excuse to shut the door in her face.

"Just thought we could get to know one another better," she said, fixing Ellie with a steely stare. "If that's okay with you, of course?"

Not at all, thought Ellie. "Would you like a drink?"

"No, thanks," Lucy replied. "Blake's picking me up in

half an hour and I have to smarten myself up. You *do* know that Blake and me—we're an item?"

"Yes, he mentioned it," she stammered.

"That's good," Lucy grinned. "He's a cutey pie—I mean, I've had loads of boyfriends, but he's the sweetest so far." She eyed Ellie closely. "So he took you to the sailing club, yeah?"

Ellie nodded. "But only because I applied for a job there," she said hastily, unsure why she was protecting Blake. I should drop him in it, she thought. He deserves it.

"A job? What for?"

"To earn money," snapped Ellie.

"Oh, sure, I forgot—poverty must be so wretched. Now then, who can we find for you? Someone dishy, with cash of course, who will spoil you rotten!"

"That's really kind but . . ."

"Now, there's Piers, he's sweet and terribly brainy. Going to be something clever in the City after uni, part of his father's firm. Loads of money. But he's definitely not your type."

She eyed Ellie up and down as if finding someone who would deign to go out with her was too much of a challenge.

"There's Miles—you won't have met him yet because he's on his dad's ranch in Montana. His stepmother is a model, she's been on the cover of *American Vogue* and knows absolutely everyone worth knowing. Then there's Jack, lovely but terribly spotty, and he hasn't got two pennies to rub together. None of them a patch on Blake, of course."

At least we agree on something, Ellie thought.

"Blake's dead clever too," Lucy went on. "He's going to do law. . . ."

"No, art, surely?"

"Oh, that—we dealt with that," she tittered. "His father had a quiet word with me—said he knew that if anyone could make Blake see sense, it was me—they absolutely confide in me all the time, you know. And as I said to Blake, fiddling about with a paintbrush and a stick of charcoal is great as a hobby, but it's hardly a proper job, is it?" She giggled. "So, when we were sailing a couple of weeks back . . ."

{ 219 }

"You sail?" Ellie cut in through gritted teeth. She had hoped that Lucy was a landlubber like herself.

"Of course—I was virtually born in a boat." Ellie thought that if Lucy giggled in that high-pitched way once more, she might be forced to throttle her. "I've got my Coastal Skipper certificate and everything. You?"

Ellie shook her head.

"Really?" Lucy's forehead puckered in a frown. "How odd. Anyway, just think, in a few weeks' time, I'll be sailing in the Whitsunday Islands."

"You will?"

"Yes, didn't Blake tell you? It was my great idea for the summer—I've got a mate with two yachts at Byron Bay and . . ."

The striking of the hall clock stopped her in her tracks.

"Oh, God, is that the time? I've got to curl my eyelashes and wash my hair and Blake . . . Well, must dash!" She ran down the hall, glancing back over her shoulder. "So you're okay with all that, yes? It's me and Blake, and you can have your pick of the rest."

She laughed but her eyes weren't smiling.

"Fine," Ellie said with a weak smile.

After all, Blake would deal with it. And by tomorrow, Lucy would know she was history. Wouldn't he? He was going to, wasn't he? Ellie tried to squelch the feeling of doubt that was rising in her stomach.

🌑 SECRET NO. 20 🌑

Love triangles are really anything but lovely

"Hi, Chloe, have a good weekend?" Abby slung her schoolbag under the chair on Monday morning and turned to her friend.

"What's it to you?" Chloe snapped. "You couldn't give a toss about me, you two-faced cow!"

"What do you mean?" Abby asked, stunned.

"How could you do that to Chloe?" Samantha Carter chipped in, coming up behind her and shoving her out of the way.

"I don't know what you're talking about," Abby gabbled, praying that it wasn't what she feared it might be.

"Taking her boyfriend off her. . . ." Samantha spat.

"Hang on," Abby cried, her mind racing. "He's not her boyfriend. . . ."

"Oh, so you do know what I'm talking about, little Miss oh-so-innocent!" spat Chloe. "You said you'd help me get Nick and then you swan off to King's Lynn . . ."

"Yes, I was with him," Abby admitted instantly. "But simply because we're friends, and I was trying to get him to ask Chloe out."

"Oh, and you had to go to King's Lynn to do all that, did you?" retorted Chloe. "Get real—I wasn't born yesterday."

Abby tried again. "We were checking out the Sunday market," she reasoned. "Listen, if you don't believe me, wait and see; he's going to ask you out."

"Really?" Chloe said doubtfully.

"Truly, honestly. It's just that he knows that Ryan fancies you, and Ryan's his best mate, and he was in a muddle over how to go about it." As Abby said the words and saw the glimmer of hope in Chloe's eyes, she knew that she'd got in really deep. She might have saved her own skin—but only if she could get Nick to ask Chloe out, and considering that the time she and Nick had spent together over the weekend had been off the charts, and that she'd felt their chemistry popping like mad all over the place, it wasn't going to be easy. "You'll see," she added, spying Nick exiting the corridor at the end of the hall.

Abby shot off after him, and as soon as she caught up, she let him know that he'd have to ask Chloe out—it was the only way for Abby to save her own skin.

The look on his face as he said no was nothing less than disgusted.

"What do you mean, *no*?" Abby cried so loudly that a

couple of year nines warming up on the tennis court missed their shots. "You have to ask her—I told you . . ."

"I don't have to do anything," Nick retorted. "If I'm going to go out with anybody, I want it to be you."

"But . . ." Abby trailed off, distracted by her thoughts. *He is so cute, the way his bottom lip goes all squashy when he gets cross.* "Just do this one thing for me. I mean, look—Ryan's dead keen on Chloe, right?"

"He's besotted."

"Well, there you are, then," declared Abby. "All you have to do is set up a few dates—you, Chloe, and Ryan. Only don't tell Chloe that Ryan's turning up, okay?"

"And then?"

Abby sighed. Some people were so slow on the uptake.

"Then, you start being really off with Chloe, Ryan gets to be extra nice to her and bingo! They're an item and you're off the hook."

Nick nodded slowly. "And then you and me . . ."

Abby winked. "Well," she murmured, "if I knew for sure that my best mate was set up with a guy, and you were still free—who's to say what might happen?"

"Well," Nick began, taking her hand.

"Don't!" She pulled it away, not daring to risk anyone seeing them looking remotely like a couple.

"Oh great—now you won't even let me touch you," he sighed. "Okay, listen, I really like you, so I'll take Chloe out, but only in a gang and only twice. No arguing—that's the deal. Take it or leave it."

"And you'll ask her today? Like soon? Very soon?"

"I guess. The sooner I get it over with the better," Nick sighed. "And, Abby? I'm only doing this because of you."

He really is sweet, thought Abby. And if Chloe doesn't go for Ryan, then I'm not sure what I'm going to do.

It was all she could think about through most of the next period (not a good thing, considering a quiz was scheduled for the following week), but luckily Abby didn't have to wait long for good news.

"Oh, my God, Abby!" Chloe cried, catching Abby's arm as she headed for the locker room after lunch. "He's done it, he's done it."

"Who has done what?" asked Abby, determined to play dumb.

"Nick's asked me out!"

"I told you he would," she said calmly.

"I know, I'm sorry I ever doubted you," Chloe gabbled. "But you have to help me."

"Hey, I've done my bit," she protested. "It's up to you now."

"Listen, you know we've got a home study day tomorrow? Well, stuff studying—come with me to King's Lynn and help me choose some new gear. Please. I haven't a decent thing in my entire wardrobe. Please."

"I've got that awful German translation to do, and that math assignment," protested Abby.

"Copy mine," urged Chloe.

"Okay, okay, I'll come," agreed Abby before Chloe could change her mind. The last thing on earth Abby wanted to do on a pleasant spring day was homework.

"Great!" Chloe grinned. "The muffins are on me."

"Mum, you have to sign this now!" Georgie thrust a sheet of bright yellow paper into her mother's hands. "And I need the check for £56," she added.

Her mother scanned the paper, and Ellie and Abby watched curiously.

"Georgie, this is dated two weeks ago," she protested. "Why didn't you bring it home earlier?"

"Just read it, Mum," Georgie urged.

"'Cromwell Community School: Trip to Brecon Beacons.

"'I hereby give my consent for my daughter Georgina Dashwood to participate in the forthcoming camping trip to the Brecon Beacons as part of her bronze Duke of Edinburgh Award.

"'In signing this consent form, parents acknowledge that pupils will undergo training in orienteering, map-reading, and camp-building that will necessitate their being in groups of three or four without full-time supervision of staff'—Good heavens, I'm not signing that!" Julia threw the booking form back at Georgie. "How can they think of such a thing? Children unsupervised . . ."

"We are *not* children!" Georgie retorted, counting to ten in her head, like all the girls did at times like this. "We're year eight, for heaven's sake. Abby went camping with the Guides when she was eleven and you didn't go ballistic about that."

"That's true, Mum," Abby chipped in. "And Ellie went to France, remember? With year eight?"

Georgie threw her a grateful glance.

"That was supervised," her mother said. "What if something happened?"

"If you would just read the next bit," Georgie ordered, "you'd find out."

Julia snatched up the paper and began reading.

"'However, each group will be equipped with first-aid kits, and marshals will be positioned at strategically placed checkpoints to ensure that any unlikely emergency is dealt with speedily and efficiently.'"

"So you see, it's fine," Georgie declared. "It's totally educational—and character building and stuff." She knew her mother was very keen on character building.

"I don't know," her mother began. "I'm not sure that your father would have approved."

"Don't make Dad the excuse! You know he'd have thought it a laugh." She swallowed hard to get rid of the choking feeling that always came when she thought about Dad. "Now do you see why I didn't tell you sooner—you always make such a big deal of everything."

"For goodness' sake, sign it, Mum." Abby grinned. "That way, the house won't smell of seaweed and yacht varnish for a few days."

"You can't say no now," Ellie added, winking at Georgie. "Think how she'd look in front of her mates—everyone would say you were neurotic."

"Which I'm not and never have been," retorted her mother. "All right, you can go. But you must phone each night and I'll give you a first-aid kit and . . ."

"Ace!" Georgie gave her mother a quick hug and headed for the door.

"Wait," her mother said. "What about this job down at the boatyard? You can't just ditch that on a whim, you know."

Georgie beamed. "It's all sorted. Adam's brother has offered to fill in." She knew the moment she'd mentioned his name precisely what would happen, and it did.

Her mother looked at Ellie, and Ellie looked at Abby.

"About this Adam . . ." her mother began.

"Who the hell," queried Abby at precisely the same moment, "is Adam?"

The only guy that's halfway on my wavelength since Tom, that's who, thought Georgie defiantly.

"Just this boy in my class," Georgie shrugged. "No one special."

She dashed out of the room before the family inquisition could really take off.

"That," she heard Abby say as she took the stairs two at a time, "means he's special."

"Get stuffed!" Georgie shouted back. "That is so not true!"

She heard the sound of muffled laughter and then Abby's voice once more.

"I rest my case," she said.

⚜ SECRET NO. 21 ⚜

Sometimes love really does find you when you least expect it
(and thus are not properly dressed)

No one told Abby the bus took three quarters of an hour to get to King's Lynn. Not only did it stop in every village and hamlet, but every few minutes someone would stick out an arm, the driver would pull up and collect parcels and then yabber for ages about the weather or some woman's bunions or the success of the village flower show. It was like finding yourself in the middle of a Jane Austen novel.

Accordingly, she was fifteen minutes late when the bus finally pulled up at the Market Square. It was pouring with rain as Abby grappled with her umbrella and began heading toward the shops. She ran across the square and past the Guildhall, dodging between the crowds of tourists and shoppers, and cursing herself for wearing a skirt as passing cars splashed mud up her legs.

"I'm looking for Top Shop," she gasped to a girl in a leather miniskirt who looked as if she might be clued up about fashion. "Do you know it?"

"Sure. The quickest way is . . ." But then she broke off and waved to someone on the other side of the road. "Just coming, sweetie!" she trilled.

"Top Shop?" Abby urged.

"Oh, sure! You just cut through that alleyway opposite, go across Queen Street, and it's facing you. You can't miss it."

"Thanks, you've saved my life." Abby pushed her already sodden hair out of her face and started running again, her head bent against the driving rain as she struggled to stop her umbrella from blowing inside out. So much for enjoying a spring day.

One minute she was running down Queen Street, relieved at finally having glimpsed the gaudy "Sale Now On" banners draped across the windows of Top Shop, the next she was facedown in a puddle of water, the contents of her bag sprawled across the cobbles, and two booted feet three inches from her left nostril. She was suddenly soaking wet.

"Hell, are you okay?" Abby was vaguely conscious of a guy's voice in her right ear. A firm hand gripped her arm and began hauling her to her feet. "I know that girls make a habit of throwing themselves at my feet, but this . . ."

"Get stuffed!" Abby yanked her arm away, brushing away tears of frustration and embarrassment with her other hand. "That is so . . . ouch! My foot!"

"You're hurt!" The guy grabbed her other arm and turned her toward him.

"Not half as much bloody pain as you'll be in if you don't—" But she stopped as she laid eyes on her rescuer. Tall, broad shouldered, huge gray eyes, wavy chocolate-brown hair, the faintest trace of Hugo Boss—it all hit her consciousness in a millisecond.

"Wow! Fiery as well as sexy—it must be my lucky day." The guy grinned at her and tightened his hold on her arm. "Hunt Meade-Holman, short for Hunter—and you are?"

"Abby Dashwood, short for Abigail," she said sweetly. "Pleased to meet you."

Ten minutes later, after he had bought her a coffee (she had declined an éclair because cream on the chin is not exactly a turn-on), some thrilling conversation, and a near kiss, she remembered Chloe.

"I've got to go," she cried, leaping to her feet and then sinking back into her seat as her ankle gave way beneath her. "Ow! Cripes!"

"You can't go yet, we're only just getting to know one another."

"I'm supposed to be meeting a friend," she began.

"Male or female?"

"Female," she replied with a smile.

"Thank God for that," Hunter sighed, looking deep into

her eyes. "Otherwise, I'd be forced to do away with the competition."

"I have to go." Abby insisted on trying not to let her delight at his remark show on her face. "I had a falling out with my best mate, and if I let her down again—which I suppose I already have by not turning up on time—well, I don't know what she'll do."

"So? The damage is done. Anyway, you've got a watertight excuse."

"Yes, but . . ."

"No buts," Hunter said firmly. "My car is parked just a couple of streets away. I'm driving you home."

Abby said nothing while a battle raged in her head. Chloe had probably given up and gone home herself, but then again she could be wandering around Top Shop waiting for Abby. Abby owed it to her to keep her part of the bargain.

"I'd love a lift home, please," she told him with what she hoped was an alluring smile, "but first, there's something we have to do."

Abby convinced Hunter to drop her by the shop, though she received a less than warm welcome a few minutes later.

"About flaming time, too!" Chloe, her arms full of clothes, glared at Abby. "You're half an hour late—hey, Abby? What's wrong?"

Abby pressed her lips together and tried a brave but weary smile.

"I had a fall," she murmured, limping a few steps to push her point home. "I've knackered my ankle."

"Oh, gosh, sorry, poor you. Is it very painful?"

"Pretty much. Hunter wanted to call an ambulance but I told him I had to get here to help you and . . ."

"Hunter?" Chloe asked. "Who is Hunter?"

Abby leaned toward her. "You promise you won't tell? I mean, seriously promise?"

Chloe's eyes widened in anticipation. "Of course," she said.

Abby jerked her head in the direction of the doorway, where Hunter was hovering, his head buried in a *Car City* magazine.

"He's my boyfriend," she whispered, wincing again for good measure as she hobbled on one foot. "New boyfriend, but whatevs. Isn't he a dish?"

"Boyfriend!" Abby was gratified to see that the word had precisely the effect on Chloe that she had planned. "So you and he—you're not—I mean, Nick and you . . ."

"Nick? How many times do I have to tell you, Chloe? It really hurts that you don't believe me." Thankfully the very real pain in her ankle enabled her to look on the point of tears without too much effort.

"I do, I do." Chloe was positively radiant as she gave

Abby a quick hug. "It's just that you never mentioned this Hunter person."

"Well, you know, it all happened quite fast," Abby said, ignoring precisely how fast it had actually happened. She rubbed her ankle pathetically.

"Look, I'll be fine," Chloe assured her, dead on cue. "You go and get that ankle sorted. But first, look, this is what I've chosen. What do you think?"

Don't tell her what you think, Abby thought, gazing at the mishmash of clothes of all styles and fabrics in Chloe's arms.

"The black's the sexiest, but the red is the most unusual." She smiled. "Depends exactly what image you're going for."

"Sexy," grinned Chloe. "Definitely sexy."

"Black, then," Abby said quickly, catching sight of Hunter out of the corner of her eye as he glanced at his watch for the third time. "And if you really don't mind, I do feel a bit faint."

"Of course I don't—and thanks, Abby. I'm sorry about—well, you know."

"Don't give it another thought!" Abby said breezily. "I'm just so happy to have been of help."

"Abby, what were you thinking of?" Julia demanded, rifling through her first-aid box for some arnica cream. "Getting in the car with a total stranger—anything could have happened! You don't know the first thing about him."

"I do now," replied Abby dreamily, resting her foot on the kitchen stool. "He's eighteen . . ."

"He looks older," her mother retorted suspiciously.

". . . his father's the local MP," Abby continued, ignoring her, " they live at a place called Fairfield Court . . ."

"Fairfield Court? That gorgeous Georgian house on the Fakenham Road?" Julia gasped, dabbing cream onto Abby's bruised ankle. "Davina took me there—the gardens are open to the public. It's an amazing place."

"Hunt left school last summer—Winchester, actually . . ."

Abby knew full well that dropping in the name of a top independent school would add to his status in her mother's eyes.

"Well, admittedly he did seem to have lovely manners," her mother conceded, pulling the wrapper off a crepe bandage with her teeth.

"Well, you'll see him again soon," Abby said quickly. "He's picking me up at seven. We're going out." She held her breath, willing her mother to think it was a wonderful piece of news.

"Going out? Don't be so ridiculous—you can't go out. I've hardly exchanged a dozen words with the boy."

"When he comes, you can do the full interrogation, can't you?" Abby said patiently, wincing slightly as her mother began binding her ankle with unnecessary vigor. "And he's taking me for a drive so I won't have to walk. Oh, Mum, he's so lovely and I think he really likes me. . . ."

Julia shook her head slowly and touched Abby's cheek.

"How could anyone not like you, darling? But don't get your hopes up." She switched into her doom-laden voice. "If everything you say is true, he'll probably turn his nose up at the way we're forced to live these days."

That was not what Abby wanted to hear. The look of fleeting surprise and the momentary frown on Hunter's face as they had pulled up outside Marsh Cottage hadn't escaped her.

"He's not like that," she retorted defensively. "Anyway, I told him all about what happened. . . ." She paused, suddenly realizing that she was digging herself into a rather deep hole. "But I made him promise not to mention it to you, because you'd get upset."

"That was thoughtful, darling," her mother remarked. "And I agree, it's best left in the past."

Absolutely, thought Abby, especially since I doctored the truth a little. So what if Hunter thought they'd leased Holly House out to a film company for a year or so while they fought Pandora in the courts? What if Julia was supposedly recovering from a nervous breakdown following

Max's death and thus, she mustn't be upset? Abby figured that by the time she had to tell him the truth, Hunter would be madly in love with her, and it would no longer matter at all. Abby had a way of justifying things.

Abby was on cloud nine. At last, after all those false starts, she was experiencing love in glorious Technicolor. She realized now that the way she had felt about Fergus, about every boyfriend she had ever dated, had just been childish infatuation, silly crushes that had nothing to do with true, adult, womanly love. Hunter was perfect; he had it all— looks to die for, sex oozing from every pore, money that kept flowing no matter where she wanted to go or what she wanted to do, and a car that was the envy of all her mates.

And thanks to Chloe, she had mates. Chloe had been out with Nick and Ryan not twice but four times and had told everyone that it was all down to Abby that she had found the love of her life. Even Amy and Samantha looked at Abby with new respect and asked her for advice on tactics for pulling guys, on top of everything else. Plus, Abby didn't even have to cope with her mother's usual neurosis.

"I think Hunter is a delightful young man," she had pronounced after Abby's third date. "Such lovely manners and such clean fingernails."

Abby knew that even the state of his digits wouldn't have counted for anything, had it not been for the way Hunter played her mother like a violin.

"Your garden, Julia," he enthused, "is quite stunning. We could do with you at Fairfield Court."

"This carrot cake is the best I've ever tasted—my mother's a hopeless cook."

"I love coming here—everything is so much more cozy than at home."

Within a week, he had Julia eating out of his hand. She didn't even complain that Abby was out three nights a week. The fact that most evenings involved a session at the sailing club seemed to set her mind at rest.

"Ellie will keep an eye out for you," she murmured by way of justification. Abby didn't bother mentioning that once they'd left for smoochy drives around the countryside or dimly lit nightclubs in Norwich, there was precious little Ellie could do. In fact, Ellie seemed to be the one person that Hunter couldn't charm.

"So what does Hunter do, exactly?" Ellie asked her one morning after Abby and Hunter had made a brief appearance at the clubhouse while Ellie was working.

"Nothing," Abby shrugged, looking up from her last-minute attempts to tackle the causes and effects of the Vietnam War. "He left school last summer and he's taking time out to decide what to do next."

"Lucky him," muttered Georgie.

"Very sensible," Julia murmured, pouring a cup of coffee. "Make sure he follows the right course."

Ellie frowned. "Well, he's had a whole year—surely he must know by now."

"Some people don't spend their whole lives worrying about tomorrow," she retorted, quoting verbatim Hunter's phrase to her from the night before. "The world is too preoccupied with work and achievement. He's trying to find the essence of him."

"Sounds like a cop-out to me," Ellie said with a shrug. "So, if he hasn't got a job, where does he get all his money from?"

"His father gives him an allowance, if you must know," snapped Abby. "He's dead wealthy and . . ."

"Just like we were once," Julia sighed. "Life is so much easier with money."

"Isn't his father the guy who is up before that Select Committee for supposedly accepting bribes about something or other?" Ellie ventured.

"Surely not?" Julia looked alarmed.

"That," spat Abby, quoting Hunter again, "is just a load of hyped-up media hysteria. Nothing's proven. Anyway, what's that got to do with me and Hunter?"

"It just sounds a bit dodgy," Ellie ventured. "I don't want you to get hurt."

"Oh, stuff it, Ellie!" snapped Abby. "I don't tell you how to behave with Blake, do I?"

"Blake?" Ellie shrugged, pushing her plate away and getting up. "What's Blake got to do with anything?"

"Clearly," Abby sighed, glancing at Georgie, "Blake has a whole lot to do with everything."

"Ellie? Blake on the phone."

Ellie's heart soared as she pushed her homework to one side. *Keep calm*, she ordered herself firmly.

"Hi, how are you?" She hoped she sounded really laid-back.

"Cool," he replied. "You?"

Time to cut to the chase, she thought.

"So did you tell Lucy?" Sugar—now she sounded too keen.

"Not exactly," Blake confessed.

"Well, either you did or you didn't," Ellie retorted, pressing the phone closer to her ear. So much for calm and laid-back.

"No, I didn't," he said. "See, she had a call when we got to the restaurant—her gran died that afternoon."

"Oh, no!" Ellie immediately felt racked with guilt for her impatience. "Of course you couldn't say anything."

"The funeral's on Wednesday," Blake explained. "She's in a right state, poor kid."

Ellie tried very hard not to feel jealous of the compassion in his voice. But he had called her "kid," which was promising.

"So when we get back from the funeral . . ."

"We?" Ellie's voice came out as a squeak.

"I'm driving her down," Blake said. "Her parents are already there, and she's too much of a mess to drive. What else can I do?"

Buy her a train ticket, thought Ellie savagely. And then she spent the rest of the evening despising herself for being so callous.

On their second date, Hunter had kissed her.

On their fourth date, he had taken Abby to meet his parents. Sadly, they were out, so they had kissed for a very long time in the sitting room on the chaise lounge, which he said was antique and worth a small fortune. And last night, on their sixth date, he had bought her a ring, a twisted silver band with a tiny green stone in the middle.

"Just to show the world you're mine," he had whispered as he slipped it tenderly onto the middle finger of her left hand and kissed her. The next day at school Abby slipped it onto her fourth finger.

"Are you engaged?" Chloe gasped.

"Not as far as the world is concerned," Abby admitted. "But between the two of us . . ."

She let the words hang in the air, and her street cred with year eleven soared overnight. If there was anything she could teach her sisters it was that spin is everything—Abby would likely end up as a VP of marketing someday.

♚ SECRET NO. 22 ♚

Sometimes the perfect guy for you isn't the perfect guy for everyone else.
And sometimes—and here's where it gets sticky—he thinks he is

"What the hell is going on?" Nick stood blocking the door to the science class, his face flushed and his sandy eyebrows knitted together in an angry frown.

"I've got to get to biology," Abby began, but Nick wasn't listening.

"We had an agreement, right? I would take Chloe out twice—twice, remember? And then you and me would get back together. Well—yes, or no?"

"Yes, but—"

"Yes, but you set me up!" he snapped. "You had already found someone better, hadn't you? Someone with a flash car, someone too stuck-up to wipe his own ass."

"Nick! It wasn't like that." Abby felt her stomach churning at the sight of Nick's ever-reddening face.

"Oh, give me a little credit!" He dropped his voice as one of the lab technicians pushed past them, glancing pointedly at his watch. "Chloe told me she saw you with Hunter Meade-Holman the day you went shopping with her—you told her he was your boyfriend."

"Yes, but I didn't really mean—"

Nick interrupted, "So even then, you were conning me and—"

"I'd only just met him that day," Abby protested. "And anyway, you took Chloe out four times, not two like you said, so I assumed you had fallen for her big-time and—"

"Is that really likely? When it's you I . . . Oh forget it," he snapped, turning away. "If Hunter Meade-Holman is the sort of guy you want, have him. See if I care—the stuck-up, self-opinionated—"

"You don't even know him," Abby began.

"Everyone round here knows Hunter!" Nick spat the words out. "He makes sure of that. No matter, though. I'm telling Chloe tomorrow."

"Telling her what?" Abby gasped.

"That I'm chucking her," he said. "That I fancy someone else."

"You won't tell her who?" The moment she had said the words she regretted them. Nick looked at her for one very long moment and then shook his head. He let the door swing closed in her face.

For the rest of the day, Abby tried to tell herself that she was blameless, that she'd never meant for Nick to fall for her, that she'd acted out of the best of intentions.

Somehow, it didn't seem to work.

The following evening Hunter sprang his surprise.

"I've got a new cat," he announced, the moment the front door had shut behind her. "She's amazing—you just have to come and see her."

Abby looked at him in amazement. He looked as excited as if he had just won the lottery. This completely proved Nick wrong—Hunter was an animal lover! How sweet was that!

"I've got a cat," she cried. "I love them."

Hunter grabbed her hand and kissed it spontaneously.

"You do?" He fired the engine and accelerated so fast down the lane that Abby had to dodge the overhanging branches of the hawthorn hedge from hitting her through the open window.

"I knew you were the girl for me! What kind is yours? Mine's a Tiger."

"Oh, Manderley's not at all fierce. She's Persian cross with next door's tabby," she laughed.

The expression on Hunt's face told her at once that she'd made a blunder.

"Oh, for God's sake!" he snapped. "I'm not talking about some dumb animal. Cat—catamaran? For sailing?"

Abby's brain went into instant situation survival mode.

"I know that, silly!" She tossed her hair and grinned at him, praying that she would look convincing. "I was just teasing."

Hunter looked slightly mollified. "So—do you or don't you sail?"

"Sail? Of course I do," she replied breezily. "Doesn't everyone?"

"Great," Hunter grinned. "We'll take her out right now. She handles like a dream—eighteen feet long, and her speed in the open water is amazing."

"Well, I'm not really dressed for—"

"Don't worry," Hunter interrupted, "you can hire a wetsuit at the sailing club." He eyed her closely. "Are you up for it or not?"

"Do you really need to ask?" Abby said, but she thought, Please God don't let me be seasick—vomit is so unsexy.

Ellie eyed herself in the mirror of the staff changing room at the sailing club. There was no doubt about it—the uniform suited her. Tight denim shorts, striped T-shirt, white deck shoes, and a lanyard with her name in mock sail stitch.

She walked through to the bar, pausing to gaze out of the huge picture windows overlooking the marina and the sand spits. From the barbecue deck below, above the sound of the halyards jangling in the light breeze, she could hear voices raised in friendly banter, bets being taken on who would win that afternoon's 470 class races. She was about to head for the bar for the lunchtime shift when her mobile phone rang.

"Ellie? It's me—Lucy."

"Lucy? How did you get my number?"

"Davina, silly. Anyway, listen—is Blake with you? His mobile phone's switched off."

Ellie shook her head and then realized that Lucy couldn't see through the phone. "No—why would he be?" she asked.

"He's not where he's supposed to be," Lucy replied curtly. "He's supposed to be taking me sailing, and he hasn't picked me up."

Sailing? You're supposed to be devastated about your gran's death.

"Perhaps he's caught up in traffic," Ellie suggested, and hated herself for covering for him all over again. "Oh, and I'm sorry about your grandmother."

"Thanks," Lucy said without much feeling. "And Blake is most definitely not with you?"

"I haven't seen him in ages," Ellie replied.

"Oh, good," Lucy sighed. "That's okay, then. Ciao!"

* * *

Abby was wriggling into her wetsuit and trying to stop the butterflies that were suffocating in her stomach when her mobile phone bleeped.

R U COMING 2 GIG 2NITE? SO XCITED. CHLOE

No way, thought Abby, wondering whether rubber-clad bums were a turn-on. Not if tonight's the night that Nick dumps her—I want to be as far away as possible.

Then again, Abby reasoned, Chloe was a friend. As Abby dragged her feet out to the dock she weighed her options. As she approached Hunter at his new cat however, her thoughts turned to the task in front of her.

The quay side at the sailing club was a hive of activity, with boats being rigged, crew yelling instructions to one another, and dinghies maneuvering out into the open sea. Abby was conscious of the strengthening breeze and the foam-crested waves and wondered yet again whether this was, after all, such a good idea.

"Isn't she a beauty?" Hunter said proudly. "She's going to slay the opposition at the regatta next week." He glanced at his watch. "Come on, let's get going. Here's your harness. . . ."

"Harness?" Abby tried to hide her fear by tying up a ponytail.

"For the trapeze, silly." He eyed her closely. "You have been out on the trapeze before, haven't you?"

Abby swallowed hard. She'd seen people at the

Brighton Marina hanging over the edge of their boats, their heads practically skimming the surface of the water, and she had always labeled them totally and irretrievably insane.

"Look, Hunt, I was just thinking . . ." She jumped as a hand landed on her shoulder.

"Abby? I thought it was you—this is amazing!"

The voice in Abby's left ear sounded vaguely familiar. "Blake!" she cried, turning around. "You never said you were coming up this weekend."

Hunter straightened up from rigging the boat and frowned. "Hi, Blake, haven't seen you in ages—you two know each other?"

"Sure," Blake nodded. "My aunt's . . ."

"Blake's aunt is keeping an eye on Holly House for us," Abby blurted out, throwing Blake a pleading look.

"Living there, actually," Blake remarked, holding Abby's gaze.

"Well, yes, obviously—you can hardly keep an eye on something if you're not there, can you?" Abby gabbled.

A look of recognition flashed across Hunter's face. "Oh I get it—during the filming?"

"Filming?" Blake frowned and stared at Abby. "I don't—"

Abby planted her left foot firmly on his toes.

"Can we get going?" she begged, clambering onto the boat. She didn't want to sail, but she reckoned the terrors of the ocean were nothing compared to Blake blowing her story about Holly House clean out of the water.

"Hunt, you're not taking that out on your own, surely?" Blake looked at them questioningly.

"No, Blake, if you look carefully, you will observe that I have Abby with me," Hunt retorted sarcastically.

"But, Abby doesn't sail," Blake replied, turning to face her. "And I don't think it's quite safe . . ."

"Doesn't sail?" Hunt's head jerked up. "Abby?"

For a moment, Abby had to fight the desire to pitch Blake headfirst into the harbor. But then as a gust of wind blew, she saw two dinghies almost capsize as they caught the cross wind, and reckoned that she had in fact been saved in the nick of time.

"Ellie said you hated the water and gave up after three lessons," Blake reminded her.

Oh-kay, she thought, glaring back at him. No need to go into all the sordid details.

"For God's sake!" Hunter hurled the rope into the boat and yanked on the zip of his wetsuit. "Why didn't you say? This whole day is turning out to be a disaster." He bit his thumbnail and then brightened. "You come, Blake—I'll show you how she handles."

"You know I can't." Blake shook his head. "For one thing, I'm waiting for Lucy, and for another, I'm not part of the syndicate."

"Syndicate?" Abby frowned.

"The boats belongs to six of the members," Blake said. "Hunt's dad is one of them, so he's okay, I guess but . . ."

"I thought you said the boat—cat—was yours," Abby said accusingly.

Hunt shrugged. "Dad's, mine, what's the difference?" he said assuredly. "Anyway, I need a drink. Want one?" He didn't wait for an answer and strode down the jetty.

"Don't worry," Blake said, as Abby turned to follow. "You're better off on dry land than on water with that maniac. He is a complete asshole in a boat."

"How dare you speak about my boyfriend like that," Abby snapped, quickening her pace.

"Boyfriend?" Blake looked gobsmacked. "You're going out with him?"

Abby nodded, crossing her arms dramatically across her chest.

"I didn't know," Blake murmured. "So is this why you've spun some dumb story about Holly House—to impress Mr. Up Himself?"

Abby was about to tell Blake where to go, but realized he was grinning at her. She shrugged.

"Okay, so I was stupid," she admitted. "But he's got this big house, and knows all these double-barreled people and I thought . . ."

"You thought you'd hang on to him if you impressed

him," Blake finished. "You won't, you know—Hunter doesn't, well, hang on for very long."

"Well, that's where you're wrong!" Abby retorted, more to convince herself than anything. "What would you know about it, anyway? You don't have a clue about love or romance or else you'd have got it together with Ellie by now!"

"Don't talk about stuff you don't understand!" Blake snapped, a flash of anger across his face.

"Look, I don't know what the problem is, but she's in the bar right now, and you're here, so for God's sake, go and see her and get your act together!"

"Leave it, Abby," retorted Blake, looking quite a bit more serious than she'd ever seen him before. "Just leave it."

"A large apple juice and soda water, please."

Ellie knew who it was before she turned around. Play it dead cool, she told herself, picking up a half-pint glass and turning to face Blake.

"Well, hi there," she said.

"How's it going?" Blake asked, nervously glancing over his shoulder.

"Cool," she replied. "Ice? Lemon?"

He nodded. "Look," he said, "about us."

"Blake, no—you've said all that needs to be said." Ellie picked up another glass.

He leaned across the bar and took her hand. "No, that's the whole bloody point," he stressed, raising his voice above the CD of Will Young playing in the background. "What I haven't said is that I think I'm falling . . ."

"Blake! Where have you been!" Lucy, purple in the face and with teeth clenched, belted up to the bar and grabbed his hand, wrenching his body away from Ellie.

"Lucy, cool it," Blake began. "You're the one who's late."

"No—you were supposed to pick me up, remember? And as for you," she said, wheeling around to face Ellie. "You liar! You said you hadn't seen Blake. And here you are with your nasty little beer-wench paws all over him!"

"I hadn't seen him," Ellie protested, cocking her fist on her hip. "He only just turned up. Looking for you. Worried because he couldn't find you."

She glared at Blake, daring him to contradict her. You deserve each other, thought Ellie.

"Well, I'm here now," Lucy said. "Take me sailing and I might forgive you."

Blake gave Ellie a pained look.

I hope she falls in, thought Ellie, slamming glasses onto the bar. Close to a very hungry shark. And I might just hope he falls in after her.

❦ SECRET NO. 23 ❦

Never turn down a date

"A gig? At the pub? Oh, Abby, it'll be dire." Hunter pulled her toward him and ran his hands down her back, resting them lightly on her bottom. Abby found this particularly rewarding since it had taken all afternoon, a lot of snogging in the sand dunes, and all her feminine wiles to pacify Hunt and make him forget her lie about knowing how to sail. "And besides, you promised we could have some real us time—somewhere romantic," he breathed, gently nibbling her left earlobe.

"I know, but . . ."

He pulled away. "Clearly you don't feel for me what you said you did." His tone was icy.

"I do, you know I do," Abby pleaded.

"So show me," Hunt whispered, cupping her face in his hands. "I'll be off to Scotland next week."

"Scotland?" Abby's heart dropped like a stone.

"My grandfather's estate," Hunt said rather grandly. "I'm going straight after the ball. I've got us tickets, by the way—so you owe me."

"How much?" Abby began scrabbling in her purse.

"Not in money, silly—in favors!" He ran his lips over the back of her neck, and shivers of electricity shot through her body.

"Well, we'll have to see, won't we? So what's this about Scotland?" Anything to change the subject, thought Abby.

"It's a great place—grouse shooting, deer stalking—and there's a dry ski slope at Glenshee . . ."

"That's something I can do!" Abby interjected. "I'm good at it—truly. And I've done clay pigeon shooting with my dad." *Ask me to come with you*, she pleaded in her head. "I'm free all summer," she added with a sigh. "And without you . . ." She let the words hang in the air.

"So make the most of me while I'm here," Hunt challenged with a grin. "Forget this stupid gig and come back to the house with me. My parents will be out. No prying eyes. . . ."

Abby's stomach lurched at the innuendo in his voice.

"Well, what if we go and get something to eat at the sailing club, then go to the gig, just for an hour, and then, I promise, we'll leave?"

"And if I say yes, you promise that you'll—you know? And this time, you won't back off?" Hunt sighed.

Abby took a deep breath.

"Mmm," she mumbled, trying to tell herself that he didn't mean what she knew full well he meant. "Come on—I fancy pizza with a whole load of chips!"

"Ellie Dashwood, you have been polishing that glass for the last five minutes to my certain knowledge!" Casey, the supervisor, grinned at her and gave her a friendly nudge. "Which one are you drooling over, then? If it's Piers, here he comes—so I'll leave you to it. . . ."

Ellie turned to protest but not quickly enough. Piers leaned over the bar and touched her arm. "Are you working tonight?"

Ellie shook her head. "No—why?" She slammed a couple of schooners down on the countertop with unnecessary vigor.

"Just that we're all meeting up at The Jolly Sailor—some new band's playing and they've got a barbecue running. Coming?"

"No thanks." Ellie shook her head.

Piers eyed her closely. "Why not? It'll be a blast."

Oh, sure, Ellie thought. Yet another hour of watching Lucy wrapping herself around Blake like a boa constrictor on speed, and standing by while my sister gets chatted up by the second-hottest guy in the room (well, possibly even the sexiest if you go for that sort of up-yourself arrogance). No thank you. "Not in the mood," she added.

"Are you in a strop about something?" Piers asked with a grin. "Is it Blake?"

"Why would it be Blake?" she retorted. "I've just got heaps to do." A weak excuse, but it would have to do.

"I just thought that Blake was rather keen—oh, well never mind," Piers murmured. "But do come to the pub—for my sake? Please?"

"What do you mean, for your sake?"

Piers sighed. "Because otherwise I'll be there, all alone, no one to talk to, and all this charm unused and going to waste and . . ."

Ellie giggled despite herself. "You're an idiot," she grinned.

"This is very true," said Piers. "I make idiocy into an art form. So you'll come?"

"Yes." She smiled. "I'll come. See you there at nine o'clock."

Later that night, Ellie stopped dead as she came out of the loo at the back of The Jolly Sailor—she'd heard a familiar voice but she didn't think she liked the sound of what it was saying.

"What on earth did you have to go and ask her for?" Blake was leaning against the bar wall, glaring at Piers.

"I thought you'd be pleased." Piers shrugged.

"You just have to interfere, don't you?" Blake grunted. "I've spent the last two months trying to get rid of—Oh, Ellie! Hi!"

Blake leaned forward and planted a quick kiss on Ellie's cheek. Act natural, Ellie told herself, clenching her hands together to stop them from shaking. Don't let him see that you heard.

"Can I get you a drink?" Blake asked, edging a little closer to her and peering anxiously into her eyes.

"Drinks? Oh, darling, thank you! Vodka and tonic, please." Lucy appeared from the corner of the room as if zapped to his side by remote control.

"Mine's a shandy," Piers interjected.

"And you, Ellie?" Blake repeated, the color in his face rising by the second.

"No thanks," she murmured. "Actually I was just leaving because—"

"Nonsense!" Piers interrupted. "You promised me you'd stay."

"And now she wants to leave," Lucy interrupted. "So let her."

There was something in Lucy's tone that set Ellie on edge, but she also got the distinct feeling that she did the same thing to Lucy. It was too good not to give up.

"Okay," she replied, giving Piers the brightest smile she

could manage. She turned to Blake. "J2O please, with loads of ice. I'm driving."

Blake pushed his way through the crowds of drinkers to the bar, Lucy close on his heels with her arm hooked through his, gazing up at him adoringly. Much as she wanted to, Ellie found she couldn't tear her eyes away from them.

"Nick, listen, please!" Abby stepped over the tangle of leads and loudspeakers and tried again. "There's something I need to say," she pleaded. "It's important."

"Like what? 'Go and get lost, Nick'? 'Go out with four of my mates, Nick'?" He grappled with his drum kit, turning his back on her just as Chloe jumped up onto the makeshift stage and shoved a plate of barbecued chicken and corn in his hand.

{ 259 }

"Hi, darling, I got you some food!" She planted a kiss on the back of his neck and Abby saw him visibly pull back. "I'm *sooooo* proud of you!"

Even Abby had to admit she was a bit cringe making.

"My very own pop hero!" Chloe practically screamed.

"Actually," Nick cut in hastily, "there is something you could do. Get me a cola—I'm parched."

"Sure!" She blew another kiss and headed for the bar.

"The moment this gig's over, I'm telling her," he muttered to Abby. "I can't pretend any longer."

Abby took a deep breath.

"Don't say anything to her tonight, please," she pleaded. "If you promise not to say anything to Chloe tonight, I'll go out with you again."

Nick gave a short, sarcastic laugh, and Abby hated herself for suggesting something so rude.

"If you remember, you are already going out with someone," he replied. "Or has he chucked you?"

Abby caught the note of hope in his voice.

"No, but . . ."

"Well, I'm not sharing you, okay? You may not think two-timing is a big deal—I do! And I don't go for cheap bribes either. Now, if you don't mind, we've got a gig to finish."

"Come on, Ellie, let's dance!" Piers grabbed her hand and dragged her onto the tiny space that passed for a dance floor.

She was about to make some excuse but then saw that Blake had turned from the bar and was watching her.

"Sure." She laughed, swaying in time to the beat and waving her arms above her head. She put a hand on Piers's shoulder and shimmied closer.

Blake was still watching.

"Answer me one thing straight, okay?" Piers asked her, brushing his lips close to her ear. "Do you fancy Blake? Because he says—"

"He says he wishes I was a million miles away, because

he's with Lucy," Ellie snapped. "I realize that now, and frankly I couldn't give a damn. As far as I'm concerned he can go to the other side of the world on a one-way ticket."

"So you do fancy him!" Piers laughed. He pulled her closer to him and glanced over her left shoulder to the bar. "That's good."

"What do you mean, that's good?"

"You're a great mover, you know," he murmured, putting his finger to her lips and then running his hands down her back to her bottom.

"At it again, are you?" Lucy appeared at her elbow, glaring at Ellie. "Can't keep your hands off men, can you?"

"What's it to you? You've got Blake, remember?" Ellie startled herself with the note of acerbity in her voice.

"My turn I think," Lucy hissed, turning to Piers.

"Hi, gorgeous!" Piers dropped Ellie's hand and winked at Lucy. And with that, she pulled him onto the dance floor, her hips already swaying to the beat of the J.Lo song the DJ had put on in between the band's sets.

Ellie was still staring after them and catching her breath, when Blake shoved a glass in her hand.

"Your drink," he said abruptly, handing it to her.

"Have a nice day sailing?" she asked sarcastically.

"Nope," Blake said, and disappeared into the Gents, leaving Ellie alone for only a moment.

A firm hand clasped her shoulder, and she turned to find

Hunter, a beer glass in one hand and a plate of sausages in the other. "Ellie, what is it with your sister? I get Abby a plate of food and what does she do? Swans off to chat up that adolescent drummer guy." He gestured toward the stage, where the band was taking a short break.

"That's Nick—he's a friend of hers," Ellie said, still watching Lucy, who was pushing through the crowd toward the bar, her hand firmly holding on to Piers. No wonder Blake looked miffed. If he was mine, I'd never treat him like that, she thought.

"The band's good, isn't it?" she muttered, in an attempt
to put Blake out of her mind and appear normal.

Hunter shrugged.

"Compared to what?" He took a swig of beer, wiped his mouth with the back of his hand, and sighed. "Frankly, this is all pretty dull, isn't it?"

"Compared to what?" Ellie snapped back at him, her bottled-up emotions finally spilling out. "Do you have to practice being so obnoxious, or does it come naturally?"

Hunter took a step backward and held up his hands in mock fear.

"Chill out!" he parried. "I was just making conversation. What's with everyone tonight? Blake's as jumpy as hell, Abby's uptight, Lucy's even more . . ."

"You know Lucy?" Ellie could have kicked herself for showing interest.

"Of course, everyone round here knows Lucy." He laughed. "I used to go out with her—well, so did Piers, and most of the rest of the crowd, to be honest." He took another gulp of beer. "Now she's with Blake, although God knows what she sees in him—no style, that guy, no style at all. Whereas Lucy . . ." He took a bite out of a sausage and glanced appreciatively at Lucy's backside perched on the bar stool. "She's a real little raver when she gets going. Mind you, I have high hopes for your sister, given time."

There was something about the way his lips transformed into something between a smile and a sneer that turned Ellie's stomach.

"Great potential," he murmured, draining his glass and dumping it on a nearby table. "Pity she doesn't sail—but she can go like the wind in other departments!"

"You . . ." Ellie bit her tongue and thanked her lucky stars that she was here to keep an eye on her sister.

✣ SECRET NO. 24 ✣

*Falling in love is the greatest adventure there is—which, incidentally,
can make it quite dangerous. After all, a broken heart can hurt
more than a broken leg*

Abby sat on the end of her bed, scribbling in her diary, the
words smudging as tears fell on the page.

Dear Diary,
*My life is over. I've been totally humiliated—and
by my own sister at that. Hunt stormed off last night,
and it's nearly midday and he hasn't phoned. We
always go out on Sundays. He thinks I'm a kid; I
knew I should have given in when he wanted to—
well, you know. I can't write it down because to be
honest it doesn't feel right—but I know that's what
guys want you to do and I kept making excuses. I
love him so much, but I was scared, and now I've
lost him forever. I should never have gone to the
gig, never have bothered about Chloe and Nick.*

She paused as her mobile phone bleeped from the pocket of her jeans. "Let it be him, let it be him," she whispered, flipping open the cover and seeing the text message alert flashing.

NICK'S CHUCKED ME. SAYS THERE'S SOMEONE ELSE. WHAT DID I DO WRONG? I NEED YOU LIKE NOW—RING ME, PLEASE. CHLOE.

Abby stared at the screen. She couldn't phone Chloe; she couldn't talk to anyone. She had her own problems to sort out, and anyway, Chloe's feelings about Nick were only puppy love, whereas her own . . .

"Abby? Hunter's here!" Julia's voice wafted up the stairs. "And he's in a hurry!"

The diary and the phone crashed to the floor as Abby leaped up from the bed and dashed toward the door, her heart beating wildly. It was when she caught sight of her reflection in the dressing-table mirror that she stopped dead. Puffy eyes, snot on the end of her nose, and mascara streaks down her cheeks—she couldn't let Hunter see her like this.

But she couldn't let Hunter not see her either.

"Hang on! In the loo!" she shouted, stuffing the diary back in its hiding place and grabbing her phone. "Give me five minutes."

This, she thought, dashing to the bathroom, never happens in the movies—no one's face ever swells up like a bloated pig when they sob. She splashed cold water on her face, blew her nose, and went to work with the concealer.

"Abby! Hunter can't hang about—what are you doing?" Julia hollered.

Abby plastered on the lip gloss, looked in the mirror, pouted her lips as sexily as she could, and flew down the stairs, ignoring the distant shrilling of her phone from the bedroom.

As Abby scrambled through the sitting room, she could hear Hunter chatting to her mother in the kitchen.

". . . so I'm off to Ballater tomorrow." She heard him say.

Tomorrow? He wasn't supposed to go to Scotland till after the ball.

"Look, if Abby's not ready, I'll have to make tracks—so much to get done. . . ."

No way, thought Abby. You can't leave.

"Hi, darling!" she cried brightly, pushing open the kitchen door and remembering the instructions for dealing with relationship crisis in her latest copy of *Heaven Sent* magazine. "What are you two nattering about?"

"Hunter's off to Scotland," Julia said. "He . . ."

"What about the ball?" Abby gasped.

"I'll probably fly down for that," he said airily. "See how the mood takes me."

"I've always wanted to go to Scotland," Abby declared wistfully. "All that walking and shooting. Just my scene."

"Oh, Abby, really!" Her mother burst out laughing. "You take a bus to the end of the road, given half a chance. And if you remember, when Dad took you clay pigeon shooting you spent half the time with your hands clamped over your ears!"

Hunter laughed, nodding in agreement.

"I guess Abby is just not your outdoors, sporty type, is she?" he replied, as if she had suddenly become invisible. "Better at indoor sports, eh, Abby?"

Abby flushed scarlet and held her breath, waiting for her mother to shout him down.

"That's right," Julia beamed placidly. "She's very good at table tennis, and a real card sharper, aren't you, darling?"

Hunter stifled a laugh and turned to Abby.

"Fancy a trip to Hunstanton?" he asked her.

"I'm all yours." She smiled sweetly. Apparently there were advantages to having a mother who had never mastered the double entendre, after all.

"I've got to stop," Georgie panted. "I'm totally out of breath."

She flopped down on the scrubby grass halfway up Pen-y-Fan, and wriggled her arms free of her rucksack.

"Me, too," sighed her teammate Harriet, unlacing her walking boot. "Thank goodness this is the last day of hiking—I've got blisters, my shoulders hurt, and . . ."

"It's ace up here, isn't it?" Georgie butted in, unscrewing her water bottle and gazing at the barren peaks of the Brecon Beacons all around her. She turned to Adam, who was poring over their OS map. "I feel like an intrepid explorer. How are we doing?"

"Well," Adam said, "we're not in the lead, but I've got an idea. If we take the higher path and then cut down by the waterfall here." He prodded the map with his thumb. "I reckon we could cut off a corner and get in front."

"Let's do it, then," urged Georgie, taking a swig from the bottle. "I bet Jeanie Cross my Mars Bar that we'd beat her lot. Come on."

"We can't do that," Harriet protested. "What if we get lost? No one will ever find us."

"Oh, get a grip," Georgie scoffed, wishing for the tenth time that day that she hadn't been lumbered with the class wimp for the day. "There are over fifty of us on this mountainside—we're hardly likely to disappear without trace. Anyway, where's your spirit of adventure?"

"I haven't got one," Harriet retorted. "I wish I'd never come—Mum said I'd hate it."

"Well, you'll just have to grin and bear it," Georgie told her, "because if we don't get going we're going to lose time points, okay?" She hitched her rucksack on her back and began striding along the path.

"No, wait," Adam called, stuffing the map in his back

pocket. "We can't expect Harriet to do something she doesn't feel comfortable with."

"Are you going soft or what?" Georgie glared at him.

Adam was going to be a sports instructor, and obviously liked being with her because she was one of the guys. And now here he was going all slushy over Harriet, who made a drama out of a small blister.

"Are we in this to win or aren't we?" Georgie snapped crossly.

Adam pulled a face and winked at her before turning to Harriet.

"Look, there's your mate Claire with Sally over by that rock," he said, shading his eyes from the sun and pointing along the path. "Why don't you join them? I'm sure they could do with someone else now that Paul's had to drop out with his sprained ankle."

The look of relief on Harriet's face was almost comical.

"Okay, then," she said. "And that way, if you never turn up at the checkpoint, I can alert the emergency services."

Georgie struggled not to laugh out loud. "Great idea, Harriet!" she said with mock enthusiasm, as Harriet slithered down the slope to join her friends and Adam walked over to join Georgie.

"I know this is supposed to be an endurance test, but we'd deserve a medal for putting up with her," Georgie declared. "That was dead clever, the way you got rid of her."

Adam grinned and pointed to the marks he'd penciled in on the map. Georgie perched on a nearby boulder and frowned.

"That's not a shortcut," she objected, peering at the map. "It's just a parallel route to this one. In fact, it could even be longer."

"I know," Adam confessed. "But it has one major advantage over all the other paths."

"What's that?"

"I get to be on my own with you," he murmured, kicking a stone out of his path.

He stretched out a hand to pull Georgie to her feet. And when he didn't let go, she decided that if he was going to be slushy, then it was only right that he did it with her and no one else.

"You don't love me, do you?" Hunter pulled into a lay-by on the outskirts of the village and turned to face Abby. "You never really did."

Abby quashed the rising panic she felt and pulled him toward her. "Of course I love you, Hunt—how many times do I have to tell you?"

Hunter stiffened and pulled away. "Words are easy," he said, flicking a stray leaf off the dashboard. "It's actions that matter."

"What do you want me to do to prove it?" Before she

had finished the sentence, she knew it was precisely the question he'd hoped she'd ask.

"Show me," he said, his shadowed eyes gazing into hers. "Come back to the house now—my parents are at a constituency rally—we'll have the place to ourselves."

"But you said you had shopping to do," Abby reminded him.

"Forget shopping," Hunter retorted. "I made that up to get you to myself."

For a moment, Abby said nothing.

"You see?" Hunter burst out. "All you want is to play little girl games. We're not kids anymore, you know, Abby. . . ."

"No," she said, her heart pounding. "It's not like that. I've never loved anyone the way I love you."

"So prove it," Hunter said, pulling her to him and kissing her rather harder than she would have liked.

"I love you, and you love me," he murmured, nibbling her earlobe and cupping her breast in his hand. "Please, Abby, I've been so patient—you can't treat me like this."

Abby could feel her throat closing with unshed tears. She did love him, but she just didn't feel ready yet.

"I can't," she whispered. "Not yet."

The force with which Hunter shoved her away from him almost knocked the breath out of her.

"Your decision," he snapped. "There's a name for girls

like you, you know that?" He leaned across her and threw open the passenger door. "I think you should get out."

"Hunt, no," Abby implored. "Don't be like that—it's not fair."

"Fair? You're a fine one to talk about being fair," he thundered. "Now, either you stop messing around with me and come back to the house, or you get out of my car right now."

She wasn't sure where it came from, but she was glad when it did—suddenly her whole being was filled with red-hot anger.

"Then I'll get out," she screamed, stepping out of the car and slamming the door shut. "When I do make love to someone, it'll be because I know they really care about me and you clearly . . ."

Her voice cracked and to her intense irritation, she could feel tears rolling down her cheeks.

"I'm out of here," he yelled through the open window, ramming the key into the ignition. He started the engine.

"No, Hunt, stop!" Abby went to open the car door again, but at the same moment she saw Hunter buzz it locked.

Her cries of "Hunter, come back" were drowned out by the noise of his car accelerating into the distance.

⚜ SECRET NO. 25 ⚜

Sometimes the more you ignore love, the more seriously it hunts you down

Ellie was lying on her bed, trying to make sense of her German homework, when her mobile phone bleeped. Even now, knowing what she did, she always hoped every text message was from Blake. She flipped the cover and squinted at the screen.

TICKETS CAME 2DAY! 6 DAYS AND COUNTING—OZ HERE WE COME! CAN'T WAIT DRLG. LUV U LUCY XXX

She felt as if her body had been frozen. She sat motionless, reading and rereading the words. It was clearly not meant for her—Lucy had obviously pressed the wrong button and sent her the message.

I'll be sailing in the Whitsunday Islands, Lucy's voice echoed in her head as clearly as if she had been sitting next to her. "Yes, didn't Blake tell you? It was my great idea for the summer. . . ."

"You idiot, you f-ing idiot!" Ellie shouted the words at

her reflection in the dressing-table mirror. "He's going to Australia with Lucy. And he didn't even have the guts to tell me."

She clamped her hands to her mouth and took a few long, deep breaths.

"That's that, then," she told herself firmly. "That's that."

Abby trudged along the lane, her eyes blinded by tears. She'd left her mobile phone on the bedroom floor, she had no money on her, and it was a five-mile walk home.

"Abby? Abby?"

She was conscious of a car pulling up beside her, but she wouldn't look around. She knew it was Hunter, but after what he'd just done, she wasn't sure she wanted to see him anymore. Of course she wanted to see him eventually again, and eventually, she even wanted to do all of the things he obviously couldn't wait to do, but not yet. She just couldn't. Was she abnormal? She knew loads of girls at school had done it, and most of them said it was amazing and life changing.

But she was scared. Did that mean she was frigid? Maybe she should just do it and get it over with. . . . Yes, then she could stop thinking about it and surely it wouldn't be nearly so big a deal once they just did it, right? Yes, that was what she would tell Hunter—that they could have sex, and that she was ready, even though she was fairly certain she wasn't.

"Abby, what's wrong? Are you hurt?"

She turned. It wasn't Hunter. It was Nick.

"Come on, in the car," Nick said, taking her arm. "I'm taking you home."

"I'm fine," she told him, shrugging him off.

"Really?" Nick looked at her skeptically. "I'd hate to see you on a bad day, then. Was it Hunter?"

She wanted to tell him where to go, she wanted to say that everything was fine with Hunter, but for some reason she couldn't. There Nick was, looking at her with big understanding eyes, so Abby simply dropped her head and sobbed. And when she felt Nick's arms go around her she didn't pull away. She just let the tears fall.

"Can someone get that phone?" Ellie shouted as the telephone in the hallway shrilled persistently. "Oh, for heaven's sake!"

She clattered down the stairs, French textbook in hand, and grabbed the handset.

"Hello? Oh, Chloe—no, sorry, she's out I'm afraid. With Hunter, yes."

She paused, trying to catch what Chloe was saying. She sounded as if she had an awful cold.

"Her mobile phone? No, you won't catch her on that, she's left it behind—typical Abby, yes. Are you okay? Oh. Right. Yes, I'll tell her. Yes, I promise. Bye." She replaced the handset just as the front doorbell clanged. "Now what? Forgotten her key as well, I suppose!"

She yanked the front door open, venting her bad mood on the creaking hinges.

"Blake!" *Look casual*, she told herself.

"Hey, Ellie."

She tried not to notice his floppy bangs and his cute new sneakers. She willed herself to keep acting normal, not look into his eyes, not to let him know how crushed she really felt. "What brings you here?"

"You, actually." Blake looked nervous. "Can I come in?"

"Well, I'm really busy and . . ."

"It won't take a minute," he said, stepping into the hallway. "I just need to explain stuff."

"What stuff?" Ellie asked, reluctantly closing the front door and waving him into the sitting room.

"Well, Lucy and me . . ."

"Oh, that! I thought you were going to tell me something interesting." She knew she sounded vicious and sulky but she couldn't help it.

"Ellie, listen—what happened was—"

Ellie interrupted. "I'm not interested in what happened. And I'm really busy, so—"

"But about you and me . . ."

Ellie took a deep breath and tried desperately to swallow the lump that was blocking her throat. "You and me?"

she queried. "There is no you and me, Blake—you've made that quite clear."

Blake stepped toward her, a pleading expression on his face. "Ellie, listen, for just one minute, please. You see the thing is, I won't be around for a bit because . . ."

"Because of your trip with Lucy?" Ellie interrupted brightly. "Great, isn't it? I'm sure you'll have a blast."

"You knew?" Blake's face paled in horror.

"Yes," she replied. "Pity you couldn't have told me yourself. All that pretense about dumping her—seems a waste of breath." Ellie thrust her mobile phone under Blake's nose. "I got this text from Lucy—clearly meant for you."

{ 277 }

Blake's eyes scanned the screen, and she saw, with a degree of satisfaction, the look of embarrassment flooding his face.

"Oh, God, no—I mean, I got the same message, but how come it got through to you?"

As the reality of the situation hit her, Ellie wondered why it had taken her so long to grasp the truth.

"Because Lucy wanted me to be damn sure that you were out of bounds," she said with as much hardness as she could manage. "Well, you can tell her from me that she needn't have bothered—I don't go snatching other girls' boyfriends."

"Ellie, I never meant . . ." Blake started and then petered off.

"Never meant what, Blake? Never meant to tell me? Never meant it to mean anything when you tried to kiss me? Never meant it when you said you were dumping her? Is that what you never meant, Blake?" Ellie suddenly realized she was yelling.

"Ellie, if you will just listen for five seconds," he pleaded, shoving the phone back into her hand. "It's because her grandmother . . ."

"Oh, yes, I forgot the grandmother!" Ellie feigned forgetfulness, slapping her forehead. "Well, she's dead now, isn't she? Or are you taking her ashes to Sydney?"

"Oh, for God's sake . . ." Blake began.

The door burst open, and Julia beamed at them while she wiped her muddy hands on her gardening apron.

"I thought I heard voices," she said. "Blake! Lovely to see you. Coffee? Cake?"

"He's just leaving," Ellie said, edging toward the door. "He's off to Australia. With Lucy."

Go on, squirm. You deserve it.

"Australia? With Lucy?" Ellie wished her mother would either construct an entire sentence or leave the room.

"Just for a few weeks," Blake said weakly. "I've got relatives out there, and my father . . ."

"Don't let us hold you up," Ellie butted in, because hearing even the vaguest outline of their plans made her feel sick to her stomach.

"I'll see you when I get back," Blake murmured as Ellie opened the front door.

"Whatever," she said, wishing he would go so that she could cry.

"Take care, Ellie," he whispered. "I'll get everything sorted, I promise."

It wasn't until she was upstairs lying facedown on her bed, howling her eyes out, that she began to wonder what on earth he had meant.

✪ SECRET NO. 26 ✪

Friendship can lead to love, but it doesn't usually work the other way around

"That was such a cool trip," Georgie enthused as the coach trundled along the M6 motorway on the journey home. "I wish it weren't over."

"Me, too," Adam agreed. "Actually, I was thinking . . ."

"Careful," Georgie teased. "You don't want to hurt yourself."

"Right, ha." Adam looked more than a little uncomfortable. "Georgie?" He dropped his voice to a whisper and leaned toward her.

"Yeah?"

"Will you go out with me?"

"Out with you?" Georgie's stomach appeared to be lodged somewhere in the middle of her throat. "As in out-out?"

"I mean, nothing heavy, just to have a laugh and hang out and stuff."

Georgie couldn't help thinking how cute he looked when he blushed.

"I don't know," she began, not because she didn't like him—she did, almost as much as she had liked Tom—but because no way did she fancy the gooey, kissy-kissy bits that boys always seemed to go for.

"I thought," Adam ventured, "that we could go to the new skateboard park over at Hunstanton."

"Oh, yes, ace!" Georgie cried at once, not entirely realizing if she was yelping for joy at the prospect of the skate park, or of Adam becoming her boyfriend. "I've got this wicked board my Dad gave me and I've hardly used it since he died."

"So, let's do it," Adam said. "It would be a bit off to let him think he'd wasted his money, wouldn't it?"

She looked at him long and hard. He was talking about Dad like he was just around the corner, like he could hear them chatting. That was so cool.

"Will you come, then?" He suddenly looked hesitant and small.

"I will." She grinned. By the time she realized she was giving him a hug, it was too late to pull back. Not that it mattered. Hugs didn't count. Hugs were quite nice, really.

Georgie and Adam let go of each other, but Georgie could still see that Adam had something on his mind.

"What is it, then?" Georgie asked suddenly. "I think there's more—I can tell."

"Well, now that we're seeing each other . . ." Adam began.

"Yes?" Georgie asked skeptically.

"There's this ball, and I was thinking—"

"A ball? Oh, come on, Adam, that's not my scene at all!" She knew this going-out thing was all wrong!

"Um, right, but it's not really a ball," Adam assured her. "More a glorified disco. I just thought the money would be useful, especially if we're going to the skate park."

"Money? You pay them, dimbo, not the other way round." She laughed.

"That's where you're wrong," he countered. "I told you my dad's got a catering company? Well, they're doing the food and running the bar for the ball, and if we're prepared to help out for the first two hours, we get £10."

"Each?"

"Each."

"Well, why didn't you say so?" Georgie laughed, and then frowned.

"What now?" he sighed.

"I guess we have to dress up, right?"

"Afraid so." Adam nodded. "I've got to put on my brother's hand-me-down tuxedo. But it's worth it for a tenner."

"True," Georgie said. "I wouldn't do it for less, though."

* * *

"You won't say anything to anyone? You promise?" Abby demanded as Nick pulled up outside Marsh Cottage.

"Of course not," he said. "Although, why you don't want the whole world to know what a slimeball Hunter is beats me."

"Just leave it, okay?" Abby said, terrified that she would start crying again. "It was sort of more my fault, really, than it seems—I'll call him and . . ."

"Abby, don't—he's not worth it," Nick began.

"You're just saying that because you want me to your-self," Abby said impatiently, opening the car door.

{ 283 }

"True," Nick murmured quietly. "Anyway, I'm here if you need me."

Abby felt guilty for snapping. After all, Nick had taken her out to lunch, walked along the beach for hours listening to her ranting and raving, and he hadn't once blown his top or got fed up. He'd told her he had broken things off with Chloe, and even though Abby felt heartbroken for herself, she felt it for Chloe, too—Nick really was a catch, even Abby could see that.

"Thanks," she said. "I mean it—thanks for today and bringing me home. I'll see you around."

She slammed the door and turned to go, but Nick leaned across and touched her hand through the open window.

"About the sailing club ball," he said. "I've got tickets, and if Hunter doesn't show . . ."

"Of course he'll show," Abby said, sounding a lot more confident than she felt. "I told you—it's just a blip."

But when she glanced back at Nick—all red-faced, and twisted-looking—she couldn't help but feel a bit of a knot in her heart.

"What's the matter with Abby?" Georgie demanded of her mother a couple of hours after arriving home. "She's hardly said a word to me since I got back, and she's playing loads of morbid songs in her bedroom and sniffing a lot."

"It's Hunter," her mother sighed. "He's leaving for Scotland tomorrow and Abby's—oh, there you are, darling!"

She broke off as Abby, crumpled tissues in hand, came into the kitchen.

"Feeling better?" Julia asked her. "How about some tea and toast?"

Abby shook her head.

"Darling, this is silly," her mother went on. "Hunter has only gone for a few days—he'll be back for the ball."

"What's he doing in Scotland anyway?" Georgie asked.

"Grouse shooting with his grandfather," Abby replied.

"He's what?" Georgie spat toast crumbs across the

table in her disgust. "How could you go out with someone who kills innocent little birds for fun? That is just the grossest thing."

"What do you know?" Abby retorted. "You eat chicken—you don't think they die a natural death, do you?"

"No, but I don't go out with the guys that wring their necks, do I?" Georgie parried, proud of herself for her quickness of thought. "Anyway, I'm thinking of turning vegetarian."

"Don't be so ridiculous," her mother snorted. "What on earth gave you that idea?"

"Adam says that you should never eat something you are not prepared to kill," she replied. "But then Adam is an animal lover and a conservationist."

"I knew it," Abby burst out, a smile interrupting her sour face. "Georgie and Adam are an item."

Her mother's eyebrows shot heavenward. "Nonsense," she retorted. "She's only thirteen—he's just a friend. Right, Georgie?"

"Right," she agreed. Telling the truth would only get her mother's blood pressure up, and besides, Abby was right after all: secret love is the most exciting.

⚜ SECRET NO. 27 ⚜

Absence can do two things to love:
make it stronger, or allow you to pretend it never existed at all

"Ellie, darling, shouldn't you be getting ready?" Julia demanded at seven o'clock on the night of the ball. "The bathroom's free at last."

{ 286 }

"I don't think I'll bother going." Ellie yawned. "I'm tired, and besides, it's not much fun on your own."

"Now, just you stop that right now," Julia admonished her. "If you don't go, you won't meet new people, and besides, do you think I want Georgie on her own at a place like that?"

Georgie had finally spilled the beans about Adam and the ball the day before, and since then Julia had been a wreck about the whole thing.

"Mum, she'll be fine—Adam's parents will be there." Ellie laughed.

"Yes, well, they will be busy, and besides, you need to get out." Julia eyed Ellie closely. "You've been looking very peaky lately—all this studying is all very well, but you need some fun. And you are supposed to be on holiday."

"Okay, okay, I'll go," Ellie sighed, knowing that her mother wouldn't stop nagging until she gave in.

"You look stunning." Chloe stood behind Abby as they gazed at their reflections in the full-length mirror in Julia's bedroom. "If Hunter does come . . ."

"He will come, I know he will," Abby assured her, twirling round to admire the sexy swing of her new black net skirt. Chloe had shown up heartbroken over Nick the same afternoon that Hunter had left Abby at the side of the road. And even though Abby hadn't exactly told Chloe that she'd already heard the other side of the story from Nick, she did offer Chloe a shoulder to cry on, and helped her hatch a plan to get Nick back. Somehow, after the afternoon Abby had spent with him, and everything that had happened with Chloe, Abby felt like she owed it to her.

"Well, if he does, he'll be bowled over," Chloe finished. "Did he reply to your messages?"

"No." Abby shook her head. "But then of course, as Mum said, there probably isn't a signal in the mountains, and I guess his grandfather won't be hooked up to the Internet, so he won't be checking e-mail."

"True." Chloe didn't sound as convinced as Abby would have liked. "Oh, God, I'm so nervous."

"What have you got to be nervous about? You look

great, you're a cool dancer, and you're going to have an entire evening in the same room as the guy you fancy." Abby smiled a bit mischievously. "Plus, we've got a plan."

"Yes, but what if it doesn't work?"

"Well, that's down to you, isn't it? I've done all I can. I've arranged for him to fetch us—and believe me, that was hard enough because he wanted to go with Liam and Ryan and all the kit in the van—"

"And he knows that I'm coming along?" Chloe urged.

Abby paused. She mustn't lie. Not this time.

"Not exactly," she said. "It's the surprise element, you see. He will never have seen you dressed up to the nines before, and it's your opportunity to sweep him off his feet." Abby cringed inwardly at her own clichés, but Chloe seemed impressed.

"That's neat," Chloe cried. "Thanks, Abby."

"That's okay," Abby replied. "Now, will you please put your face on and let's get downstairs? He'll be here any minute."

After a few more minutes of lip gloss application and another layer of perfectly tinted bronzer, Abby and Chloe swooshed down the stairs in their gowns. Before they'd even reached the bottom step, the doorbell clanged.

"Just in time!" said Abby as she dove for the door.

Upstairs Ellie was playing music a bit louder than she usually did, so Abby had the unusual good fortune of slipping out without her mum quizzing the boys on their every intention for the evening.

"Hey, Nick!" said Chloe enthusiastically as they shuffled out of the house.

"Hey, Chloe," Nick said, and then turned to Abby a gave her a withering look.

They drove to the ball in near silence, and as soon as Chloe disappeared to the Ladies room at the sailing club, Nick grabbed Abby's shoulder. "If you think you're going to get me to start up again with Chloe, let me tell you right now it's a nonstarter."

"I don't," Abby assured him. "I was wrong about you two—you're not suited anyway. She just needed a lift, that's all. Honestly."

"That's okay, then," Nick muttered. "Ryan will be all over her anyway. Got to go—we're on in ten minutes." He gave the thumbs-up sign to Liam and Ryan, who were beckoning him urgently from the stage. "Hang on to my car keys and wallet, will you? I hate clutter when I'm drumming."

She shoved them into her new oh-so-chic quilted clutch bag. "Good luck," she whispered, and gave him a quick kiss on the cheek.

"Thanks." Nick's fingers went up to his face, and when he smiled, Abby noticed how his whole face relaxed. "See you during the break, yeah?"

"Yeah." Abby smiled.

"Lovely to meet you, Georgie, dear," Adam's mother cried, shoving a plate of canapés in her hand. "Now, hand these round, will you? Start with the VIPs, in the captain's corner, and then do the rest of the crowd. Refills in the back kitchen, okay?" She darted off to stir a vat of soup.

"Come on," Adam said. "The sooner we get rid of all the appetizers, the sooner we get our ten quid!" He kicked open the swinging door with a foot to let Georgie through.

"Wow," Georgie breathed.

She gazed at the room, which had been transformed into an underwater world with sea green voiles hanging at the window, huge silver fish covering the dim lights, and piles of seaweed and shells stacked around upturned lobster pots at every table.

"Doesn't it look amazing?" she gasped, turning to Adam.

"So do you," he mumbled, his face flushing. "Really— you do."

"I feel stupid," she admitted, tugging at the spaghetti straps of her lavender shift dress and gazing down at her legs, the bruises from skateboarding not totally hidden by her pantyhose. "I don't really do dresses."

"Well, you should," Adam said. "You look like—well, pop starry or something."

Georgie squirmed and fiddled with the sequined necklace that Abby had lent her.

"Get real," she muttered, shoving the dish of canapés under the nose of the first person she passed. "Oh, it's you." Georgie grinned up at Ellie, who was chatting to a guy in a maroon tux.

"This is my sister, Ellie," Georgie said, turning to Adam. "The one I was telling you about with the complicated love life."

"Georgie," Ellie hissed.

"This is your little sister?"

Georgie realized then that the guy with Ellie was the one who had turned up at the house with Blake weeks before. "Remember me? Piers?"

"Oh sure," nodded Georgie. "Say—you two—you're not . . . ?"

"Georgie?" said Ellie.

"Yes?"

"Go serve your canapés, okay?"

After collecting some food on a plate from the buffet, Piers and Ellie settled into a table alongside another few guests. But before long, the other partygoers began drifting toward the dance floor again, and Ellie found her mind drifting off as well.

"Ellie? Come back—you were miles away." Piers touched her arm across the table, and Ellie jerked her thoughts away from mental images of jet planes taking off, and back to the dance floor of the sailing club.

"Sorry," she said. "What were you saying?"

"Just that it's a pity Blake's not here," Piers commented, picking chicken off a drumstick with his teeth. "His name's on the prizewinners' list."

"It is? What for?"

"Winning the Open Laser Challenge," Piers answered. "Of course, it was all down to the superb quality of the guy at the helm."

"Who was that?" Ellie said, pushing coleslaw salad around her plate.

"Me." Piers laughed. "I'm surprised Blake didn't tell you."

"Why would he tell me anything?" Ellie asked. "It's not as if—"

"Not as if you're crazy about him?" Piers teased, eyeing her closely as she fiddled with her earring. "No, of course it's not."

Ellie wanted to shout him down and tell him where to go, but she was so close to tears that she didn't dare open her mouth.

"I'll tell you one thing," Piers went on, "you'd be much better for him than Lucy. Those two aren't remotely suited, you know."

"Don't you think so?" Ellie tried to sound disinterested.

"No way," Piers asserted, topping up his wineglass.

"Lucy needs a guy who knows how to chill, someone with a bit of spunk."

"Blake's got spunk," she cut in.

"Oh, sure, like a warthog's top of the glamour stakes." He laughed.

"I thought he was your friend," Ellie snapped.

"He is—he's a great guy, just not Lucy's type. He'll kill her spirit and . . ."

"Well, it doesn't seem to bother her, does it?" Ellie retorted, giving up all attempts at eating as she pushed her plate away. "She is flying halfway round the world with him as we speak, isn't she?" Ellie visibly cringed at the idea of { 293 } Blake and Lucy sitting in first class together, sharing an iPod and drinking ginger ale.

"Jealous, are you?" Piers smiled at her.

"Of course I'm not jealous!" Ellie spat right back at him.

"That's good," Piers commented calmly as she scanned the room for a sign to the loo. "Since it's your fault he's gone."

"My . . . ? How do you make that out?"

"Come off it, Ellie," he protested. "There's only so many times you can give a guy the brush-off before he gets the message."

"What are you on about? Like I'm expected to two-time another girl?"

"It wasn't like that," Piers began. "It's complicated."

"No, it's not," Ellie said. "It's dead simple. Blake wanted to be with Lucy and I don't give a damn." I'm getting like Abby, she thought, quoting old movies in times of stress. "Get the message?"

Piers grinned. "The message as in you're crazy about him and he's besotted with you? Oh, sure I get it. The question is, what are we going to do about it?"

Ellie wheeled round and began pushing her way to the loo. She had to get there before the tears came. No one, least of all Piers Fordyce, was going to see her cry.

"Ryan's singing better than ever," Abby said to Chloe as the band broke for the interval and Chloe came storming toward her. "He's quite cute, isn't he? He's dead keen on you."

"How could you do that to me?" Chloe demanded. "I saw you—you kissed Nick!"

"I gave him a good-luck peck," Abby protested. "A peck doesn't mean a thing."

"I suppose," Chloe sighed. "Ryan just gave me one before going on as well, but I just don't feel it for him, you know? He's much nicer than I thought at first, but he's not Nick, is he? I mean, if you didn't have Hunter . . ."

Which right now I don't, thought Abby.

". . . which one would you choose? Nick or Ryan?"

"Nick," Abby said before she could think straight. What? It was the truth.

"See what I mean?" replied Chloe. "No contest, is there?"

But before Abby could find a way to temper her reply in Ryan's favor, she was distracted by the double doors that had just swung open with a party of latecomers. And at the back, towering above the rest, and with his arm around a tall, chestnut-haired girl with a plunge neckline and a cleavage to die for, was Hunter.

☙ SECRET NO. 28 ☙

You'll never forget your first kiss

"It's nice out here, isn't it?" Georgie said, listening to the jangling of the halyards on the boats lined up by the jetty. When they had finished serving the guests, Adam had suggested they come outside, and now Georgie was glad he had. "Do you go sailing?"

"No," Adam said. "But I thought I might give windsurfing a go—or water-skiing. Cheaper and less complicated, I guess."

"I fancy that," Georgie said. "We could do it together."

Adam put his hand on her shoulder.

"There's lots we could do together," he said, and his voice was so husky that Georgie wondered if he had caught a cold.

But when he pulled her gently toward him and kissed her, ever so lightly, on the lips, all thoughts of his state of health evaporated on the spot.

* * *

Hunter had his hands around the girl's waist as Abby sashayed up to them, puckering her lips and blowing a kiss in his direction. She took a giant gulp of wine to give her courage, and she realized she'd just emptied her third glass.

"Hi, darling—how was Scotland? Missed you big-time," Abby trilled as she approached.

"Oh, it's you." Hunter seemed amused but hardly overwhelmed by passion.

"And who is this?" The girl clinging to his arm spoke with a soft Scottish burr and looked at Abby as if she had crawled out from under a rotting log.

"I'm Abby," Abby said as charmingly as she could. "I'm Hunter's girlfriend."

"How extraordinary," the girl said. "I'm Fiona, and I'm Hunter's girlfriend. Now, one of us must be wrong, and it surely is not me." She turned to Hunter, who was watching them in amusement. "Is this the kid you were telling me about? The one with the crush on you?" she asked.

"Yes, this is Abby," he said in the tone of voice one might use when talking about a rather senile old lady. "Abby, meet Fiona. And yes, she's my girlfriend."

She put out a hand to grab a chair because for some reason the floor was moving like waves on a rough sea.

"You . . . you can't . . . I'll do what you wanted . . . you . . ." Abby's voice cracked.

"Sorry, sunshine," Hunter said, sidling up to Fiona. "I need someone a bit more sophisticated than a schoolgirl, if you catch my drift."

"Ladies and Gentlemen, please make your way to the podium—the prize-giving is about to take place." Everyone turned as the announcement boomed from the speaker system.

"Come on, Abby, let's go," Piers urged, suddenly appearing at Abby's side. They didn't know each other well, but Piers was quickly developing a soft spot for the Dashwood girls. "He's an idiot—don't let him get to you."

"Leave me alone," Abby shouted. "Hunt, listen to me. . . ."

"Hysterical as well as immature." Fiona grinned. With that, she wound her arms around Hunter's neck and began kissing him passionately.

Whether it was the effects of the wine or simply the fact that she realized she had nothing else to lose, she didn't know; but before she could think, Abby had grabbed Piers's glass and thrown the burgundy contents all over Fiona. Abby watched, pleased as the red liquid ran down Fiona's neck and into her milky white cleavage. It looked, she thought with satisfaction, very much like blood.

"For God's sake!" Hunter leaped back as droplets of wine splattered his dinner shirt. "What the hell's going on?"

"She's crazy!" Fiona wailed. "This dress—it's ruined. It cost me £300."

"Well, it was a waste of money," Abby yelled. "It just makes you look like the tart you are!"

"Abby, what on earth's going on?" She heard Georgie coming in from the patio, and felt someone pulling her back. She wrenched herself free.

"Get lost!" Abby shouted, pushing past Hunter and Fiona. Fiona grabbed her arm.

"Not so fast," she began. "You'll pay for this."

Abby swung her arm, hitting Fiona on the cheek with her handbag. With that, she ran across the room, burst through the doors, and sped as fast as she could, blinded with tears, into the car park.

"Go and find Ellie," Piers ordered Georgie urgently. "I think she's in the loo. I'll go after Abby."

Georgie rushed to the ladies' room and found Ellie, both hands resting on a washbasin, staring at her reflection in the mirror.

"Come quickly," Georgie gabbled. "It's Abby—she hit this girl and now she's run off."

"Hit what girl? What are you going on about?" Ellie gasped, as Georgie grabbed her hand and pulled her through the swinging doors.

"I just came in from outside, and Abby was yelling at this girl, and then she threw wine over her, and now she's run off. And Piers thinks she's been drinking."

Ellie pushed through the crowd gathering for the prize-giving, ran to the door and out into the night. A blast of cool, salty air hit her burning cheeks, and she struggled to focus in the unaccustomed darkness.

"I can't see her," Piers said, panting up to them. "I went down to the jetty, but she's not there. The state she's in, if she fell into the water . . ."

He didn't bother to complete the sentence.

They were all laughing at her. Abby could hear them in her head, imagine them staring after her as she ran through the car park. She could hear someone calling her name, saw a dark shape striding along the jetty, but she couldn't face anyone. She had to get away. She ran across the car park and that's when she saw it: Nick's battered old car.

And she had the keys.

Her hands shook as she fumbled in her bag. If she sat in the car and kept her head down, she'd be safe. No one would find her.

She opened the door, shut it as quietly as she could, and sat, catching her breath and choking on her sobs.

"Abby, Abby!" The shouts were coming nearer.

She stared at the keys in her hand. She wouldn't go far. Just down the road, away from here.

She could only just reach the pedals and she struggled to remember what to do. She'd driven her dad's old car up and down the drive before. She'd even had a go behind the wheel of Hunter's car down by Holkham beach. Surely, if you could drive one car, you could drive any car.

She pressed the accelerator and the engine revved. As she let the hand brake off, she caught sight of a familiar figure run wildly from the door of the club.

Ellie.

She had to go. Now.

She pressed the pedal harder and the car lurched wildly forward.

🐞 SECRET NO. 29 🐞

*There is no worse combination than a broken heart and too much
champagne*

"We've got to find her," Ellie cried, looking frantically
around.

"I'll get Adam and go round the back," Georgie said.
"You check the boathouse and look behind . . ." Her words
were drowned out by the spluttering of a car engine.

"That's Nick's car," Ellie said. "Stop him—tell him to
look out for Abby. She might be trying to walk home."

Piers sprinted toward the car, Ellie hard on his heels,
shielding her eyes from the headlamps as the vehicle swung
sharply around.

"No!" Piers gasped.

The car reversed wildly, hitting the bumper of a blue
Mercedes and then bouncing off the bonnet of a Ford
Fiesta.

"For God's sake, what's he doing?" Ellie shouted above
the engine noise. "Nick, stop!"

Piers grabbed her arm and spun her around to face him. "Ellie, it's not Nick," he stressed urgently. "It's Abby."

"But Abby can't drive," she stammered. "She wouldn't." But Ellie knew: *she would*.

Nick's car was lurching toward the exit, swerving haphazardly from side to side.

"Get your car, follow her," Ellie pleaded. "Quickly."

Piers shook his head. "I can't—I've had too many drinks. Don't worry, I'll find someone else to drive my car."

"Hurry," Ellie sobbed as Nick's car disappeared out of sight. "Please hurry."

Abby hadn't realized it would be so dark. Even with the headlights on, she could hardly see where she was going, and the tears streaming down her face weren't helping. A motorcyclist came toward her, blaring his horn, and she swerved, narrowly missing a ditch.

The road from the sailing club was really no more than a track, rutted in places and sprinkled with shingle. She hit a pothole and rammed her foot down. The car sped forward. She drove on. The shingle gave way to tarmac and the lane widened slightly. Ahead of her was the main road, traffic thundering past, headlights piercing the darkness.

She began to pull out into the road but the speed of the traffic scared her. Headlights streaked by her in every direction.

And then, a sudden, piercing light blinded her. A horn blared. A huge, black shape with silver bars bore down on her. For a split second she saw a face frozen in terror.

Then she felt herself spinning, tipping, falling.

A searing pain shot through her body. Someone screamed.

And then she fell into a huge, black, silent pit.

"What took you so long?" Ellie said as Piers ran up to her with Nick behind him. "She's been gone fifteen minutes."

"The speeches were on," Piers panted. "And everyone I asked had had a drink. Then I found Nick."

"Which way?" Nick grabbed Piers's car keys and jumped into the driving seat.

"She turned left," Ellie sobbed, climbing into the back with Piers. "Are you sure you're okay to drive?"

"Fine," Nick said. "I've been on soda all night—always am when I'm playing." Nick jammed the keys into the ignition.

Please, God, Ellie prayed, let us find her. Let her be okay.

"What about Georgie?" Piers asked suddenly.

"Adam's parents are keeping an eye on her," Ellie said. "I've told her not to phone Mum, at least not yet. Not till we've found Abby."

Nick accelerated gently up the shingled lane.

"Keep looking," he said. "She might have parked up in a lay-by."

They didn't speak for several minutes.

"The main road," Nick said finally. "Which way?"

Afterward, Ellie would never remember who saw it first. Was it her, when she screamed at the sight of blue flashing lights? Was it Nick's "dear Jesus" that had tipped her off? Or was it Piers, who shouted "Stop!" and then put his hand over Ellie's eyes?

What she *would* remember for weeks to come was the sight of twisted metal, the image of the other driver on his knees on the side of the road, and the voice of the burly police officer: "She's trapped. We're going to have to cut her out."

A siren wailing. Then jolting. And pain. Someone crying.

"Mum, Mum," over and over.

Then faces, coming and going. All in a blur.

"You're in hospital now."

Familiar voice. Mum.

"I'm here, darling. Right beside you."

Hospital. Going to see Dad. Dad's getting better? No. Dad is dead. Hospitals are where people die. Pain everywhere.

And then a prick in the arm. And nothing.

It was happening all over again. Just like before. Sitting,

waiting, in the Relatives Room, wanting them to come but dreading what they'd say.

"Oh, why are they taking so long?" Ellie said for the tenth time. "The police can tell us about your car, but no one says anything about my sister. . . ."

Nick swallowed.

"The police—they asked me if I wanted to press charges," he said. "Like I care about the damn car. All I care about is Abby."

Ellie smiled faintly and nodded.

"You do, don't you?" she murmured, shivering with delayed shock. "You really care."

Nick turned, and Ellie saw he was struggling not to cry.

"I love her, Ellie." He got up and paced the room. "If anything—" He paused as the door flew open and Julia stood, tears streaming down her face.

"Do you ever pray?" Georgie sat in Adam's kitchen, cradling a mug of hot chocolate and staring at the clock.

"Sure," Adam replied. "I mean, there has to be someone in charge, doesn't there? Otherwise we'd all have messed up eons ago."

"Yes, but when Dad died," she began, stuttering over the word, "we all prayed like crazy and it didn't make any difference."

"You don't always get what you want, I guess," Adam said, stifling a yawn. "But it can't hurt to ask, can it?"

"So will you—I mean, could we . . . ?" Georgie ventured.

"Pray? Sure." Adam wiped his nose with his sleeve and put his mug on the table. "Look, God, Georgie's sister had a car crash and we're all dead worried about her. You can cure anything, so if possible, could you get to work on Abby right now? She's in King's Lynn hospital, but I guess you know that. Thanks for listening. Amen."

Georgie stared at him.

"That didn't sound like a prayer," she protested. "That was just like normal talking."

Adam shrugged.

"That's just the way I do it," he said.

Julia's tearstained cheeks looked brighter under the fluorescent hospital lighting.

"Oh, God, Mum, what?" Ellie froze.

Julia flung open her arms and hugged her. "She's going to be fine," she wept. "Oh, Ellie, she's going to be all right."

ᴀ SECRET NO. 30 ᴥ

*Surviving a broken heart requires that same thing as recovering from
any injury—time and love. (And a little ice cream doesn't hurt)*

"I don't want to see anybody, Mum." Abby blinked back
the tears and squeezed her mother's hand. Two days had
passed but still everything hurt. "Promise me, you won't let
anyone come."

"But, darling," her mother protested, shifting her position on the chair beside the bed. "You said that yesterday,
and Ellie and Georgie so want to be here. . . ."

"No, Mum!" Abby shouted. "Yesterday I kept praying
I'd remember what had happened. Now I can—and I realize that amnesia is no bad thing. I just want to die."

Julia stood up and leaned over the bed.

"Now, Abby, you listen to me, and you listen good,"
she stressed. "I don't want to hear that kind of talk again,
you understand me? I know you feel dreadful about what
happened, and I know you wish you could wind the clock
back. But you can't."

Abby's tears flowed faster.

"Everyone's going to hate me," she sobbed, shifting her plastered leg gingerly. "Even you are getting cross."

"Only when you say silly things about dying," Julia murmured, her voice breaking. "And no one will hate you—if you think that, you underestimate your sisters and your friends."

"What friends?" Abby retorted. "They're not going to want to know me now, are they?"

"Oh, really?" Julia replied, plunging her hand into a large carrier bag at her feet. "So that's why there's a card and some chocolates from Chloe, a couple of magazines from Piers, and a note from Nick? He's come by here waiting for you to wake up quite a few times, you know."

Abby stared at the pile her mum had made at the foot of her bed.

"And Hunter? Is there anything from Hunter?"

Julia shook her head.

"Hunter's not a friend, darling," she said softly. "The one person Hunter adores is Hunter."

Abby closed her eyes.

"I was taken in by him too, you know," Julia said. "But Piers and Nick have been putting me straight."

"You've seen Nick?" Abby asked, opening her eyes. "He must hate me. That letter must be legal papers suing me for stealing his car!"

"Darling," Julia said patiently, "he didn't leave the hospital on the night of the accident till four in the morning—he hardly seemed concerned about his car. In fact, he blames himself for not telling you straight what Hunter was like."

"He tried." Abby sniffled. "I just thought he was jealous."

Her mother smiled. "He does seem very fond of you," she admitted. "So let him come—he'll cheer you up."

"I couldn't even if I wanted to," she said, just to put an end to her mother's nagging. "Chloe would kill me—she's got a thing about him and . . ."

"Chloe wants to come, too—she said Ryan would bring her tonight."

"Chloe? Ryan?" Abby asked, running her hand along her cast. "Mum, you've got it all muddled up—Chloe can't stand Ryan."

"Oh, really?" her mother smiled. "So is that why Chloe came round holding hands with a rather nice-looking boy whom she introduced as Ryan. Lovely lad. He said my carrot cake was the best he'd ever tasted. . . . But then, I've heard that before—haven't I? Now then, will you have visitors?"

"Do I have a choice?" Abby sighed.

"No." Her mum smiled. And as if on cue, there was a light *tap tap tap* on the door.

"Hello?" Nick came in the door. "The nurse said you were awake, so . . . Oh, hi, Mrs. Dashwood."

"Hi, Nick," Julia said mischievously as she slipped out the door behind him. "I'll just leave you two alone."

"Nick, I'm so sorry," Abby began, "but I'm afraid I can't—"

"Let me guess, see me?" Nick asked, sounding much less perturbed than Abby would have expected. "Well, you have to."

"Why's that?" Abby asked, surprised by Nick's assertiveness.

"Because you've got a broken leg." Nick smiled at her. "So, I'm afraid you can't get away." Nick sat down at the chair next to the bed and took her hand. "Abby, I love you. And I know you love Hunter, much as it makes me want to puke to say it." { 311 }

"Nick—" Abby tried to interrupt.

"No, Abby, listen," Nick said. "I know you think Hunter is great, but he's not, and besides, the rumor is that he's going back to Scotland with that girl." Nick paused, but Abby didn't interrupt. "And I'm here. So how about you give me a shot, eh? For a few weeks, until your leg heals and you can run away from me if you want to?"

Abby was very quiet, and Nick's hopeful expression dropped. "What about your car?" Abby finally asked.

"To hell with the car. What about what I just said?"

"Well, it's just that . . ." Abby stammered, "what with Chloe and all . . ."

"Forget Chloe. This is about you and me, Abby!"

Abby looked at Nick, who was looking at her with more love than Hunter ever had, and suddenly knew what she had to do. "Just let me sort a few things, okay?"

Nick twisted his mouth up, unsure whether or not this was a good sign. "Okay," he said. "I guess that's okay." Nick turned to go but before he left he bent over Abby, and very gently, he kissed her.

Abby's eyes were open the whole time—she couldn't believe he'd just done that! But then again, it was quite nice, really. Abby realized she could imagine doing quite a bit more of that with Nick. He left without saying another word.

Abby lay back on the pillow and closed her eyes. How could he be so nice after everything she'd done? And he was quite cute, really. Plus, he had seen her all goobery with runny mascara over another guy and he still liked her.

"Abby, you've got a visitor." The nurse stuck her head around the door a few minutes later. "I'll tell her to come up."

"No," Abby began, but the nurse had left. Who else could it be?

I'll pretend to be asleep, she thought, but as she screwed up her eyes, the door flew open and Chloe burst into the room, flowers in one hand, and started talking before Abby could even say hello.

"Oh, God, Abby, if I hadn't forced you to get Nick to drive us to the ball, you wouldn't have had his keys and . . ."

"Hey, come on," Abby said, the saliva drying in her mouth. "I was the dumb idiot who took the car and ruined the party and caused so much worry. Everyone must hate me."

"Certainly not! Because of you, I've got a boyfriend." Chloe flopped down on the bed.

"Ouch! Not on the bed." Abby winced as a pain shot through her leg.

"Sorry." Chloe jumped up and started pacing the room. "It's Ryan."

Abby was gobsmacked. "But, Chloe, you've been rotten to Ryan. You loathe the guy."

"I know, but that was before the ball. You see, after you drove off, I was crying, and he comforted me. He said you'd been drinking . . ."

"Don't." Abby winced at the memory.

"Well, anyway, we got to talking, and I said you were my best mate in the whole world and that if anything happened to you, I couldn't bear it. . . ." Chloe said animatedly.

"You said that?" Abby sat up a bit in bed.

"Of course, it's true, so why wouldn't I say it?" Chloe asked. "Anyway, we started looking for you with a lot of the others."

Abby groaned from embarrassment.

"Anyway, the next day Ryan phoned me and we went by your house to find out how you were doing, and then we went for a drink, and he said that Nick had been up all night and was sick with worry. That's when I knew."

"What?" Abby asked.

"That no matter what I did, Nick wouldn't fall for me because he'd already fallen for you," she said surprisingly brightly. "Okay, it hurt a bit at first, but then Ryan and me talked some more and then he asked if maybe I'd like to meet up again, which we did, and then tonight—"

"So you like him?" Abby interrupted, trying to get a hold on Chloe's long-winded report.

Chloe nodded, her eyes bright and her normally pallid cheeks flushed.

Abby paused and took a deep breath. "More than Nick?"

Chloe bit her lip.

"Not entirely," she whispered. "But I think I could. I mean, it's early days and everything, but it's a lot nicer being with someone who really wants to be with you. I mean, when I saw how totally devastated Nick was about your accident, it hit me that he would never feel that way about me. And Ryan—well, he's quite hot, isn't he?"

"Chloe, you promise you're not still angling for Nick? Promise on your honor?"

"I swear it—why?" Chloe looked concerned.

"Because if you don't mind, I think I might rather like to have him," Abby confessed.

☙ SECRET NO. 31 ☙

*Sometimes a kiss says more than words can
(no matter how good a talker you may be)*

"I'm so bored," sighed Abby, lying on the sofa ten days later as Nick drew cartoons on her leg plaster. "I feel like one of those Victorian invalids who die in darkened rooms for want of sunlight and stimulation."

Nick burst out laughing. "Abby, you're so dramatic," he teased. "You want to go out? Let's go, then."

"I can't," she protested. "I can hardly walk on those awful crutches, and thanks to me you don't have a car. Mum's out serving tea to the old ladies, Ellie's down in Brighton seeing old schoolmates . . ."

"Wheelchair! My great gran's old one is still in our shed. Wait here. Oh, well, I suppose you don't have a choice, do you?" He grinned at Abby. "I'll be back in an hour."

"Is that Georgie?" Nick asked as he pushed Abby in the wheelchair down the jetty. "With that guy by the row boats?"

Abby shaded her eyes against the glare of the late afternoon sun. "Yes," she said. "I can't see who the guy is, though."

"Must be Adam, I guess," Nick remarked.

She shook her head. "He's gone to Liverpool to see his grandparents," she told him, cupping her hands to her mouth. "Hey, Georgie—over here!"

Georgie waved and ran along the jetty toward them. "Hi," she panted. "Hey, wheelchair—neat idea. Can I have a go?"

"No, you can't," retorted Abby. "I'm the invalid, re-member?"

"As if you'd let us forget," Georgie teased. "Anyway, you'll never guess who I'm going rowing with! Tom!"

"Tom?" Abby shielded her eyes again. "What's Tom doing here?"

"Surprise visit," Georgie said. "He missed me."

Abby couldn't help seeing the smug look on Georgie's face.

"But what about Adam?"

"I like Adam. I do," replied Georgie calmly, "but Tom and I have been rather close for quite a long time."

Abby could see the twinkle in Georgie's eye. She smiled at her little sister, who suddenly seemed rather grown-up.

"And," Georgie went on, "I reckon Tom and I have

always had a bit of something special, don't you think?"

Abby smiled. "You know, Georgie, I do."

Ellie fumbled in her jeans pocket for her door key, slipped her shades over her eyes to cut the glare of the sinking sun, and kicked the gate open with her foot.

"Hi."

"What the . . . ?" She jumped back, dropping her bag, her heart pounding as a figure stepped out from behind the laurel bush.

"Sorry—I didn't mean to scare you."

Blake. She stood motionless, her mind in turmoil. He was in Australia—or, at least, he was *supposed* to be in Australia.

"I had to come to see you," he said, taking a step toward her. "Then when I got here, I didn't have the nerve to ring the bell."

Ellie exhaled deeply. "I'd have thought," she said, ramming her key into the lock, "that compared to flying round the world at the drop of a hat, bell ringing would be a doddle. Aren't you meant to be somewhere else?"

"Not anymore," he murmured. "Look, can I come in?"

No you can't, Ellie muttered silently in her head. *No way.* "Yes, of course. Come on." The truth was, no matter what she tried to make herself think, Ellie's feelings for Blake were not so simple.

As Ellie led him into the kitchen and flipped on the hot water, Blake took a seat at the kitchen table.

"I told her." Blake handed her the empty mug she'd just absentmindedly set in front of him, his eyes holding Ellie's gaze.

"You told who, what?" She knew full well he meant Lucy, but she wasn't about to let him off that easy.

"I told Lucy. About how I really felt. About you." Blake spoke in sentences that quite resembled Julia's in times of stress.

"You did?" A surge of joy flooded Ellie's heart, and she turned toward the coffee machine to hide a smile. She was suddenly doubly thankful that the rest of the family was out of the house and not bursting into the room.

Blake nodded. "In Hong Kong. I wanted to go to see this amazing exhibition that was on—about Asian art, you know? Anyway, Lucy kept on and on about how it was pointless, since any idea of me being an artist was stupid. And that was when . . ." He hesitated, chewing his bottom lip. "Well, I flipped. Told her that no way was I doing law, that I'd probably be penniless for years till I got established, but that I'd be happy and that was all that mattered." He laughed dryly. "I told her straight out that I didn't want to be on the trip with her in the first place," he confessed.

"So why were you?" The image of Blake and Lucy together on the other side of the world—even if it was of them fighting—was cooling the feeling she'd had a moment before.

"It was arranged ages ago," Blake said. "Lucy's parents and my lot got together and decided it would be an ace idea, in the way that parents do, and they paid for the air tickets and everything."

"And then when Lucy's gran died, you felt you couldn't back out, is that it?" Ellie asked, with a touch more acerbity in her voice than she intended.

"Well, yes . . ." Blake nodded. "I know it was pathetic, I know I took the easy option—but if you'd been just a bit more encouraging . . ."

"Hang on a minute, don't you go blaming me!" Ellie protested. "I'd been perfectly cl—"

"Oh, no, you certainly hadn't!" Blake said to her, more loudly than she'd expected him to. "But let me finish for once, will you, Ellie?"

Ellie nodded, taking a seat across from him.

"I told her that if she wanted money, status, and all that hip lifestyle, she should be with Piers and not me. Which I always knew was the truth and I think they both did as well."

Ellie shook her head in bewilderment. "I don't get it," she stammered. "Where does Piers come into it?"

As she asked the question, snippets of the conversation she'd had with Piers at the ball filtered back into her

confused brain. *He's a great guy, just not Lucy's type . . .
he'll kill her spirit . . .it's your fault he's gone . . .only so
many times you can give a guy the brush-off. . . .*

Blake leaned forward and reached out for her hand.
Ellie edged back into her chair. *Not so fast, buddy.*

Blake retreated, but kept talking. "Before I went, I told
Piers how I've wanted to be with you ever since I met you
that evening at your old house," Blake began.

"Come off it," Ellie protested. "You had heaps of oppor-
tunities . . ."

"Sure I did, and what happened?" Blake raised his
voice and Ellie saw him clench his fists. "You ran off—
remember that night on the beach? You wouldn't let me get
near you. Whenever I tried to talk to you about the real reason I was going to Oz with Lucy, all you could say was
'There is no you and me! Australia's wonderful at this time
of year!' Hardly the sort of thing a girl who's keen on you
comes out with, is it?"

Ellie swallowed. "I thought—I mean, you two were an
item and I . . ." Ellie paused before remembering something. "At the bar that time, I heard you say to Piers that
you'd been trying to get rid of me for months."

"Not *you!*" Blake practically laughed. "Lucy! I'd been
trying to get rid of Lucy for months! Ever since I first met you,
in fact," he added, his voice softening. "So can we start
over? Will you come out with me?"

"What about Lucy?" Ellie asked—she knew she wasn't cut out for any more confrontations with her, and after all of this back and forth, she wanted to be damn sure things were over between her and Blake.

"If you'd *ever* let me finish"—Blake grinned—"I'd have explained. Lucy's in Australia. Waiting for Piers."

Ellie's protests were cut short by the touch of Blake's lips against hers.

"I love you, Ellie Dashwood," he breathed. "And even if you say no, I'll pester you until you change your mind."

"But—"

{ 322 } It was when he kissed her for the second time that she decided that saying no would simply be a waste of breath.

EPILOGUE

"You like it?" Blake asked, a worry crease set between his eyes.

Ellie nodded her head and brushed the tears from her eyes. "Mum, Abby, Georgie, come and look!" she called.

"What is it?" Julia gasped as she and Georgie dashed into the sitting room, followed by a slightly limping Abby. She clamped her hands to her mouth and stared at the painting lying on the coffee table.

"It's all of us—you, me, Abby, Georgie," Ellie breathed. "And Dad."

Even Georgie let out a little throttling sound in her throat.

"Oh, Blake—it's beautiful." Julia beamed at him.

Blake smiled.

"I sketched Max while I was living with him and Pandora in London," he explained. "He was laughing at

Only Fools and Horses on the TV. I added the rest of you later."

"We'll hang it next to your painting of Holly House," Julia declared. "We'll start a Blake Goodman gallery, and when you're world-famous, we can say that we knew you in your early phase!"

"Look," he said, fumbling with a button on his shirt-sleeve. "You guys know that I'll be starting at art school next week in Brighton, and living at Holly House. And, well, I know it's awkward, but Pandora's going away for a couple of months—some crystal therapy course—and I wondered if you'd like to come? You know, visit your home?"

For a moment, no one spoke.

"Not me," Julia finally replied brightly. "I've got so much to do here, what with being on the Garden Society committee, and playing in the bridge tournament. . . ."

"Um, I think I'll stick around here at weekends," Abby agreed. "You know, with Nick playing at gigs and stuff . . . ."

"Yeah," said Georgie, "Tom's coming up again for a visit, and I've already got my hands full with Adam, so . . . 'fraid not. Thanks, though."

"Ellie?" Blake's voice was hardly more than a whisper.

"I don't think so." She smiled into Blake's anxious eyes. "This is our home now," Ellie said softly. "I reckon we're finally fine where we are."

And with that, everyone slowly nodded. Ellie was right—this was home now, and with the picture of Holly House smiling down on them from the wall, the new portrait of all five of them together again, and a year's worth of secrets of love finally uncovered, it finally felt that way.